I0748725

WHEN ANGELS CRY

ALSO BY ROBERT LANE

The Second Letter

Cooler Than Blood

The Cardinal's Sin

The Gail Force

Naked We Came

A Beautiful Voice

The Elizabeth Walker Affair

A Different Way to Die

The Easy Way Out

Searching for Dali

Kiss it Goodbye

WHEN ANGELS CRY

A JAKE TRAVIS NOVEL

ROBERT LANE

ISBN: 9798993329918

Mason Alley Publishing, Saint Pete Beach, Florida

This is a work of fiction. Although some incidents of this story may appear to be true and factual, their relation to each other and implications derived from their occurrences are strictly the product of the author's imagination. Names, characters, places, and incidents either are the product of the author's imagination or are used fictitiously. Any resemblance to actual persons (living or dead), localities, companies, organizations, and events is entirely coincidental. This book was created with 100 percent human content. No part of this work may be used for AI production. Cover design by James T. Egan, Bookfly Design.

Great sorrow dies in silence.
—John Donne

WHEN ANGELS CRY

FORTY-SEVEN YEARS AGO

Mine eyes have seen the glory

He sat in his car outside the school halfway between the streetlights to maximize the darkness. What was this, number seven? Nine? *My, how the good times roll.* He was comfortable alone in the dark, for he'd always felt alienated from the world. As if all of society were hostile to him. He twisted the radio dial just a tad. "Dust in the Wind." *Finally. A song that says something. How much can you take of "I miss you"? "I love you"? "My life is blah-blah without you"?*

This one was pretty. Hell, they were all pretty, but those dimples. *Focus. You got a job to do.*

Two nights ago, she'd been with a dude her age. He assumed it was the boy/man who knocked her up. *What did Doc say she was? Barely seventeen. Guy looked to be about the same.* The two of them sipping sodas in a McDonald's—over 25 billion served—like they were on some goddamn Hollywood set. They were plotting. Planning. He could tell. She laughed. That upset him. The only time he heard people laugh was when they laughed at him. *Hey, elephant ears, can you hear me?*

You still washing sheets at that sleazy dump your mama works at? Hey, I'm talking to you, short-shit.

The boy and girl had reached across the table and joined hands. Oh, sweet Lord, that had brought a typhonic wave of hurt. A twisting knife inside. He never recalled a single person holding his hand. Almost five billion people in the world. Close to fifty billion fingers. And not one set of human fingers had ever interlocked with his. Even when the doc had him flat on his back and they did their dark thing, sweet as it was, their fingers never touched.

Fucking dust in the wind.

They had walked out of the Golden Arches into a moonlit evening. Her head high. A timid wind teasing her strawberry hair, as if nature Herself wanted to caress her. There is nothing in the universe—no autumn, no spring, no flaming star, no winter storm or mourning dove—that does not bow to a young woman in love.

But this night was windless. This night she was alone. The moon cowered behind clouds.

He tossed the wrapper from a Baby Ruth bar onto the empty passenger seat. *Damn candy bars, you can feel your teeth rotting with every bite. Might gas up on the way home. Grab a burger, too. Wonder who Johnny's got on tonight?*

Five minutes passed. Six. She should be out any minute now. He never arrived too early. That only increased the odds that someone might identify him. He also never used the same car twice. To do this job properly, you had to be a multitasker. Needed to know how to hot-wire a car. Better yet, spot one running while some dimwit dashed into a store.

She walked out of the school. *Right on time, baby. Why the hell she doing night classes anyway?* He was relieved it was dark. The last assignment the doc paid him for had been in freakin' broad daylight. Doc was all panicky. *She's threatening to go to the police.* That job was pushing it. He knew you never wanted to rely on luck. It changed sides faster than a wink.

He nudged the gas pedal with his foot. He always started slow. Easy. No need to bring attention to yourself. *Christ, look at her. She's practically floating.* He glanced at her picture taped to the dash. *If only you knew.*

She started to cross the street.

His foot smashed the gas pedal.

She glanced up.

PART I

BACK SEAT SEX

CHAPTER 1

The day we got a puppy was the day I concluded my search for Archie Williams's daughter, who had been dead for forty-seven years. The dog was a goldendoodle that Kathleen and the girls named Woodruff. Archie's daughter was . . . we'll get to that.

Before we go any further, though, you should know this. More than anyone I've known, Archie Williams was a man who, as his wife Bobbie Lee pointed out, loved love. The whole fairy tale. God bless Archie Williams. The world marched forth every day, but his heart was stalled on the palm-leaved boulevards of his youth where his heart had experienced the first thrust of love. Youth had discarded Archie, but Archie had not discarded youth.

I often think of how, on that puppy/daughter day, Woodruff's unbridled and contagious enthusiasm was so disenfranchised from my mood and the message I was to deliver to Archie. Isn't that the way life swings, though? No sooner than it finds a pretty melody, it convulses into a dissonant key, and you wonder, *Where did the melody go?*

For the record, I didn't want the dog. Argued against it. But the older I get, the less my vote counts. Both our girls, Joy and Sophia, had been hounding (get it?) me for some time, and Kathleen had recently joined their campaign. Our nanny, Bonita, was also in favor. She never used to have voting privileges in the family. She sure as hell does now, though I've jumped miles ahead.

"Blue or beige?" Kathleen said. She popped out to the screened porch holding a jacket in each hand. She jiggled them both.

"Beige."

"You always vote beige."

"Blue."

"I think I'll wear black."

She twirled and headed back into our house, leaving me alone in the screened porch that fronted Boca Ciega Bay on the west coast of Florida. An old schooner sailed past, trailing a dinghy behind it. A front had blustered in during the night. The Gulf would be a tempest, and I hoped the crew of the schooner knew their business. Even those who were accustomed to rough waters, seasoned in harsh weather, are surprised and often ill prepared for the storms they voluntarily encounter.

We were attending a fundraiser at the home of Archie and Bobbie Lee Williams. It was for early childhood education awareness, a topic Kathleen was passionate about. Morgan, our neighbor, was attending as well. Morgan and I operate Harbor House. It's a home for families in need of temporary housing as well as women who sought refuge from abusive relationships. Whose lives had once brimmed with promising melodies and who now struggled out of bed every morning, hoping to hear that song again. Business was booming. We found ourselves on everyone's list of invitees. It would be good to hobnob with charitable-minded people. Morgan was good at stuff like that. I, not so much. But there was another reason I was attending.

A friend, Yankee Conrad, had called last week. Yankee had a long relationship with the CIA, where he served, as far as I could ascertain, as minister without a portfolio. I'd done several freelance jobs for him. Decades older than I, Yankee indicated he was an old college roommate of Archie Williams, and was worried about him. Yankee explained that Archie was under stress from work, health, and family. The holy trinity. Archie owned a pharmaceutical company. He had two children whom he had legally adopted from his second wife. Those adult children had joined him in the business years ago. The oldest, Abigail, was chief operations officer. Her brother, Lester, was VP of finance.

Archie had told Yankee he wanted to add another person as a beneficiary of his estate, a daughter he'd never met. Best yet, she'd been dead for forty-seven years. Or was it forty-six? But Archie had reason to believe she was alive. Yankee had suggested to Archie that I might be of assistance in finding her. Yankee, after telling me this and upon my questioning, insisted that Archie was of sound mind. Yankee had scored us the invitation to Archie's shindig and alerted Archie that I would be there.

I had questioned Yankee as to what effort Archie had made in finding his not-dead daughter. I was particularly interested in whether he'd solicited help from his adopted children.

"I sense that engaging the help of his children would be counterproductive," he'd told me. "Any added beneficiary would only dilute their share of his estate. They would have a vested interest in Archie failing. As far as any previous effort, his first call was to me." He'd also informed me that his old roommate had pancreatic cancer. Stage two. Lucky to catch it early. The Vegas line was fifty-fifty.

Morgan came in through the side door. Hadley III, our cat, darted in with him. She liked Morgan. Whenever he came over, she made herself known. I had fed her every day for the last twelve years, but she largely ignored me. I'm not complaining. Just pointing it out.

I poured Morgan a glass of red wine. The simple act calibrated my compass. Wine is a portal, the cork a door to another place and time. That particular bottle was from the boot of Europe. Its magic nose conjured images of a dark-haired woman with tanned skin who, for a solitary moment, had locked her eyes with mine in a crowded piazza on a summer night long ago. We bumped into each other two days later in a confectionery store. She flashed a smile of recognition that melted every piece of chocolate in the store. Maybe in the world.

"Did you see the boat go out?" I asked Morgan, snapping back to the present.

"That schooner is docked downtown," Morgan said. "They're on a practice run."

"They got all they can handle."

"That's what they want."

Kathleen returned to the screened porch wearing charcoal gray. Was that even an option? I took a sip of wine and thought wouldn't it be grand if we ditched the Williamses and hung out at home?

"No," Kathleen said when I voiced my idea. "Besides, fuddy-duddy, you're supposed to meet this Archie fellow, right? Hand it over." I passed her my glass. It went straight to her lips. "I've read up on Archie and Bobbie Lee Williams," she continued. "I'm looking forward to meeting them."

"I'm looking forward to seeing their house," Morgan added. "I've fished the mangroves in that area, and it's an impressive residence from the water."

"I'm looking forward to the hors d'oeuvres," I said.

And with that, the three us departed the quiet waters of our house and set out to sea.

CHAPTER 2

The Williams home sat behind opened iron gates pilfered from the fourteenth century. I pulled under the portico. One man opened Kathleen's door and another mine. Morgan, hidden in the rear by the tinted glass, was on his own. I tossed my truck fob to a man and told him to give it a good wax. You know he never heard that line before. The castle exterior of the house was more suited for the moors of Scotland than the west coast of Florida.

"Just plain ugly," I said as we approached the front door, a piece of oak that nature took two centuries to create.

"Let's not be judgmental," Kathleen said.

"Better look up and make sure they don't pour boiling oil on our heads."

"You should see it from the water," Morgan said. "The only thing missing are cannons pointing over the bay."

A man robotically swung open the front door for us. The inside could hardly be more incongruous with the outside. Light marble floors radiated brightness. A towering wall of windows overlooked the Gulf. The place swirled with people and disharmonious voices. I stifled a yawn. Why do people insist on starting parties at eight o'clock in the evening?

"Hi, I'm Bobbie Lee Williams," said a woman standing in the hall. "I'd like to thank you for coming and supporting early childhood education."

Her voice, which carried a hint of a southern accent, sprinkled the air with sugar. Her engaging face was highlighted by dimples placed by the tip of an angel's brush.

"Thank you for opening your home," Kathleen said. "It's beautiful."

"The inside, yes. The outside looks like a medieval fart."

I coughed out a laugh. "I wouldn't go that far."

"How far would you go, Mr. . . . ?"

"Travis. Jake Travis. It just needs a little attention."

"Attention, Mr. Travis? It needs—"

"Jake."

"It needs a bulldozer," Bobbie Lee said.

"I got a better idea."

"Oh?"

"A bomb. It's much quicker."

"Jake," Katheen admonished me.

Bobbie Lee laughed. She shot Kathleen a look. "Is he your man?"

"Straight off the clearance rack," Kathleen said.

"Better keep him on a leash," Bobbie Lee said with a twinkle in her eye. She could charm the leaves off a tree. "They don't make 'em tall and straight anymore."

"I'd like to thank your husband as well for hosting the event," I said. "Could you point him out?"

"Look for a man whose goal in life was to be Hugh Heffner."

"Purple robe and a pipe?"

"Don't forget the slippers."

"What's that make you?" I said.

"I," she said with a quick curtsy, "am the last bunny. Archie and I are the happiest couple in the world."

"That can't be."

"And why not?"

"I regret to inform you that my wife and I occupy that spot."

Bobbie Lee reached out and touched Kathleen on the back of her hand. "We need to get to know each other." She shifted her attention back to me. "Archie's outside, likely discussing business with his two adult children, neither of whom is potty-trained. And not to contest your point, Jake, but Archie and I are neck and neck with you and Kathleen." She looked at Kathleen. "I need to do the mingle thing. Give me a few minutes. I'll circle back."

She flirted into a crowd that had gathered at the front door.

"Clearance rack?" I said to Kathleen.

"She didn't seem too impressed with Archie's children."

"She's wife number three and a self-admitted bunny. I doubt forging a lasting relationship with the children of one of her husband's previous marriages is high on her list. Yankee said Archie snagged Bobbie Lee off a dance pole at a gentlemen's club."

"Seriously?"

"I never joke about dance poles," I reminded her.

"No, you do not. I like her."

"Based on?"

"Intuition." She pecked me on the cheek. "You hop out to the patio and give my best to Hugh." She looked at Morgan. "You game to meet new and fascinating people?"

Morgan hooked out his arm "Always."

Kathleen wrapped her arm in his, and they scooted off. I headed outside in search of Hugh Hefner. And let's not forget those hors d'oeuvres.

CHAPTER 3

Hugh—Archie Williams—was in contentious conversation with a woman and a man who, judging from pictures I'd seen, were his two children Bobbie Lee had referred to. The three of them stood by the edge of the pool. A sea breeze rippled the surface, and the underwater lights danced over their bodies like a 1920s motion picture.

Archie gestured in the air and spoke forcibly to the woman, who retorted in a clipped voice. She looked like she could walk into the North Pole in a sleeveless dress and be comfortable. Her hair was cut short, and her copper wire lips barely parted when she spoke. Her figure indicated she ran ten miles a day and ate every third Thursday. Her neck was long and hard and void of any sensuality. She reminded me of a popsicle.

I rudely stepped into the conversational circle, bringing an abrupt truce. I introduced myself to Archie and thanked him in earnest for opening his house. His eyes flashed a twinkle of recognition. The man next to Archie, a colorless face wearing a blue sport jacket, shuffled his feet to show his disapproval of my effrontery.

"Yankee's man," Archie said, bobbing his head. "It's good to meet you. You'll want to thank my wife. She's the one who does the heavy lifting."

Archie was a pale man who looked as if he'd been carved from a marshmallow. But he exuded the striving confidence of someone who had mastered their circumstances, unlike most men, who are mastered by their circumstances. I put him a couple of decades older than Bobbie Lee.

"I've met her," I said.

"Of course you have," Archie said. "She's fanatic about greeting people as they enter."

"A perfect hostess."

"A perfect wife."

The woman groaned. I turned to her. "Are you interested in early childhood education?"

The man next to her snickered.

"I am not," she said in a clipped voice. In contrast to the man, who held a drink, her hands were loose by her side.

"You live around here?" I said to her.

"I do not."

"Am not and do not."

Her eyes registered me for the first time. "What can I do for you?" she said.

"You know, I didn't catch your name."

"I didn't toss it."

"Ready when you are."

Her lips curled in a barely discernable smile. "Abigail Williams."

"Archie's little girl?" I shot a glance at Archie. I sensed he was enjoying the show. But she'd tired of my act, as had I.

"If you would excuse us," she said. "We were having a conversation before you rudely intruded."

"He's here to see me, Abby," Archie interceded on my behalf.

I shifted my attention to the man. "You must be Lester."

"My sister's being kind," he said with a breath of arrogance that I suspected masked his insecurity. "If it were up to me, I'd walk away for no other reason than your boorish behavior."

"But it's not, is it?" I said.

"What's not?"

"Up to you. Lester."

Lester squirmed in his skin and gave me a smirk. Abigail snickered, and that told me what she thought of her brother. Archie's eyes darted between his daughter and son. "Mr. Travis and I have a few things to discuss. I believe we've settled everything."

"We're good," Lester said.

"We'll continue our conversation at a later date," Abigail said. "Free from interruptions."

"I don't see the point," Archie said.

"Not here," she said, punching out each word.

He waggled a finger at her. "This is still my company." He shifted his attention to me. "I'll see you at the bar." He sauntered away.

"We'll talk later," Lester said to his sister. "Maybe—"

"Take a hike, Lester," Abigail commanded him.

Lester looked at her like a puppy that has missed the paper. He gave a huff and trudged away. That left Lady Popsicle and me.

"Do you ever think things would be easier in your life without your little brother?" I said.

She leveled her eyes at me. "Don't encourage Archie."

"Pardon me?"

"He told me why you're here. That his old college roommate recommended you. He's tilting at windmills. Searching for a daughter who died nearly half a century ago. I need him focused on the business."

"Perhaps we could talk sometime," I said.

"What are we doing now?"

"In more depth."

"Don't flatter yourself. You're in over your head."

"Ah, but I'm so fond of deep water."

"Call my office and make an appointment. That's how civilized people operate. Good evening, Mr. Travis." She turned and marched away. A woman with a purpose but no destination.

I found Archie at the bar chatting with a tall, elegantly dressed man. After a minute or so, Archie excused himself and came over to me. "That was quite an entrance you made back there."

"I thought it might be good to get things off to a fast start. I hope I didn't offend you."

"Not at all," he chortled. "I appreciate a man in a hurry. But unfortunately, I need to beg off tonight. The chemo plays with me, and I get exhausted without notice. This is Bobbie Lee's doing anyway. I've asked her to invite some couples, including you and your wife, to dinner in two nights. I'll be feeling much better. I'm eager to explain what I need a man in a hurry for."

"I wish you the best in your fight against cancer."

"Oh, I'll beat it," he said, though more to himself than to me. "Stupid thing doesn't even know that if it kills me, it, too, dies. Pleasure meeting you. I look forward to engaging with you more tomorrow."

"Tomorrow or in two nights?"

"I misspoke. Day after."

He took a step but then stopped. "You handled Abigail well. She likes hard men."

He disappeared into the crowd. I placed my empty glass on the bar. "Bourbon and ice," I said to the bartender.

"Hard liquor for a hard man."

I stifled another yawn.

"Late for you?" she said, handing me my drink.

"It is. I'm usually in bed by ten."

"I can make that happen."

"I'm married."

"I'm game."

"And fast."

"Three is more fun than two."

It was time to either advance or retreat. Rule Number One in Jake's Book for a Happy Marriage: Run away. Retreat. I raised my glass. "You're beautiful and dangerous, and I'm leaving now."

I turned and went searching for Bobbie Lee but couldn't find her. I did manage to secure beef tenderloin on buttered toasted sesame bread, which complemented my bourbon. Ten minutes later, after tossing down a half dozen of the bite-size treats, I bumped into Kathleen.

"Bobbie Lee is upstairs hustling pool," Kathleen said. "I spent more time with her."

"Any juice?"

"She says Archie's under tremendous stress. Did you meet him?"

"I did. He excused himself. Said he was not feeling well. Might have gotten tomorrow mixed up with the day after it. Apparently, we're being invited back here in two nights for dinner."

"We are. She knew he wouldn't be up to it tonight, but it had been on the calendar for a year, and she thought it would be good for you to meet his two children. His diagnosis is favorable, but the outcome is far from certain."

"Did she give any indication that she is aware of her husband searching for a deceased daughter to add to his will?"

Maybe Archie shared everything with Bobbie Lee. Maybe he didn't. It was a question I should have asked Yankee but had not.

"She did."

"How'd you draw that out of her?"

"Just asked her."

"That'll do the trick."

"She seems fine with it. Even supportive. Oh, one more thing. She said that in the event that Archie's daughter is still alive, Abigail would rather kill her than forfeit part of her inheritance."

"Was she joking?"

"Aren't jokes supposed to be funny?"

CHAPTER 4

Two nights later, Kathleen and I were discussing Bobbie Lee and Archie as we passed under the toll booth that led off the island. I was perturbed by the repeat trip and had to remind myself that the first night had been for a good cause. It was hardly Archie's fault for being exhausted after chemo. I'd just inquired if Kathleen knew who else would be in attendance that evening.

"No names, but Bobbie Lee did say there's a business angle to everything. She indicated she'd try to clear the others out early so that you and Archie would have plenty of time to talk. Joy's cough didn't seem as bad today."

Joy, eight, was the oldest of our two girls. Her sister, Sophia, was five.

"I hope we don't get what she had."

"I doubt she's contagious anymore," Kathleen said.

"They're born contagious."

"You think Archie and Bobbie Lee really met when she was a pole dancer?"

"That's what Yankee said."

"Wonder what it's like. To curl around a pole, practically naked, while men ogle at you."

"I wholeheartedly support any career decisions you make."

"I'll bear that in mind."

"You'll be baring a lot more."

"Ha."

"Wear glasses," I said. "On the pole. And a hat. One of those Liza Minelli deals."

"You've given this some thought."

"I've made some notes. Minor sketches. Do you know dogs can pass the common cold to children?"

"That is so not true. You're shameless."

"Just looking out for my girls."

Kathleen had taken our enthusiastic daughters to a pet store that afternoon. They'd returned empty but were flushed with excitement. Giggling while landing sideway glances at me. Joy telling Sophia to "sush" when she started talking about where it would sleep. Here's what followed.

Me to Kathleen: "Did you buy one?"

Kathleen in her Scarlett O'Hara voice, which she doesn't do as well as she thinks she does, but I'm not telling her that: "Whatever are you talking about, my darling?"

"It will make a mess in the yard."

"I want to look back one day, and it's all just one big, fat, glorious mess."

Was she speaking figuratively? I'd retreated—Rule Number One, remember?—into the sanctuary of the study and researched Archie Williams.

Archie had founded his company as a wholesale distributor. He had tacked on a start-up biotech company in the early 1990s. Against the urging of investment bankers, whom he inherently distrusted, he shunned going public and kept the company private. But after a couple of big hits, the pipeline was bare.

Both Abigail and Lester joined out of college. They had been with the company for close to thirty years. Archie had no biological children, except for his stillborn daughter, who he apparently had reason to believe was still alive, which is very different from stillborn. His first two wives lived in the area. Neither had any ownership in the company. I doubted Bobbie Lee did, either. Her prenup likely ran a thousand pages. Or one: nothing. I wanted to interview the two ex-wives. They might know more about his lost daughter or lead me to someone who did. Other than them, I really didn't have a direction to start until I engaged with Archie and asked him the obvious question.

Why would he think someone who was dead was alive?

CHAPTER 5

I punched the doorbell as Kathleen ran her hand through her hair. I straightened my belt buckle so that it lined up with the row of buttons on my shirt. It was a new, and somewhat puzzling, habit I'd picked up.

"No glasses," Kathleen said. "And not a Minelli cabaret hat."

It took me second. "Oh?"

"A hat with black ribbon and a rim so broad no one sees my eyes. My face always shadowed."

"I dig that. And—"

The door swung open. A woman in a maid's outfit invited us in. "Mrs. Williams will greet you in a minute. She's just checking on the kitchen."

Less than a minute later, Bobbie Lee appeared like a rainbow waltzing into a room.

"It's sooo good to see you," she exclaimed.

I couldn't decide if she was one of the most genuine and pleasant persons I'd ever come across or an accomplished fraud. Kathleen claims I'm too cynical of people. I counter that I'm skeptical, not cynical. She warns me not to fence words with her. I don't learn.

Bobbie Lee and Kathleen exchanged a quick hug. "And you brought your man," she tacked on, giving me a look. "I understand you ruffled Abigail's feathers. Good for you. That woman, as we used to say, needs to be plucked. We're going to have a great time. Archie dreads dinner parties. But then he tells me later what fun he had." Her eyes darted between Kathleen and me. "Do you guys have anything like that? Something one of you craves but the other feigns indifference only to come around?"

"I can't think of anything," I admitted.

"My girls and I want a dog," Kathleen said. "So does Jake, but he doesn't know it."

"Oh, I love dogs." Bobbie Lee looked at me disbelievingly. "And you don't? Really?"

"It's not that I don't like them," I said. "It's that—"

"I had a dog growing up," she continued. "Sally. We named her after Charlie Brown's sister. She loved the water. Would jump into the lake and swim every day. When she died, we found her by the shore."

"That's touching," Kathleen said.

"It is," I concurred. "It's just that—"

"Give it up," Bobbie Lee said, cutting me off verbally and physically as she touched my arm. "You know you're going to get one, so why not enjoy the process? You're just like Archie. You have to be reminded of what's important."

"I'm sure Archie knows how lucky he is to have you," I said.

"Don't patronize me," Bobbie Lee said with a twinkle. "And for the record, he tells me how lucky he is and how much he loves me every time we have sex."

"That's a reaffirming thing to hear before you go to sleep," I said.

"Oh, we're dead on our feet at night. We're daytime fornicators. Okay, Bobbie Lee, time to shut up. Pretty soon I'm going to be telling you which end of the kitchen counter we favor. We broke it in right after we remodeled. When they tell you a twelve-inch overhang is fine? Pity them, for they have no imagination. Follow me. Let's play grown-up. It's such a . . . challenging game."

We trailed her through the kitchen. My eyes lingered on the quartz countertop. I peeked underneath. Thing would hold a Mack truck.

Two other couples were sitting in the living room, as we were the last to arrive. The elements of the twenty-four-hour clock, along with the cardinal directions, have always eluded Kathleen—when I'd first met her, she was surprised to learn that Alabama did not lie under Georgia. I was hoping for an early dinner so that I could move on to the main event. The leading edge of fatigue had checked into my body. I'd hit the beach running at six that morning. That had been followed by a twenty-minute punch-a-thon with the hanging bag in the garage. A girlfriend from a different life had painted a happy face on it with her lipstick. The girlfriend was long gone, and the lipstick followed a few years later.

I often find myself looking where things used to be.

After the prerequisite thirty minutes of wine-sipping chitchat that only served to reinforce my belief that I'm not missing anything in this world by staying home and reading to my girls, Bobbie Lee ceremoniously stood. "Time for dinner, sinners," she announced. She herded us into the dining room where we settled behind name tags placed around an Arthurian table. The couples were separated. Kathleen was on Archie's right. I, at the opposite end of the table, was on Bobbie Lee's right. A woman, Rachel, was to my left. Rachel wore too much perfume. She had the annoying habit of dropping the tone of her voice at the end of each sentence as if to convey that everything was beneath her station in life.

Bobbie Lee kept the conversation balanced. When Rachel's husband—I'd forgotten his name before Bobbie Lee had finished introducing him—prattled on for too long, she would politely cut in and redirect the conversation. Archie endured it, although I sensed he was fonder of his drink than the guests. We exchanged glances several times, both eager to get to the main card.

One couple, God bless them, cut out early. Bobbie Lee didn't protest. But Rachel, who laughed like a polluted monkey, didn't pick up the cue, nor did her yapping no-name husband. He owned a commercial building company. Want to know his story? I didn't either but had no choice. The more he drank, the more he talked, and the more he talked, the more he drank.

Bobbie Lee politely noted the hour and that she had a Zumba class at seven thirty the next morning. Rachel apologized for staying so late, her snotty tone indicating anything other than penitence. Bobbie Lee assured her that the hour was fine and thanked them effusively for "sharing your evening with us." When talking with people, Bobbie Lee possessed the innate gift of treating that person as if they were the world to her.

That left Kathleen, Bobbie Lee, Archie, and me. We plopped down in the living room, and I struggled to identify the song playing over the speakers. I have a lazy left ear, courtesy of a bomb in Sandland fifteen years ago. Fifteen years. Can that be right? Like the lipstick smile on my punching bag that is no longer there, I am puzzled by the wide gulf that has developed between the present and the leaf-pile of yesterdays.

"Where'd you get the talker from, dear?" Archie asked Bobbie Lee.

"He's tight with the county permit board. If you want that variance for your new office, you need him."

"I don't want a new office. That's Abigail's plan."

"I know. But this way, you can at least say you're open to considering it with her."

"But I'm not."

"I know you're not," Bobbie Lee said. "But an open mind does wonders for a relationship."

"And the others? What about the lady with the pearls who kept burping and saying excuse me?"

"She's the one who gifted fifty thousand dollars to the Early Learning Coalition of Pinellas County. She was here two nights ago."

"Thousand dollars a burp."

"Archie. She wasn't that bad."

"Keep up the fine work." He shifted his attention to me. "You got yourself a keeper. Your first try?"

"Excuse me?" I said.

He jutted his head at Kathleen and smiled. "She your first wife?"

"She is."

"Lucky man. For me, third time was the charm."

"Tell us about yourself," Kathleen said to Bobbie Lee. "You're gifted in getting others to talk, but you deflect questions about yourself."

Bobbie Lee winced. "Am I that obvious?"

"Not to that boneheaded motormouth," Archie chirped in.

"It was not obvious," Kathleen said. "You're an accomplished host."

Bobbie Lee dipped her head. "Thank you. I appreciate you saying that. I do work at it. I was married at eighteen. Divorced at nineteen. Married again at twenty-two. Same guy. Same result. I did odd jobs until I discovered that a few nights a week on the pole yielded more cash than forty hours behind a desk. Archie strolled into the Havana Club one rainy night years ago, and we've been together ever since."

"Lust at first sight?" I quipped.

Archie laughed. "That is how the species survives. I was driving downtown. It was pouring. There was this clown on the sidewalk, its face smeared in color. Must have been leaving a gig somewhere. I was in front of the Havana Club. I'd never been in it before. Wouldn't have even noticed it if it weren't for the wet clown. I swear he pointed at the club, like he was signaling me to go in. I was lonely. Wanted a woman to share my life with. Thought I'd go in and get me one. What's that saying? You want a woman with a past and a man with a future. I might be a little old for half that equation, but I'm living yesterday's future right now, and that counts for something."

"He came up to me at the pole." Bobbie Lee took over. The lights from the chandelier brightened her face. Light always found her. "His hair was wet. I thought he was going to stick a C-note in my string. Instead, he told me to 'Get off that pole and let's have dinner.' Said he needed a woman in his life and I needed a man in mine. Something about the clock was ticking, and we'd already missed so much together, but we still had so much in front of us."

"He told you the clock was ticking?" Kathleen said.

"I know. Hardly a compliment, right? But he was being honest. I was touching my young thirties. It was time to get off the pole. And he was . . . *so* convincing. So sure of himself. Of us."

"Archie," Kathleen gushed. "Every woman's dream."

"Tell them what you said," Archie said to Bobbie Lee.

"I don't remember."

"Yes, you do."

Bobbie Lee dipped her head. "I said, 'You just love my tits.' And you said that when you came in, my back was to you, and that's when you made your decision."

"Is this true?" I asked Archie.

"I decided to marry her before I ever saw her face, or tits."

I shifted my attention to Bobbie Lee. "Speaking of pole dancing, if Kathleen were to ever consider such a profession, what do you think of her donning a wide-brimmed hat?"

"You looking for a few extra dollars?" Bobbie Lee said to Kathleen.

"My husband's mind is prone to winged fantasy."

"Here's the problem with the hat," Bobbie Lee explained. "It gets in the way of the pole. You'd always be knocking it off."

"I didn't consider that," Kathleen said.

"What is your profession?" Bobbie Lee asked.

"I'm a professor of literature."

"I can see how that wouldn't come up. But really, kids?" Bobbie Lee's eyes danced between Kathleen and mine. "I love the way you two birds think. Now, tell me about you guys, and pleeeease make it the unedited version."

"I approached him at a hotel beach bar," Kathleen jumped in. "I lied. Told him I was looking for my husband when I was really looking for a man who wanted to kill me because my ex-husband—we were divorced—ran books for the Chicago mob. They were afraid he confided information to me. Jake and his friend Garrett killed four men on a deserted stretch of Fort De Soto, faked my death, and changed my name so the mob would stop hunting for me."

The room exploded with silence. Kathleen had just divulged what we'd pledged never to mention. That a grave marker north of Chicago, where the wind never ceases, had her name etched in it. What was she thinking? Why now?

"Is that right?" Archie said to me, his tone both incredulous and cautious.

"First time I heard any of this," I said.

Another round of silence passed, and then Archie burst out laughing. He looked at Kathleen. "I don't know whether you're bullshitting me or telling me something you shouldn't have said."

"What do you think, Arch?" Kathleen demurred in a silky voice. She got like that sometimes, a stranger unto even herself.

"What do I think?" Archie leaned forward, fully engaged for

the first time that night. "I think some people you never trust, some take years to trust, and some you trust intuitively. Your secret's safe with me."

Bobbie Lee grabbed Kathleen's arm. "Come. Let me show you the castle. Perhaps you can suggest new ideas by which to squander Archie's money."

The women chatted their way out of the room. Archie turned to me. "Better be right."

"About what?"

"Trusting you. It was you I was referring to. Let's go to my study. I'm afraid I've made a hell of a mess with my life."

"Is this about your stillborn daughter whom you believe to be alive?"

He didn't wait for a reply but headed to the front foyer and the circular staircase that snaked its way to the second floor. I obediently followed as Linda Ronstadt sang "Long Long Time." No one could resurrect the pieces of a broken heart and weave them into a timeless melody like Ronstadt.

Until Archie Williams rode into town.

CHAPTER 6

The night had transformed the wall of windows in Archie's second floor study into mirrors. A desk with two chairs in front of it anchored one end of the room. The remainder of the space was filled with a couch, a table, more chairs, a fireplace, and a bar with two stools. Paintings hung on the walls. I approached one that looked like jazz on canvas. It was an eruption of form and color that translated into a woman dressed as a clown. An angel clown, for she had wings. The clown's sad eyes sat atop a dimpled face. A plunging neckline added a jolt of sexuality.

Clowns and I don't get along. Years ago, I had one die in my arms. He'd been stabbed multiple times. Even before that, the ancient tradition of clowns had vexed me.

"An alluring angel clown," I mused, keeping my eyes on the painting. "I haven't seen one in years."

Archie chuckled. He had positioned himself beside me. His sport coat, a snazzy blue blazer with black lapels, remained buttoned. "I'd be second-guessing our relationship before we even got started if you said you were tired of them. Bobbie Lee did that. Every painting in the room."

I glanced around. A half dozen oil paintings of various sizes hung on the walls. "She's good."

"She has a real talent. This, though"—he dipped his head at the clown—"is her magnum opus. You see it?"

I studied the face in the painting. "It's her, isn't it?" I said. "Bobbie Lee." It was hard to be certain, as the face was smeared with makeup and thick paint. But the dimples gave her away. "Why did she dress herself up like a clown for her self-portrait?"

"You'll need to ask her. Funny thing is, her eyes, her dimples, remind me of Lisa's. Or at least what memories I have left."

"Lisa?"

"My high school love. Deceased mother of my daughter who I thought was dead and is not and who you are going to find for me. I top the night off with a shot of rum on ice. May I fix one for you?"

"You may."

We walked over to a bar cart, the eyes of the clown drilling my back. Did Archie marry Bobbie Lee because she reminded him of Lisa, his high school girlfriend? I pondered whether Bobbie Lee considered that as well. After that, I wondered if I could talk Kathleen into wearing a wide-brimmed hat to bed. But, as with the pole, wouldn't the hat be awkward on a pillow? *How would we—?*

"To the women in our lives," Archie said, extending his hand to me.

The hat would fall off, and then we'd laugh and—

"Mr. Travis?"

I took my drink from his outstretched hand. "To the women."

We clanked our heavy glasses. "That was a nice story you told about meeting Bobbie Lee."

"It was a lucky day for us both."

"How did you really meet her?"

He raised his eyebrows. "Our version is close enough. I brought her home. In the morning, I asked her how much I owed her. She said I could pay her a thousand bucks to leave, or she could stay. We had breakfast, talked about everything. I knew I had one in a million. Smart like no one's business, and she never let a minute slip by without a smile. Despite two wives, she conjured emotions I'd not felt since Lisa."

"Tell me about Lisa."

"What did Yankee tell you?"

I summarized what Yankee Conrad had said. How Lisa had died shortly after giving birth to a stillborn girl, and now Archie was searching for his stillborn daughter. It sounded even worse when saying it out loud.

"You a spook?" Archie said.

"Excuse me?"

"CIA. The Agency. Yankee and Constance both got recruited out of college. You even look like a younger version of Yankee."

Constance is Yankee's wife.

"I am not."

"But you've done work for him."

"I have."

"You're a spook. You just don't know it. I need help locating my daughter. Think you're up to that?"

"Just to clarify," I said, "she was stillborn."

"That's what I was led to believe then and believed until recently."

"What changed your mind?" Hopefully not the cancer drugs.

"I received an anonymous letter. I know what you're thinking. Abigail told me it's someone preying on a man's sentimentality. But the letter mentions something that only Lisa and I would know. Lisa died not long after giving birth. Killed in a hit-and-run. Never caught the guy."

I asked him what Abigail's and Lester's reactions were regarding his search for a lost daughter.

"Somewhere between tolerable and accusing me of engaging in a wild-goose chase."

"Are they threatened by the prospect of having your estate diluted?"

"That's Bobbie Lee's line of thinking. I don't think so. Or, I should say, I don't want to think so."

"With all due respect, a letter that references bits of truths is not conclusive proof."

"It is, however, reason to investigate."

"I'd like to see it."

He walked behind his desk, opened a drawer, withdrew an envelope, opened it, and handed me a letter. "It's postmarked Saint Petersburg," he said. "Two weeks ago."

Dear Mr. Williams,

I am writing to inform you that the child you had with Lisa Trowbridge did not die. I know you thought she was stillborn. That is what Dr. Ziegler told Lisa. He sold the baby. I saw him hand the baby out the back door.

Lisa was a fine girl, and she would want you to know that your Little Strawberry is alive. I am sorry I did not speak up earlier.

Best of luck to you.

I handed it back to him. "Little Strawberry?" I said.

"Our nickname for our unborn child. Few knew about it. It tells me that whoever wrote this knew Lisa."

"She was a patient of Dr. Ziegler," I said, as much as to myself as to Archie.

"She was. Are you familiar with the name?"

I searched my memory. "Ziegler babies, right? Wasn't there some investigation into him years ago regarding selling babies?"

"Ziegler ran a clinic that was notorious for abortions and missing babies. Look him up. He's long gone, but the fact that Lisa was under his care adds legitimacy to the letter."

Or someone whose ultimate goal was to blackmail Archie dropped that in the letter to authenticate their position.

"And Lisa?" I prodded him. "A high school fling or more?"

"I've got a couple of decades on you, but you'll learn. Your mind gets crowded with memories. They battle each other for relevancy. Here are two that will outlive me." He paused, took a drink, and gazed out the window, but nothing was there except our reflections. "I can still see her sitting across from me when we met at Vacation Bible School." He turned back to me. "We were ten, eleven? There was never another for either of us."

After a solemn silence I said, "And the second?"

"We went to Busch Gardens for prom. My friend Jerry Shark drove. He had a nicer car. That night on the way home, Lisa and I could hardly keep our clothes on. I felt bad for Jerry and his date, sitting in the front. God, I never wanted a woman more than I wanted her that night. The best sex you'll never have is in the back seat of a car while someone else is driving. The sound of the pavement, the night rushing by outside the window. The heat, the panting, the kissing, and the groping," he said, punching out each word. "The disheveled clothes, the tangled legs, the desperate tongues."

He gave me a hard look. "Men are mortal; memories live forever."

I remained silent. What else to do when a man speaks with the passion of a Beethoven symphony?

"Lisa got pregnant at seventeen," he said with resignation. "Stupid. But I've forgiven myself for that." He skipped a beat. "Stupid. Just stupid."

Didn't sound to me like he'd forgiven himself.

"We wanted the baby," he continued. "Her mother called me and said the doctor had to induce her. Something about being the best thing for the baby. But that the baby, a girl, was stillborn. She claimed the doctor did all he could to save her."

"Did you question those words then?"

Archie arched his eyebrows. "Why would I? I was eighteen. I didn't question doctors. Would never occur to me that a mother, even a bad one like Lisa's, would lie. And, for the record, I don't think she questioned the doctor, either. Or lied.

"Lisa moved in with her aunt in Bradenton. She always got along better with her than with her own mother. The pregnancy and its aftermath had put a sizeable gulf between Lisa and her mother. She enrolled in a new high school. She took night classes so she could graduate on time. She'd dropped out of school when she was showing."

"You kept in touch," I said.

"Of course." He snorted at the implications of my statement. "I'd drive down after school to see her. About a week, maybe ten days, after she moved in with her aunt, she told me she was having a recurring dream, but it wasn't a dream. She'd heard her baby cry. Said she saw Little Strawberry and she looked healthy. Sounded healthy. But someone took her, and the doctor said she'd died."

"Was it a dream or not?"

"That's the question, isn't it? She insisted it was coming back to her. In bits and pieces. Visions. Sounds and images."

I asked him if either set of parents got involved.

"Lisa and I both came from impoverished families. My mother was a single parent working two jobs. I'd gotten my girlfriend pregnant. My mother had little sympathy for me, and I didn't want to burden her more than she already was.

"I planned to move out after I graduated. I found an apartment. Off Central. I've forgotten the exact street. The unit number is long gone. But I still see that empty room where I envisioned Lisa and I living. It's waiting for me. For us. That image, that room, sticks to me like glue. And her voice." He settled his eyes on mine. "If you lose someone, you must listen to her voice every day, or it will disappear. Did you know that?"

"I did not," I lied.

Linda Ronstadt's plaintive voice had moved on to "The Sound of My Voice," as if the playlist was tracking our conversation.

"She asked if I believed her," he continued. "I said of course I did. We made a pact to find Little Strawberry. Lisa was dead three days later. Eighteen years old and the kingdom of my days was past. I surrendered myself to the mindless pursuit of money. I ran through two marriages, and both those women deserved better than me, or at least a better version. It wasn't until I met Bobbie Lee that I rediscovered myself. The light came back on."

Archie was a troubadour of love. But if I were going to find his daughter, I would need facts, not romantic reminiscing.

"Did you ever search for your daughter," I said, "based on what Lisa had told you?"

"She knew it was coming," he said.

"Who knew what was coming?"

"Death. Lisa wrote a poem about the death of a lover. Like a premonition. But the poem's lost."

I let that go. I repeated my question whether he'd previously mounted any effort to find his daughter.

His eyes shot up to mine. "I heard you. No. I'm ashamed to say I did not. I began to doubt what she said. Didn't even know where to begin. But that was just the bullshit I fed myself. She was gone. It was over. I realize now what a great disservice I did to both Lisa and myself. What a spineless chickenshit I was. Now"—he paused as if to make sure I was on board—"I'm a man in a hurry. That's why you're here."

"What about her high school friends? Do you have names?"

"I wish I did. My memory's no good since I started on the chemo. Katie was her best friend. But I haven't a clue what became of her. We're not talking yesterday."

I thought of something I should have questioned earlier. "Did you verify that your daughter was dead?"

"Of course."

"By medical records?"

"Yes."

"You deserve more credit than you give yourself. That's pretty conclusive."

"Not considering it was Ziegler."

"His name wasn't poison at that time," I reminded him.

"You're being kind, but you're right. You see the similarities, don't you?"

"Pardon me?"

"My daughter is a little like your wife."

"In what manner?"

"Their headstones are both premature. Find my daughter, Mr. Travis. She's alive. I know it."

CHAPTER 7

I'd just finished taking a picture of the letter Archie had received when Bobbie Lee and Kathleen breezed into the room.

"Well, lookee here," Bobbie Lee said. "Two stuffed shirts sipping rum in a wood paneled study." She cuddled up to her husband and kissed him on the cheek. "Here's an idea. Let's switch. I'll leave you with Kathleen, if you promise not to trade her in for me. I'm stealing Jake. He thinks we should detonate our humble house, dear. That that would be much simpler than bulldozing it. Isn't that right, Jake?"

"That's the last time I share my thoughts with you," I said.

"No, you'll just learn to say things you can use to your advantage." A table lamp goldened her face as she talked. She grabbed my arm. "Come on, handsome. Let me share my vision of what to build after I blow this fortress sky-high."

I was eager to continue my conversation with Archie, but it would have to wait. Bobbie Lee was an irresistible force. I followed her down a hall lined with framed penciled drawings. "Is this your work as well?" I said.

She turned her head. "Archie told you that I draw?"

"He did. You're talented."

She stopped, faced me, and gave a slight bow. "Thank you. I paint, draw, whatever each morning. I'm good for about two hours, then I can't stand it anymore."

"The pole dancing brought in enough cash to allow you to pursue your passion and work in the mornings."

"You nailed it."

I thought about asking why she did her self-portrait as an angel dressed as a clown, but something unidentifiable held me back. I never did ask her.

She continued to parade us through a maze of rooms until they all started to look the same. I told her that. Her shoulders slumped. "I know," she said. "What's the purpose of it all when Archie and I each have our own space and a communal space that together amount to a fraction of the house?"

"It's a corporate house."

"Bingo." We had stopped in the kitchen. My eyes wandered to the massive island countertop. Certainly, they would turn the pendant lights off, wouldn't they? "That's what I thought the first day I set foot in it."

"Was that the day you volunteered to waive your fee and stay?"

Bobbie Lee planted her hands on her hips. "My, you two boys covered some ground. Can't a girl have a secret anymore?"

"You're both lucky to have found each other."

"And don't we know it. That story about faking Kathleen's death and killing four men on the beach—is that true?"

"No."

"Yes it is."

I didn't say anything.

"Ooo-kaay. Remind me to stay on your good side. Moving along, what else did you and Archie confess?"

She swiped back a strand of her hair from her eyes. I haven't told you about her hair. It was a wave of strawberry blonde that stopped six inches below her shoulders. The color was a perfect match to the island of shy freckles above those killer dimples. Bobbie Lee was ripped out of a summer edition of a 1950s *Better Homes and Gardens* magazine. She was a man-killer, in the old-school sense.

I said, "Your husband wants me to find a stillborn daughter from a love affair he had long ago. Is there a direction you can point me in?"

She gave that a moment. "To understand Archie, know that he is a man who loves love. Lisa might be gone, but he's forever reserved a chamber of his heart for her."

"That's fine with you?"

"One hundred percent. I'm not greedy. I'm certainly willing to help; it's just that I know nothing from that time. But you can assist me."

"How so?"

"Protect him. I'm afraid someone's trying to blackmail him. I suggested that to him, but he's brimming with hope that he can find his lost daughter."

I pointed out that the letter made no demands for money.

"Not yet. But my guess is that's yet to come. If that is the case, find that person and shut them down. Fast. The higher Archie's hope soars, the harder he falls."

"Lisa was a Ziegler patient," I said. "Are you familiar with his story?"

"Wasn't. Am now. All that does is grant credence to Archie's fervent search. Don't get me wrong. Nothing would make me happier than seeing him wrap his arms around a child he's never had the opportunity to know. It's just that . . . he's so excited. He's trying to temper his expectations, but they leak out."

I asked her what she could tell me about his children. She confirmed that both Abigail and Lester were adopted when he married his second wife. That Archie considered them his children and had always treated them as such. I explained that before charging ahead and looking for Little Strawberry, I wanted to protect my flank. See what, if anything, Archie's children knew and, more importantly, if they would create any problems for me.

"If I were you," she said, "I'd march right in and confront Abigail. She is what she appears to be. Lester, not so much."

"How's that?"

"He's secretive. Withdrawn." She pointed a finger in the air. "If I wanted to know Lester, I'd talk to those who know him."

"Any suggestions?"

"You might try my old haunt, although I've haven't been there in years."

"I don't follow."

"The Havana Club. Where Archie and I met. We have a party every year for current and ex-employees. I hear Lester is a heavy hitter there. The type who rents a table on a regular basis. Talk to the girls at the Havana Club. He has a favorite. Just be discreet." She gave me a flirtatious smile. "Take it from an ex-pro. Guys spill everything to near-naked woman they barely know."

And that's how I ended up in a strip club the next evening when I should have been at home reading bedtime stories to my girls. A man has to do what a man has to do.

CHAPTER 8

At nine forty-five the next morning, Bonita ushered the girls into her car and carted them off to some art class that I should have known more about. Kathleen blew a kiss as she whisked out the door to the college. Their twin departures vacuumed the house of noise. I had an appointment with Abigail at eleven and planned to investigate Lester at the Havana Club that evening. I wanted to make sure neither of Archie's two adopted children were inclined to sabotage my efforts to find Archie's daughter. With luck, one of them might even be of assistance, but I wasn't banking on that. I poured my third cup of coffee and settled behind my computer.

Dr. Wayne Ziegler had worked as an obstetrician in Saint Petersburg from the early 1970s to 1981. According to articles, he performed abortions prior to *Roe v. Wade*. He was also accused of coaxing women out of having abortions by exchanging money for their babies. He would arrange an adoption, pocketing unknown dollars for himself. For those couples who could not conceive and were unable to adopt, Dr. Ziegler was an answer to their prayers.

But age has a way of wearing on one's conscience, and

unanswered questions have a tendency to float to the surface. Women stepped forth with wild tales. *Yes, now that you mention it, we always wondered why it was so hard to adopt through normal channels and so easy through him. He told me my baby had died, but I swear I heard it.* Rumors gained traction. Had the doctor informed birth mothers that their child had died but then sold the baby to unsuspecting couples? As the questions flooded in the front door, Ziegler slipped out the back. He was last seen in Key West.

When DNA kicked in, brothers and sister were united. Parental linage established. But the victories were sparse, and each one came with a thousand defeats. Too much time had passed. Too little was known. Too many of the players had died.

Too many silent voices.

Then a woman named Heather Kirkland came forth over ten years ago. She maintained that Ziegler had told her that her baby was stillborn, despite her insistence that she'd heard the baby cry. She went on the warpath to find her little girl and expose Ziegler for the monster he was. She had been lucky, as the couple who adopted the child had always harbored suspicions about Ziegler. They had made as much of an effort to find Heather as Heather had made to find her daughter.

"He preyed on vulnerable and guilt-ridden girls," Kirkland said. "I was fifteen. My mom was stoned on even days and drunk on odd ones."

Kirkland found her daughter, and soon other victims of Ziegler stepped out of the shadows. Most were under eighteen when they delivered. Some as young as fourteen. Many came from broken homes and were steered to him by their parents. Days and weeks after delivery, when the haze lifted, many who were told their child was stillborn remembered hearing their baby cry. They claimed that Ziegler lied to them and sold their baby on the black market, though there was no proof of any such act.

That would be Archie's position.

Records were spotty. Lips were sealed. Years rolled by. People died. The whole affair looked like it could morph into a giant time drain, and I wasn't going to swirl around in that bowl. I decided I'd give it everything I had—for a few days. Unless I got a substantial lead on Archie's daughter, I'd graciously withdraw.

I called Heather Kirkland and asked if we could meet. We set up a time for the following day. I checked my phone. Time to scoot.

THE RECEPTIONIST IN THE lobby at Williams Pharmaceutical announced to someone that I was here, hung up, and informed me that Jonathan would be down to see me. Thirty minutes later, a man led me to the elevator that we rode to the third floor. He escorted me into a corner room with a large table in it.

"Take a seat," he instructed me.

"You don't need them anymore?"

"Really?" he said with a smirk and left the room, closing the door behind him.

Ten minutes later, I stood as Abigail marched into the room. A man with an earpiece followed behind her. He took a seat at the opposite end of the table. Abigail remained standing.

"Archie's looking for a lost daughter he thought was stillborn and now believes is alive," she said. Abigail was not one for the niceties of cultured conversation. "And he thinks you're his ticket. Do I have that right?"

"I'm doing it as a favor. Your father's college roommate, a man named Yankee—"

"I know all that. Did it ever occur to you that someone is trying to take advantage of a man with cancer? Shake him down for money?"

"There's been no request."

"Not yet."

"Bobbie Lee raised similar concerns."

"Really? I didn't realize that floozy had a brain."

"She voiced a similar assessment of you."

Abigail landed a cold stare.

"Can you at least pretend to help?" I said.

She puffed out her breath, then sat and leaned across the table. "Archie is a hopeless romantic," she said. "A man with a bear hug on the past. I wish him luck in his quixotic search, but there's nothing in which I can be of assistance."

"I understand that, if successful, he plans to alter his estate plan to include her."

"A most absurd thing. A person he never knew."

"You have little incentive to aid him in his search."

"What are you suggesting?"

"Nothing. I'm pointing out the obvious."

"It's his money to do with what he wishes. His fantasy doesn't concern me. I have a business to run."

I told her I'd read that Alpha Healthcare was interested in acquiring the company. Their founder and CEO, Julian Sensenbrenner, had skirted criminal charges for years. Bilking Medicare and Medicaid. Archie, according to the article, was not in favor of the transaction. I wondered, at the time, if that had been the point of contention when I'd interrupted them the first night at Archie's house.

"That is an issue between Archie and me," Abagail said.

"What if I find his daughter and she gets a vote?"

She snorted. "That will never happen. Archie's assured me she would never be entitled to vote. Are we finished?"

"Is there anything you can recall that might aid me in finding your father's lost daughter?"

"No."

"Anything, any person who might have struck you as odd? Something from his past?"

"No."

"Have you ever heard of the Little Strawberry?"

"You peddling fruit now? I have a busy day. If, for some inexplicable reason or twist of fate, I come across information regarding Archie's lost daughter, I will share it directly with Archie."

She stood. I did not.

"I'm sure your father will appreciate that," I said.

"He raised me," Abigail said defiantly. "He is not my father."

"Then I should double my efforts."

"Why is that?"

"The man deserves a daughter."

She marched out of the room as if she'd already forgotten who I was.

CHAPTER 9

At six thirty in the evening, I stepped inside the Havana Club in downtown Saint Petersburg. According to Bobbie Lee, who had made a phone call on my behalf, Lester Williams would be at the Havana Club that night. He arrived at seven and was gone by eight.

I'd checked Abigail off my list. She would neither help nor hinder me. I didn't see her as a threat to sabotage her father's—excuse me, Archie's—quest. I accepted her at face value. Her life was business, and annoying peripheral items held no interest for her.

The Havana Club was a classy joint in a sleazy business. Tops never came off. Not that it mattered; in this case, thread count meant you could literally count the threads. There was no touching. You paid for dances. More for a girl to sit at your table for a few minutes. Cash only. A beautiful woman, who, if only for a moment and a Franklin, made a man feel good about himself. A woman whose eyes never left him. A woman in whom he could see whatever he desired to see. His dreams. His soaring ambitions and dark fantasies. But do not touch, for she is not real.

I paid the twenty-dollar cover to an old man on a backless stool who looked like a permanent fixture. He instructed me to "Enjoy the show."

"Just one?" the woman behind the counter said when I presented myself at the hostess station.

"Just me. How about that table over there?" I pointed toward a table in the back where I could observe the stage. I also didn't want Lester to spot me when he came in.

"I can get you closer," she demurred in a tone that suggested more confidence than she had. Her bulging Botox lips were glossy and moist. If she floated on her back, they'd be the last thing to sink. Can lips have a US Coast Guard flotation rating?

"That table will be fine," I said.

A waitress named Chanel introduced herself. I ordered a bourbon on the rocks. The lighting was subdued but not dark. A single pole ran down the center of the stage, which had mirrors on three sides. A woman wrapped herself around the pole. A posse of young men had gathered at her feet, drinks and cigars cluttering the tables. They wore suits and shiny shoes. Corporate warriors. Opposite me on the far side of the room was a circular platform with a pole in the middle and empty stools surrounding it. The walls were decorated with pictures of Havana. Hemingway was in one, smiling away in his seat at the El Floridita, his tenth daiquiri of the day nestled in his hand. He looked happy. He was less than ten years from blowing his brains out with a side-by-side shotgun.

Lester Williams strolled in at 7:05 p.m. I adjusted my seat so that he didn't have a clear view of me. He claimed one of the stools that surrounded the small stage, took a placard off it, and sat down. Unsolicited, a waitress brought him a drink. Ten minutes later, a woman climbed onto the round stage in front of Lester. She slithered around the pole a few times before plopping on Lester's lap. They talked. Laughed. The rest of the vacant stools also had placards on them. Lester paid to reserve the other seats so that he had a private show.

After a few minutes, the woman left. Lester stood and strolled over to a corner booth. The waitress who had served him approached the circular stage he'd just vacated. She lifted all the placards off the other stools. They were no longer reserved. Lester came in at the same time, took the same seat, and talked to the same girl. Although it had been my intention to question him, I called an audible and changed my plan for that evening.

The woman who had danced for him slid into his booth. She had changed into a slinky dress. They sat there like high school lovers, side by side, barely enough room between them to hold the air they needed to breathe. She dipped her head when he spoke. He kept his hands folded in front of him. I pretended to be looking at my phone and took a couple of pictures, something I knew was frowned upon in such establishments. They talked for twenty minutes. He slid her a wad of bills. She snuck in a peck on his left cheek, stood, and walked away.

Lester sat there for a few mindless minutes before ambling out the door. Home to his wife. His three children. His life that, on some level, left him deeply unfulfilled. Maybe he should get a dog.

I dropped some bills on the table and went outside to the warm, moonless night. The Havana Club had a rear door. I assumed the woman who Lester had cuddled with would exit through it, as I'd not seen any employees use the front door. I positioned my truck on a side street so as to view the door and still keep an eye on the front of the club. I hoped she wouldn't keep me waiting.

Fifty-eight minutes later, she walked out the door. At least I think she did. She was no longer a blonde but had short black hair. She had a spring in her step as she took the corner and headed west on Fifth Avenue. She must live in the area. I jumped out of the truck and caught up with her at an intersection where she was waiting for a walk signal.

"I wonder if we could talk about Lester Williams," I said.

She shuddered. "Jesus, you startled me. Who?"

"Lester. The man you reserve a seat for. Who you talked to in the booth."

"Don't know who you're talking about."

I pulled out my phone and brought up the picture. I showed it to her. "This guy."

The light signaled that we could cross, but she made no movement. I didn't want to come across as threatening and was glad that there were other people strolling the streets.

She glanced at the phone and then at me. "What kind of dirtball takes pictures in there? What do you want?"

I rushed out that I'd been asked by Lester's father to locate a missing daughter. I wasn't worried about her squealing to Lester. He would not want his weekly rendezvous to become public. I stuck my phone in my pocket and introduced myself. "Can I buy you a cup of coffee?" I spread my hands. "Anyplace you want. Bright and crowded."

Her face scrunched in concern. "He told me that his father was looking for a lost daughter. Why not approach him directly?"

"I've been advised that it might be best to learn a little about Lester first. I was informed that his situation is delicate."

"I don't know how I can help. Or why I would want to."

"Maybe you can; maybe you can't. I'd just like a few minutes."

"What's in it for me?"

"A hundred."

"You haven't answered why."

"Thought I just did."

"I'm not taking money to squeal."

"And I'm not asking you to. My interest is solely in finding his father's daughter."

"I pick the place."

"I pick up the tab."

"Thirty minutes. I got to get home."

"Deal. What's your name?"

"Really? My name?"

I spread my hands.

"What's the name of the first girl who ever wobbled your knees?" she said.

It took me a second. "April."

"You can call me April."

CHAPTER 10

April and I sat next to each other at a bar in an Italian restaurant a block off Central Avenue. The bartender inquired if we wanted menus. I said no. April said yes.

"I'm always famished after work," she said. "I barely eat during the day. Trust me, you don't want to pig out on spaghetti, put on a thong and then try to convince men you're masturbating on a cold pole while what you're really doing is pinching your cheeks so you don't fart."

"I'm going to take your word on that."

"You're down to twenty-nine minutes."

April ordered a salmon salad and a glass of red wine. She downed her water before the salad came and asked for a refill.

"How long has Lester been seeing you?"

"First of all, when we met, he was Michael."

"Michael?"

"You don't get out much, do you?"

"Married. Two girls. A cat."

"No dog?"

"Not yet."

"Everyone has a dog."

"Do you?"

"Duh."

"Apparently one is in my future."

"You never do real names. Men come to escape. They check their name at the door."

I asked her when Michael became Lester.

"You mean when did we break the wall?"

"Is that what you call it?"

"Call it whatever you want. Year ago, maybe? He'd been a regular for about six months. One night, he spilled it all. Name. Family. Business. The whole kit and caboodle."

"What do you discuss?"

"Tell me again how this has anything to do with his father finding a lost daughter?"

"I never told you in the first place."

She cracked a smile. "I know."

"I might talk to Lester. I thought a little background material—"

"Yeah, I get that. But you can't say anything came from me. You got that?"

"Understood."

"I'm serious."

"As am I."

"How did you know he'd be here?"

When you spin a story, you can't anticipate everything. April came in as I was formulating a reply. "She knew, didn't she?"

"She?"

"You know who. Lester said his dad married a dancer who used to work at the Havana years ago. She still knows some of the girls. What's her name? Some southern thingy. Though I don't think she started with that name."

The bartender topped off her water glass. "Thank you." She

squirmed on her stool so that she faced me. She rubbed her knees together.

"They come to forget about life for a while," she said. "Like the song 'Piano Man.' They see everything they ever wanted. What they believe they deserve and will solve all their problems. All of life's answers in a curve of a neck. The slope of a breast. The soft valley of a stomach. They sip their watered-down drinks and envision long legs rising up on either side of them while they pound away at their dream.

"Lester asked if he could reserve the stools, you know, that surround the small stage. The manager, Lydia—Christ on a stick, she'd go ballistic if she ever found out you took pictures—said no way. Those stools are money. Lester paid up. He rents all those stools every Thursday for one hour. I dance for him. We relocate to the booth. We talk. He leaves. I'm his therapist."

"Why does he need a therapist?"

"Because he's a human being?"

"Can you narrow it down?"

Her salmon salad came. She laid waste to it.

"When I give up the pole gig," she said when she came up for air, "I'm going back to cheeseburgers. I work admissions at UCF, but my husband split, and I got a daughter to support and a mortgage. The pole brings me an unreported fifteen hundred a week. My mom sits for free."

"I wasn't asking."

"Sure you were. Everyone wants to know. You, with your wife, two kids, cat, and dog yet to be and the rest of the world are just too polite to ask. Lester's a big part of that dough. Understand?"

"He'll never know we met."

"He might have been interested in my belly button when he first came in, but that's not what brought him back. We talk."

"About?"

"He's got sister issues. From what he says, she's a real Cruella de Vil."

"Abigail?"

She looked at me as if registering me for the first time. Her eyes were tired. It was the end of a long day, and I felt bad keeping her out.

"Yeah," she said. "Funny, I just always assumed he made her name up. She's soulless."

It was my turn to sit a little higher. Maybe I should not have written Abigail off so casually. "Did he expound on that?"

"He said she never liked their father, despite him adopting her and Lester and treating them like gold. Lester considers him to be his dad. She does not. They have no contact with their—you know, biological father."

"What does he tell you about the business?"

"We don't talk much about it. He comes to forget about life, not relive it, remember?"

We were quiet for a moment. A couple entered, considered the empty stools next to me but opted for a booth.

April flicked her eyes up at the bartender. "I'm finished. Thank you."

The bartender swept away her plate. I inquired if Lester said anything else about his sister.

"Like I said, he and his sister were adopted. He likes Archie. That's who he calls his father. His sister is seven years older. Different story with her. She was ten when her mom married Archie. She rebelled. Lester said Archie moved heaven and earth for her. Couldn't ask for a better man."

"Did Lester discuss any issues at work?"

"We covered that."

"Just making sure."

"Give it up."

"Did he ever mention that his father was searching for a lost daughter?"

"Just recently, he said his dad—that's what he calls Archie, says his sister gets pissed when he calls him that in her presence. Anyway, he said his dad told them he was hunting for a daughter he had long ago. He thought she was dead but apparently got some notice or letter that she might be alive. Pretty weird, right? I mean, either she's dead or not."

I asked if Lester ever mentioned the name Little Strawberry.

"No."

"What else did Lester say about Archie's quest?"

"Not much. He wants to help him, you know, search, but sister Abigail told him to drop it. Thinks the whole thing just distracts them from business. He put it out of his mind."

"Why's he so submissive to her?"

She stared at the amber bottles behind the bar. Age was just starting to creep into the corners of her eyes, the edges of her red lips. She turned to me. "I'm telling you only because I care for Lester. You understand? I mean, I take his money, but . . ."

"But?"

"It just can't always be about money. And I'm not taking any of yours. Got it?"

"Got it."

She twirled her hair. "She owns him."

"How do you—?"

"Abigail set him up with a hooker when he was fourteen."

I nodded as if I understood because that's what we do when we don't understand.

"Despite my 'Piano Man' comment," April explained, "the regulars never bring anything light into the club. They haul in the heavy baggage. Their personal problems. Their disappointments. Their one shot of glory they missed, as if telling a nearly naked girl will bring it back.

"Want my take on the whole mess? From that day forth, he's been trying to figure out the world." She puffed out a breath that lifted her bangs. "Eating salmon is like chewing air. Somewhere in the world, someone's having french fries."

We made idle chitchat for a few more minutes, but she had nothing else to help my cause. As we got ready to leave, she said, "It's stories like theirs that keep the lights on."

"Excuse me?"

"Lester's dad coming in and leaving with a girl. That's every dancer's dream. Every man's fantasy who walks through the door. Almost be better for both parties if it never happened. Who needs that shit, right?"

Did April see Lester as her knight on a white horse? Was she his Guinevere?

"It's not a bad drug, is it?" I said. "A guy gets a woman to talk to. The woman gets money."

April looked at me with sadness in her eyes. "It's still a drug. It wears off. Both sides vow to quit, but you can't."

"You know what I think?"

"What?"

"You're supporting your little girl. You're a great mom."

She gave a solemn shake of her head. "You just proved my point. Men see what they want to see. You don't even know my name. Go home, dog-man. Go home."

You'll be the final judge, but I've often wondered if it would have been best if I'd never met April.

CHAPTER 11

The following morning, I set out to see Heather Kirkland, the woman who had exposed Ziegler for telling her that her baby was stillborn and had managed to reunite with her daughter decades later.

Heather lived in a tidy tree-lined neighborhood fifteen minutes north of me. She invited me in, offered me coffee, and said I better like rocket fuel because she didn't have cream or milk. On the way to her house, I decided that neither of Archie's two adopted children would likely sabotage his efforts. Abigail was consumed by the business, and Lester, per April, had true affection for the man who had adopted him and whom he called Father. I wouldn't waste my time with him.

We settled in a room crowded with pictures of wildlife but no people. I'd just finished explaining why I was there. That I was looking for a woman, a Ziegler baby who was born to Lisa Trowbridge nearly fifty years before. That I had reason to believe Ziegler sold the baby. That the father, whose health was failing, dearly wanted to know if he had a daughter.

Heather sat upright in a chair that was too large for her. A thin gold necklace hung low on her blue blouse. It had a small stain on it, and I wondered if it was something she'd tried to get out or was unaware of.

"He was an ugly man," she said. "I was indecisive as to whether I wanted my baby or not. He told me a child was a wonderful thing and encouraged me to have it. He paid for my room at the clinic. The day I delivered, he told me the baby was in danger. He drugged me. Then he told me my baby was stillborn. But she wasn't. What he did was wrong. Preying on girls like me. That's why I stood up.

"Thing is? It took the woman who adopted her to make it happen. How many women are going to be suspicious of how easy it was to get a baby from Ziegler, let alone step forth decades later? I was lucky. DNA test proved positive. We talk, my daughter and I, maybe a couple of times a month, but nothing can bring back lost years."

I asked her if Ziegler had an assistant.

"He did. A fat woman named Belle, with an *e* at the end of it."

She'd punched out the word *fat* as if it were poisonous. I asked her to tell me about Belle.

She shrugged. "Pretended to be nice but looked right through you like you weren't there. That's what I remember. She never saw me as a person. Took me a long time to come to terms with that. She had a son, too. At least, I got the impression he was her son. Little man with shifty eyes and a pencil-thin mustache."

"You spearheaded the effort to expose Ziegler," I said. "You're to be commended for that."

"Thank you. But they never caught that scumbag, and that rattles me."

"Are there any names, contacts you can direct me to?"

"What year did this happen?"

I told her.

She let out a low whistle. "Time marches on, doesn't it? I

heard Belle died years ago. By its nature, Ziegler's operation was not one to include a lot of people. I don't think it would have been to his advantage to keep meticulous records."

"Perhaps a name or place you overheard?"

"Have you dropped by the source yet?"

"The source?"

"The Cardinal Inn on Twenty-Second North. He operated his clinic there. In the back. Had its own entrance."

"I'm sure it's changed hands by now." But as I spoke those words, I chastised myself for not considering it.

"Don't be so confident. I believe the same family owns it. Seedy place then. Little less seedy now."

"Do you think they knew what was happening under their roof?" The question wasn't even half out of my mouth when I realized the answer.

"How could they not? I do have a name for you. Jenna Cappabianca. She's been cutting her own path from the other side."

"How so?"

"She adopted a Ziegler baby but had her doubts," Heather explained. "Jenna tracked down the birth mother and introduced her son to his mother. After that, she went on a crusade. Started looking for others and keeping a database. Lot of people give me credit for exposing Ziegler, but she's done the heavy lifting. You need to give her a call. She's the one in the trenches."

Our conversation hit a dead end. I thanked her for her time and promised to keep in touch. Ten minutes later, I pulled into the parking lot of the Cardinal Inn, a two-story motel that had just received a fresh coat of yellow paint. But that didn't hide the sagging gutters, the sun-blanched parking lot, and the neon sign suspended in purgatory, somewhere between classic art deco and sad neglect.

CHAPTER 12

The young woman sitting behind the counter had blue hair on the right side, pink on the left, and a streak of black down the middle. I'd just told her I was looking for anyone who might have recollections of Dr. Ziegler. And yes, I realized it was long ago. Her phone rested in front of her. She kept glancing at it.

"We don't disclose who's staying in the motel," she said.

"He's not a customer," I explained. "He worked out of the motel performing abortions."

"At a motel? Yuck."

"I understand the motel has been owned by the same family for generations. Are any of them here?"

She flicked her eyes to her phone. "Any of who?"

"The owners. Your boss."

Staring at the phone.

"Hello?" I said.

She looked up, irritated that I was still there. "You need to talk to Charlene. She owns the place."

"Is Charlene here?"

"Sure."

"Where might I find her?"

"Doing laundry."

"And where might that be?"

She tilted her head and cut me a sassy smile. "Maybe the laundry room?"

"Imagine that."

She looked down at her phone. "What's a five-letter word that begins and ends with *d*?"

"Dread."

She typed on her phone. Her eyes shot up to mine. "Go outside. Take a right. End of the building. He really do that? Abortions in a motel room?"

"He did."

"Yuck."

The laundry room was open. A woman was stuffing sheets into a commercial dryer.

"Charlene?" I said.

She looked up. "Yes?"

I gave her my spiel, which I was already tiring of hearing. As I prattled on, I wondered if I could cut out of the gig early. Tell Archie I was not the man for the job. Some cock-and-bull story about his interests being better served by engaging someone else. But Yankee Conrad had asked me as a favor. I gave myself a mental slap.

"That was long ago," she said, echoing words I would grow sick of hearing. She wore tight jeans, red tennis shoes, and a Jimmy Buffett "Summerzcool" T-shirt. "My grandfather owned the motel then. Died standing in his office. Or sitting. Does it matter? He's long gone, and so is Ziegler."

"I know it's a wild-goose chase," I said, giving her my best aw-shucks voice. "But I promised this man I'd do what I could. He was told his daughter was stillborn and now has reason to believe she was one of the babies Ziegler sold."

"I don't need that publicity."

"And it's the last thing you'll get from me."

"What's the birth mother say?"

"She died not long after giving birth."

She tossed a sheet on a wood table. "You can't wash them forever. Sooner or later, you got to get new ones. Listen, Mr. —"

"Jake Travis."

"Listen, Mr. Jake Travis, I'm the third generation to own and operate the Cardinal Inn. I run a clean motel. No hourly rates. I keep my prices high enough to ward off the druggies and low enough to be competitive."

I complimented her on the exterior paint job.

"Thank you."

"I'd love just a few minutes of your time."

She pushed out her breath. "Fine. Come into my office."

She took three steps to her right, opened a door, and entered a small room with a wood desk under a window. "Have a seat."

I searched around for what she was referring to.

"Go ahead and place that stuff on the floor. I'm looking at new drapes. Ugly ones are cheap; pretty ones are expensive. What a racket. Like it costs more money to make something pretty."

I picked up a bundle of fabric that had been camouflaging a chair. I placed it carefully on the floor so as not to disrupt the order. Charlene reached into a metal file cabinet and struggled with some files. She extracted a worn manila folder and handed it to me. Radio Margaritaville played over a speaker behind her desk.

"Here you go. Everything I got about the infamous Dr. Ziegler. You know he was never caught, right? Slipped out of here over forty years ago, and no one's seen him since."

"I'm looking for any records he might have kept." I held up the folder. "Anything like that in here?"

"Nope. That's police stuff. They never charged him with anything."

I opened the folder. It appeared to be mundane reports. I decided to get a copy from a friend, Detective Dennis Rambler. I didn't want to assume what I held in my hands was the complete report on Ziegler.

"You've been here your whole life?" I said, circling back to her comment that she was third generation.

"I have. We do everything ourselves, except the yard work. Grandpa hired it out to a young man who did it until he was an old man. I got a service that does it now. Got someone to do laundry, but she's off today."

I asked if she'd heard any stories or rumors growing up.

"No. We tried to distance ourselves from our past, not embrace it. Pity, really. It's a nice piece of property with a good history. That asterisk mark hurts. I don't like it crowding out everything else."

"Did your grandfather know what was going on?"

"One can assume. I know you're supposed to like your family and all, but if you got some bad apples, you got to call it like you see it. You don't choose your family."

I asked her what she knew about the layout of Ziegler's clinic.

"At that time, we had three rooms that you entered from the back. He took all three and operated his clinic there. They had connecting doors. Only one door led into this office. That was so he wouldn't disturb the rest of the guests. We've reconfigured it since then. It's nothing like it used to be."

"I understand he had an accomplice. A woman named Belle."

She leaned forward. "She's gone, too. But her son lives—or did at one time—not far from here. He used to come around asking questions about the Ziegler babies."

"Do you have his name? Where he might be now?"

"You're a real question machine. Nathan someone. Lemme see that."

I handed her the manila folder. She flipped through it.

"Naw. Hoped it might be here, but no one thought to ask about Ziegler's assistant's maybe son. Whiting. That's his last name. Funny, I don't recall that being Belle's last name. Seems to me there was some question as to whether he was her son or not. He's got to be pushing seventy by now. Only person I know from that time who might still be kicking."

"Any idea of where I can find him?"

She humped her shoulders. "He lived in his mother's house, which was close by."

"Got an address?"

"First house on the right when you turn onto Oak Street. But don't get too excited. He sold it long ago, and no, I don't know where he moved."

I gave her my card and thanked her for her time. I jumped in my truck and navigated to the first house on the right after turning onto Oak Street.

CHAPTER 13

"Nathan Whiting?" I said, although I knew the man in front of me was not Nathan Whiting. I'd come up behind him as he trimmed a hibiscus bush. He ceased his work, turned, and eyed me from under a wide-brimmed hat that needed to be retired.

"He doesn't live here anymore. Hasn't for going on twenty years."

"Do you know where I can find him?"

He lowered the cutters and took two steps toward me. "Why are you asking?"

"I want to talk to him about his mother's job at the Cardinal Inn. It's just around the corner."

"I know where the Cardinal Inn is."

I went on to explain that I'd just come from there. I tacked on that I apologized for intruding and didn't wish to take up any more of his time. My hedge trimmer took off his hat and wiped his brow. He squinted in the sun, an orange blob of heat, and put the hat back on his head.

"When I bought the house, he claimed he came into some money—his mom died or something like that—and always wanted to live on Treasure Island. Said he always liked the name when he was a kid, and that was his dream. Nice fellow. A little off, if you know what I mean. Sorry. That's all I know."

I climbed back into my truck, hit the ignition button, punched it into gear, and navigated to Treasure Island. I was on track to talk to every person in Tampa Bay. I couldn't keep up that pace for very long.

CHAPTER 14

Like much of the land that Ponce de Leon beached on after dropping anchor in 1513, the name Treasure Island was invented to promote and sell real estate. The developer buried wooden chests in his strip of sand, pretended to discover them, and voilà, the gullible flocked forth with open wallets. They started calling it Treasure Island. The toe of sand I live on is slightly less underhanded. Its current name translates to Vineyard by the Sea. Because Florida is wine country, right? Its predevelopment name was Mud Island, and it is still labeled that on nautical maps.

It wasn't hard to do a property search and find a Nathan Whiting who lived in the area. His characterless, single-story block home was on a canal. A car sat in the driveway, but no one answered when I repeatedly rang the doorbell. I peered through a side window into a cluttered garage. No wonder the car was outside. I opened the fence and marched around to the backyard. It wasn't easy. A large hibiscus bush not only crowded his house but also made it difficult for the neighbor to even walk around their house.

A man sat in a weather-peroxided center-console fishing

boat on a lift. He eyed me as I crossed his property, rising to his feet when I stepped onto the dock. He didn't rise far, for he was a short man. His ears looked like twin radar disks sticking out of his head. He had a timid mustache, which, considering his age, was more an embarrassment than an asset. I introduced myself and told him I had tried the front door and was hoping I'd find him in the back.

"This is private property," he said. His fingers were long and bony and held fishing line. An open tackle box rested on the floor of his boat.

"I apologize for trespassing. Are you Nathan Whiting?"

I thought I saw a flash of fear in his eyes. But his shadowed face was hard to read under his tattered Rays baseball cap.

"Maybe. What can I do for you?"

Maybe.

I explained what I was there for. That I was looking for a man's daughter who I had reason to believe was a Ziegler baby. That's about as far as I got before, shadowed or not, his face darkened and his eyes narrowed.

"I don't know anything about that. Can't help you."

"The birth mother's name was Lisa Trowbridge. Is that familiar to you?"

"No."

"I understand your mother—"

"She's been gone a long time, and I won't tolerate any bad language about her, understand?"

I spread open my hands. "I'm not criticizing anybody. I'm just looking for a dying man's daughter."

"And I'm just cleaning out my tackle box. Sorry I can't be of help."

"Do you know if your mother or Dr. Ziegler kept records? Names?"

"I told you I don't know anything about any of that. Never knew the man. Never met him."

"You never met him?"

"You heard me."

"Your mother worked for him."

"Yeah? That was her life. I had my own. Always have. Sorry I can't help you."

He seemed eager to disassociate himself from the Ziegler babies. I can't blame him, but that didn't explain his nervousness. His jitters. I took a different tack.

"I'm not looking to dredge anything up. I'm just trying to reunite a man with his daughter. Anything you saw or heard would be helpful."

"Didn't see or hear nothing."

"Ever hear the name Little Strawberry?"

He rolled his tongue in his mouth. "Wish I could help you," he said in a tone that indicated he couldn't care less if he helped me. "But my mother never talked about what she did at work. My mother was innocent. Her job was to deliver babies, and she was good at it."

"It's what happened to the babies after they were delivered that interests me."

"I've answered your questions."

"And I appreciate your help. Do you know of—?"

"You can get off my property now."

"Of anyone who—"

"I said, get off my property."

I handed him my card. "If you think of anything."

Without taking his eyes off me, he flipped my card into the water.

CHAPTER 15

I was beat. Flogged. I needed to get off the hamster wheel.

I pulled into the Drunken Clam and grabbed a stool, half in the restaurant and half out. I knew the waiter, as he used to work at the pink hotel. We chatted about the twin hurricanes and how they had disrupted people's lives longer than you could anticipate. I ordered a hand-pattied beach burger, fries, and iced tea. No clams. The burger was swell, the fries were hot, and the waiter refilled my iced tea without me having to ask. I closed my eyes, inhaled the salt air, and emptied my mind of the morning carousel of characters I'd met.

After the last bite of the burger, I dialed back in.

First up was Jenna Cappabianca, who Heather Kirkland had told me about. She was easy to find when searching under Ziegler babies. As Heather had mentioned, Jenna appeared to be thick in the mire of solving Ziegler baby mysteries. I messaged her, then opened my notes app and dictated what I knew.

—Abigail, frightening but harmless. Buried in business.

—Lester, good son. Would not act counter to his father's interests.

—Heather Kirkland, initially broke open Ziegler baby case, told me to seek Jenna Cappabianca.

—Jenna Cappabianca, waiting for reply.

—Charlene, runs motel now. Eager to distance herself from past.

—Nathan Whiting, lying little twerp. No way does he not know more.

—Drunken Clam, better than I remembered.

—Dog, I'll be the one cleaning up its crap for the next fifteen years, and don't you doubt it. Be firm or suffer the consequences.

I studied my list with swelling pride. Here's a tip: Make a list. It's a great way to fool yourself into thinking you've accomplished something.

I scrolled through my phone, reading more about Ziegler. The police had investigated him but never brought charges. Without a crime to pursue, all they could do is kick dirt and ask questions. The lead detective was a man named Josh Arnelli. I looked him up. Retired. I called my friend, Detective Rambler.

"I need a favor," I said when he picked up on the second ring.

"No."

"Won't take but a minute."

"Do you ever sense our relationship is one-way?"

"Think of all the goodwill you're sandbagging."

"You can't eat goodwill. Please don't tell me you have a body."

I had the habit of seeking his help when someone was murdered, and, for reasons we don't have time for, I was involved.

"Not yet," I quipped. "But the day's young."

"Let's hear it."

I explained that I was looking into the Ziegler babies. That I wanted to talk to the detective who handled the investigation, and would he call Josh Arnelli and grease the rails for me?

"I know him," he said with unexpected enthusiasm. "Good man. Old school. Give me a minute."

Rambler called back five minutes later.

"He's at Home Depot carping about the price of garden hoses. He's free after that and said to text him. I'll send you his contact information."

"I appreciate it," I said as I stuck a crispy french fry in my mouth.

"How's the family?" he asked.

"They want a dog."

"And you don't?"

"Not wild about it."

"My wife came home with some little poodle concoction couple of weeks ago. Didn't even ask me."

"I'm sorry to hear that."

"Thing is? I like the little guy. Ralphie. Dogs don't have past and future. No baggage. They're flippin' happy every minute. You ought to see him when I walk through the door. So excited he literally pisses on the floor. Want some advice?"

"I'm not feeling it."

"Don't fight it. It just makes you look stupid. Give my best to Arnelli."

He hung up.

I took a final drink of iced tea and swirled an ice cube around in my mouth before cracking it with my teeth. I slipped off my stool and skipped to my truck. I didn't really skip, but I had a spring in my step. At the rate I was moving, either I would find Little Strawberry soon or I would exhaust all the players. Either way, I was not going to sacrifice endless days to Archie's infatuation with his past and his ceaseless desire to find a daughter, who, for all anyone knew, even if she were alive, didn't want to be found. Did he even consider that?

CHAPTER 16

Detective Arnelli and I met at the Bay Pine location of Doc Ford's Rum Bar. We dragged back adjoining barstools overlooking an inlet off Long Bayou. A great white egret executed a masterly landing on the edge of the water. I asked Arnelli if he came there often, as it had been his choice.

"I sit over there." He dipped his head toward a table of three men. "We bitch about our doctor appointments and solve the world's problems."

"How's that last part going?"

"Can't get anyone to listen to us," he said.

"If only."

"You got it."

I thanked him for carving time out of his doctor-juggling, world-problem-solving conference. He was a jovial man and seemed unlikely to have been a detective. He wore baggy cargo shorts and a fatigued Tommy Bahama T-shirt—something about a daily workout with a corkscrew. His eyebrows were a FEMA disaster zone and made me think of the man whacking hedges at Whiting's former residence.

"Rambler said you're digging around the Ziegler babies," he said. "That's a few miles ago. Why the interest now?"

At least he didn't say "a long time ago." I explained to Arnelli what led us to be sitting next to each other on a triumphant Florida afternoon.

"What can you add?" I tacked on when I'd finished.

He put down his Hammerhead beer. I took a gulp of iced tea. I'd wrestled with alcohol once and now rarely touched it before five. Since I'm passing out tips, here's another one: You will not win every battle, but know which ones you cannot afford to lose.

"I'd just started on the force," Arnelli said. "You know there were never any charges filed, right? We knew funny business was going on at the Cardinal Inn, but we investigate crimes, not comedy clubs. There was no evidence that any law was being broken. Rumors and innuendoes don't count.

"Then Heather Kirkland came forth," Arnelli continued. "Accused Ziegler of telling her that her child was stillborn when it was not. That was what—close to fifteen years ago? Since I retired, the years no longer carry numbers. We looked into it. But Ziegler had long vanished. We tracked him to Key West, a second floor rental on Waddell. That's where the lead went cold."

"I ran into Nathan Whiting today. Belle's son."

"Belle, she was Ziegler's assistant?"

"Correct."

"I don't think that was her real name."

"Do you recall what it was?"

"Sorry. Nor do I recall her having a son. Was he involved?"

Arnelli delivered his last question in a cautious tone, afraid he had missed something in his investigation.

"Claims he wasn't. He denied knowing anything or even meeting Ziegler."

"His mother, Belle, was the good doctor's right hand. Now

that I think about it, I seem to remember she had a teenage son. I don't think we ever had any reason to question him."

"What about the owner of the Cardinal Inn? Charles Buford."

He cast a frown at his beer. "You're familiar with it, right? Two—maybe it was three—rooms in the rear had doors to the back parking lot. Motel guests wouldn't see him or the patients come and go. But Buford maintained he didn't get involved in his customers' business. Said Ziegler paid on time, and that was all he cared about."

"No complaints?"

"You got to remember," he said, taking offense to my statement, which was not intended to be judgmental. "Ziegler also had happy patients and clients. People who wanted to adopt and found their rainbow pot because of him. Also, no security cameras back then. Buford denied ever hearing a baby cry that Ziegler later claimed as being stillborn. Then he died."

"Buford?" I recalled Charlene telling me that.

"Heart attack. Hit the floor one day." He took a swig of his beer. "That was the end of questioning him. The whole thing stank like roadkill you couldn't see."

I asked him if there was anyone I should be talking to. He indicated he couldn't think of anyone. That it was possible, even probable, that he'd talked to other characters, but if so, those names had long deserted him.

He drained his beer and raised a finger. The bartender switched out drinks for him.

"Two a day's my limit," he said as if he owed me an explanation. He dipped his head at my iced tea. "You making me feel bad?"

"Just holding off till after five."

"I hear you. It bugs me. All that going on right under our noses. But the perps, Ziegler and his assistant, Belle, are gone. Win some, lose the rest." He took a long pull of his frothy beer.

"This daughter you're looking for—did you ever find her mother?"

"She was the victim of a hit-and-run a few months after she gave birth." I'd told him as much when I gave my synopsis earlier. Perhaps he'd forgotten.

"That's right. You told me that." His eyes wandered out over the water. He stared straight ahead as if the past was staring back at him. "That bugged me. Still bugs me."

"What's that?"

He turned to face me. "We tried contacting the birth mothers; they were, after all, the best source to bring charges against Ziegler. But a lot of them had died within a year of giving birth. More like three to four months."

"Complications from giving birth?"

"They had the bad habit of stepping into speeding cars."

We were both quiet for a beat.

"That's not really a habit, is it?" I pointed out.

"No, it is not. And that's what thirty years on the beat will do to you. Making light of tragedy."

"Think they were related?"

"Who knows? We never had the resources to follow up. Oh, we questioned a few people, let the press know we had suspicions in hopes of getting a tip, but bigger cases came in faster than we could solve them."

I wondered what could be bigger than multiple dead women, but I swallowed the question. Instead, I went with, "What did your gut tell you?"

He waited a beat before answering. "I don't really recall. It's been a few days."

I didn't question his sudden amnesia. He grew sullen and seemed more interested in playing with his beer than drinking it. I thanked him for his time and handed him my card. When I walked out, he had settled back into the sanctuary of friends, tackling the world's problems while juggling doctor appointments in an effort to squeeze a few more quality years out of his body. Maybe I will go back to drinking before five.

I got in my truck but left the door open to allow the heat to escape. I checked my watch. I'd told Kathleen I'd be home around five. She had office hours at the college until five thirty. Bonita had to scoot by five. I still had time for my next two appointments. It would be a lot for one day, but I was determined to run this thing hard and then, success or not, retire from the field of battle.

I was about to close the door when Arnelli came huffing up to the side of the truck. "Forget something?" I said.

He placed a hand on my door and took a moment to gather his breath. "The hit-and-runs," he said. "The birth mothers being gunned down. We boggled it. We didn't look hard enough. There's something's there. No way they're not connected."

He turned and sulked away, his shoulders burdened and slumped with the weight and misgivings of the past. I wished he hadn't told me what he had just said. I pretended to believe it meant nothing, but I knew it changed everything.

CHAPTER 17

Arnelli's closing remarks were torturing my mind when I pulled into Theresa Bond's driveway. Traffic had been thicker than I anticipated, and I was already regretting my decision to create such a marathon day. What was I thinking? Too late now.

Theresa was Archie's second wife and Abigail and Lester's mother. I'd called and explained that I'd been retained by Archie and would appreciate a few minutes of her time. She'd protested, stating that she hadn't seen Archie since "What was that show—you know, with the bartender with the head of hair? *Cheers*." I'd assured her I would only be a few minutes. She assured me that was all she'd grant.

I wasn't certain why I thought she could help. But when you're looking for clues, you start by casting a wide net. Maybe Archie said something to her about Lisa. Mentioned Little Strawberry. Perhaps he'd told her things he'd since forgotten. Someone wrote Archie the letter. I needed to find that person.

As I knocked on the red metal door, I considered that Archie was a dysfunctional romantic. He was grasping at the past and dragging me along for the ride. Did the cancer spur his quest, or, as he claimed, was it the anonymous letter he had received? What if he snapped out of it? Called me off and confessed he didn't know what came over him, but he didn't care anymore? I didn't see that happening. Archie impressed me as a sincere man who sought redemption for his heart. Who wanted to know his daughter because who wouldn't want to know their daughter? But even if Archie did toss in the towel, Arnelli's comment about multiple murders had taken root in my mind.

The door opened. Theresa Bond said, "I told you I don't know how I could possibly help you. We've been separated for decades."

"Pleasure meeting you, ma'am," I shot back with more bite than intended.

"You understand what I said?"

"I do."

"No. You do not. Why do people say that?"

She turned and walked into her Lakewood Ranch home. "Have a seat," she said over her shoulder. She fluttered her hand to indicate she couldn't care less where I sat.

I flirted with the idea of leaving but followed her in and settled into a chair with zero back support.

"That pole dancer paying you?" she said with distaste. Theresa Bond had short hair and high cheekbones. She wore jeans and a white shirt with the top three buttons undone.

"Bobbie Lee?"

She gave a me a smug smile. "Oh please. What kind of name is that? Is she?"

"No. I'm here because Archie wants to—"

"I know all that. He's smitten with her. She reminds him of Lisa. Why do men invariably return to their youth?"

I wanted to keep the conversation focused. "Do you recall Archie saying anything during your marriage regarding Lisa and his lost daughter?"

"No."

Silence.

"Did he ever mention a daughter lost in childbirth?"

"You're not even in the ballpark."

"Oh?"

"My ex-husband never mentioned his old flame. Never peeped about some lost daughter. I found out later from Abigail, and it all made sense."

"What made sense?"

"His distance. Looking back, I see now I never had his heart, assuming he had one."

"How did Abigail feel about all this?"

"Ask her."

"I did."

"And?"

"Less than thrilled."

She humphed. "She's fearful it will cut into her slice. Listen, I don't mean to be ungrateful to Archie. He adopted my children. Treated them as his own. He was a good father to them. Lester idolized the man. Still does. But as a husband, he wasn't there. He worked twelve hours a day. When he came home, he beelined to his study and then to bed. A great father, a great businessman, and a lousy husband. Two out of three aren't bad, except when you're the third, and then it sucks."

We bantered some more, but she had little to offer. I thanked her and left. I hadn't made any progress, but each negative brings you closer to a positive. There's zero proof of that, but it sounds good and keeps you moving.

LAUREN SILCOX, ARCHIE'S FIRST wife, lived in Rotonda, Florida. It was less than an hour from Theresa's house but would put me late in getting home. I was exhausted from the rolodex of people I'd talked to, but I was eager to check more names off my list.

Like Theresa, I wasn't sure Lauren could be of assistance, but better to receive answers to questions that don't help than to never ask them and wonder if you've missed something. There was always the chance I would get a spark of information that would ignite a bonfire. And that's what happened. But it wasn't a bonfire. It was a wildfire. There's a small but significant difference. One, you control. The other, you do not.

CHAPTER 18

In contrast to Theresa, Lauren Silcox, Archie's first wife, was pleasant and accommodating. She informed me, in a tone that conveyed warmth and sincerity, that she'd be happy to meet. She worked in an art gallery and gave me the address. My second wind—or was it the third?—kicked in, and my positive attitude followed.

The Back Room Art Gallery had a brass bell above the front door and a massive counter along the rear. On the wall behind it were rows of sample frames. A woman stood behind it, measuring a print laid out on the counter. She glanced up at me. "Be with you in a minute," she said.

I browsed around the studio. One painting caught my eye. It was of two girls frolicking on the beach. They were about the same age as my daughters.

The woman behind the counter popped her head up. "Hi, there. May I help you?"

I introduced myself and said I was looking for Lauren Silcox.

"Search no more." She marched around the counter and extended her hand. "I'm Lauren. Pleasure to meet you, Jack."

"Jake."

She snapped her fingers. "Right."

She had a cheery smile and chestnut eyes. She wore a loose long blouse with puffy sleeves. Her tight whitewashed jeans flared around her ankles. She reminded me of Bobbie Lee. Had Archie married Lauren and later Bobbie Lee because they both had traits similar to Lisa?

"There's a patio out back in the shade," she said. "Let's talk there. I get cooped up in here. If someone comes in, Tinker Bell will let me know."

She led me to an intimate courtyard, jungle lush with colorful hibiscus, waxy crotons, and a hedge of eureka palms along the back. A stretched canvas provided shade for a wrought iron table and four leaf-speckled chairs. A gecko scurried over the top of the canvas, its shadow betraying it.

"Sooo," she began after we sat down. "You're searching for Archie's daughter. Is that right?"

"I am."

"The one who was stillborn?"

"You know about her?"

"Not as much as I thought if she's alive."

"We don't know that."

"What do we know?"

I explained in more detail than I had when I called her. That Archie, who had cancer, had reason to believe his daughter from long ago was not stillborn but had been sold. She interrupted and asked what his prognosis was. I told her and continued to explain that Lisa had been a patient of Dr. Ziegler.

"The Ziegler babies," she said. "I knew, of course, when we were married, that he'd lost both his child and Lisa. But Ziegler's name at that time didn't mean anything or raise any suspicions.

"Archie's really a wonderful person," she continued. "We

had a true bond. A spiritual connection. He was an artist, like me. I doubt anyone but me knows that. Saw that side of him. But he changed. Became a different person. He took a job with that pharmaceutical distribution company, and within a few years, he was running it. I mean, he shot out of bed at five a.m. and I never saw him before seven that evening. He became obsessed with money. No, that's not correct. He became obsessed with losing himself in the pursuit of money. I don't think he cares a bit about money."

"I read that he started the company."

"Archie? No. He took a job and vaulted to the top. Became the classic workaholic. Five years into it, I folded up my tent. He was not the man I married. All because of Lisa. He worked to forget her. In the process, he shut me out. Denied who he really was. Archie Williams committed an act of treason against his soul."

I asked her if he discussed Lisa and the loss of his daughter.

"Rarely. Never, really, after the first year or so. You should be talking to Lisa's friends at that time."

"Archie's memory is failing him," I said.

"Of course. Chemo brain, right? I might be able to help you."

"How so?"

"Sit tight."

She went inside and came back a moment later holding a high school year book. "Your lucky day. I didn't even know I had this here until digging through a box looking for something else. Lisa and I went to the same school. That's how Archie and I knew each other. I was a year ahead of her. I didn't really know her." Lauren flipped the book open and handed it to me. "Lisa," she said. "Bottom row. Second from the end."

I stared at a pretty girl with the confident and sinless smile of youth.

Tinker Bell rang. Lauren popped up. "Take your time." She went into the studio.

I flipped through the pages.

Dimpled-faced Lisa with the soccer team.

Lisa in debate club. One of two girls.

Lisa working in the front office.

Lisa, editor of *Brief Candle*, the school's poetry publication.

Lisa eating in the cafeteria. Two of the girls at the table looked familiar. They were also on the soccer team. One was also the other girl on the debate team.

"Jake?"

I looked up to see Lauren standing above me. I'd not heard her return. "Yes?"

"I said, is there anything there to help you?"

I turned the book around and pointed at the two girls at the cafeteria table with Lisa. "Do you know them? They appear in several pictures with her."

"Remember them? Yes. But I didn't really know them. Cliquish high school years, you know?"

I wiggled out my phone and took pictures of the yearbook.

"Are you going to try to contact them?"

"I am."

"That one there?" She pointed to the girl next to Lisa in the debate club picture. I'd noticed they'd also stood next to each other in the soccer team picture. "I seem to recall they ran together. You might want to start with her."

I found the individual pictures of the two girls who appeared with Lisa the most. Katie Phillips and Diana Bennet. Katie was in every group picture that Lisa was in.

Katie, maybe.

CHAPTER 19

It had been a doozy of a day. Heather Kirkland led me to Charlene Buford, who led me to Nathan Whiting. I'd followed Whiting up by meeting with retired detective Josh Arnelli and topped the day off by interviewing both of Archie's previous wives.

When I got home, I shed the world and took care of the girls. When they snuggled up to me, an open book on my lap, if only for that unholdable moment, I was a hero. Afterward, I joined Kathleen and Morgan on the screened porch. A sea breeze whistled through the screen, agitating the solitary candle that Kathleen lit every evening. A waxing gibbous moon glowed on the hushed bay, and a sailboat slid past the end of the dock, its Bethlehem mast light guiding the way. A sleeping osprey on a dock piling cast a gargoyle outline against the night sky, and I thought of the shadow of the gecko scrambling across the top of the canvas at the Back Room Art Gallery. I also thought of the mess I'd need to hose off in the morning. Keeping the dock clean had become a daily responsibility. With the girls old enough to venture the hundred feet over water on their own and neither being fond of shoes, Kathleen wanted the dock to be shipshape. I didn't blame her, as I didn't want the girls to navigate land mines of bird crap every day.

I'd messaged Katie Phillips on Facebook but hadn't yet received a response from her. She still lived in the area. I had heard back from Jenna Cappabianca, the woman Heather Kirkland suggested I contact. She was on a cruise and would be happy to meet when she returned in three days. She advised me not to get my hopes up, admitting that uncovering Ziegler's secrets was more difficult than she'd imagined.

"I like it," Kathleen said. "They're the same age as our girls. Or close enough." She was referring to the painting I'd purchased from the Back Room Art Gallery. It rested in front of us, leaning against the support between the screens. "Where are we going to hang it? It's getting a little crowded."

It was not the first painting I'd hauled home.

"Maybe I'll add a room, a wide hall, just for paintings."

"Huh," Kathleen said in a tone that indicated favorable inclination to my comment, which I'd intended as a joke. That was not good.

"How's the hunt for Archie's daughter coming along?" Morgan asked.

I glossed over the day. Upon hearing my words, I sank in disappointment over how little progress I'd made in finding Archie's daughter or who wrote the letter. Worse yet was Arnelli's comment regarding the subsequent deaths of Ziegler's patients. That was far more—

"I don't buy that no one knows about Lisa's baby," Kathleen said, slicing into my thoughts.

"But is that someone alive?" Morgan said. "Both players, Ziegler and Belle, are gone."

"You said Belle's son, Nathan, pleaded ignorance?" Kathleen said.

"He did."

"Believe him?"

"No," I admitted.

"And?" Morgan said.

"I'll pay him another visit. But it would be good to have more information before doing so. If I catch him in a lie, he might be more cooperative."

Hadley III came in through the cat door. She considered the three of us and jumped on Kathleen's lap.

"You do know I'm the one who feeds you," I said to the cat.

"Meow."

Kathleen stroked the cat. "Patty came by today."

"The duck?"

"Mm-hmm."

Years ago, we'd adopted a duck. But Patty the Duck had an independent streak and was prone to going AWOL for large swaths of time.

"She ate out of both Joy's and Sophia's hands. I think she's come home for good. It's a cruel world out there. Her feathers looked a little scraggly."

"Too bad you're so hot on getting a dog," I said. "I'd shudder at the sight of the girls witnessing the brutality of nature."

"That's a cheap shot."

"I'm just looking out for Patty. We took a vote today. It was three to nothing in favor of not getting a dog."

"Liar. Who voted? Wait, let me guess—me, myself, and I."

"All legitimate."

"Ha. Stuffing the ballot box. Help me out here, Morgan."

"We could never have a dog growing up because we lived on a sailboat," Morgan said.

"And you turned out just fine," I said.

"Always regretted it," he said, clarifying his position, though not in my favor.

"There you go," Kathleen said triumphantly.

I reached over and finished her glass of wine.

"Hey, I wasn't done with that."

"I act petty when cornered. What am I missing at Harbor House?" I asked, eager to redirect the conversation.

"We got a family of five moving in tomorrow," he said.

"I'll be back in rotation in no more than three, four days," I said.

"Why's that?" Kathleen asked. "Is there something you didn't share with us?"

"No. Other than I signed up for a bottomless well of characters who might know something or someone, but they really don't remember, and why don't you talk to so-and-so? The past is a five-hundred-piece puzzle with half the pieces missing."

"Take it as far as you can," Kathleen advised, "so you have no regrets."

"You said that many of the women were victims of hit-and-runs?" Morgan said.

"So Arnelli told me, though he seemed reluctant to admit it."

"Where do you even go with that?" Kathleen asked.

"I don't know."

A gust of wind harmonized through the screen. It exercised a gradual decrescendo followed by an impressive crescendo.

"It's like the wind is a symphony," Kathleen said.

"It's the sound of angels crying," Morgan said.

"Oh, that's even better," Kathleen enthused. "Tell us."

This is what Morgan said.

"Growing up on the sailboat, the wind would howl through the halyards. All ranges of tone and chords. Majors and minors. Harmony and discord. Notes that exist only on the sea at night. Music with no instrument and no source. When I was young, it spooked me.

"My mother told me not to be afraid. She explained that angels rode the night winds. They circled the globe searching for separated lovers. And whenever they were successful and lovers were united, the angels cried in joy and happiness. That nothing was more joyous than lovers, once lost, finding each other. The music I heard was angels crying in joy. When I'm on a sailboat at night, and the wind plays the halyards, I know that somewhere, lovers, once lost, are reunited."

"Somewhere, tonight," Kathleen mused.

No sooner had she uttered the words than they were lost, feathered into the wind. The three of us sat in such quiet that a whisper could have passed as a shout. We've always been comfortable in the binding sound of silence.

After uncounted breaths, Morgan announced he was done with the day. If I were an artist, I would capture Morgan's silhouette as he crossed the lawn beneath the star-speckled sky, the moon filtering through the palm fronds. I would paint the wind. A baby's laugh. The air between a woman's smile and my eyes. But my hands are clumsy and useless when holding a brush.

My thoughts drifted to the Cardinal Inn and how Charlene said the family always hired out the yard work. That a young man did it for years until he was an old man. Would he still be alive? I made a note to call Charlene in the morning. One more character with a foggy memory.

Kathleen stood and plopped down on my lap. She cozied into me and nuzzled her head into my shoulder. Her mouth rested below my ear. Her breath was warm, moist. Our breathing slowed and became syncopated.

"Archie is still in love with Lisa," she said.

"He's glorifying her memory," I said.

"Memory will hallow all we've known but know no more."

"Is that you?"

"Lincoln."

"I'm hoping to get lucky tonight, and you're quoting Father Abraham?"

She snuggled deeper into my shoulder. "Silly. You're already lucky. When should we tell the girls they're adopted?"

Really? She knew not to bring up serious subjects late at night. I reminded her of that.

"You need to change," she said in a dreamy voice.

"I don't want to change."

"That's what you need to change."

"Tomorrow," I said.

"Tell them?"

"I'll change."

"Uh-huh."

Her breathing slowed, and my eyes closed. Of all the images of the day, the one that survived was of Rambler entering his home and his dog, Ralphie, pissing on the floor in the sheer excitement of seeing him. Once again, I was bedazzled by my mind's total disregard of grand thoughts. Or, as I was beginning to suspect, did I just not recognize them?

I made a note to think about it. Tomorrow.

CHAPTER 20

Diana Bennet, one of the girls who appeared to be friends with Lisa, lived in Jacksonville. According to her social media posts, she worked in the human resources office at a hospital. Katie Phillips, who seemed closer to Lisa, hadn't gotten back to me yet.

At eight thirty the following morning, I called Diana. I gave her the reason for my intrusion. She said she couldn't talk then and would call me back in twenty minutes. I decided to squeeze in fixing breakfast for my girls. That was going splendidly until Diana called back ten minutes later while I was scrambling eggs.

"Wow," she said. "Lisa Trowbridge. I haven't thought of her in years. What can I do for you?"

"Don't forget the cheese," Joy said.

"Tons of cheese," Sophia added.

When I scrambled eggs, the girls swarmed me to make sure I got their orders right. I put a finger to my mouth to signal them to be quiet. I asked Diana what she recalled about Lisa's pregnancy.

"Not much. She dropped out of school. There were rumors

and all. She was pretty tight with her boyfriend. Archie, like the comic book. I forget his last name."

"Williams," I said.

"That's it. Once she fell for him, we didn't—"

"Piles of cheese."

"—really hang around much. Lisa's mom—she never had a dad—well, she did, but he split when she was young. Anyway, her mom wasn't real supportive. I felt bad for her. Getting pregnant and no one to help her. No one to turn to. That had to be rough."

I inquired if she knew anything about a man named Nathan Whiting or a woman named Belle.

"No. I don't recognize either name."

Joy planted her hands on her hips.

"Did Lisa ever mention having a daughter?"

"Not to me. Her child was stillborn, and then Lisa was run down by some maniac they never caught. Like all in three months or something. Her last day she showed up to high school? That was the last time I ever saw or spoke to her."

"Would Katie Phillips be of help?"

Joy twirled a finger in the air, signaling me to wrap things up. I ignored her and ran the spatula through the eggs. My shoulder ached where I had the phone pinched between it and my head.

"You know about Katie?" Diana asked.

"I do."

"Well, that's who you should be talking to," she said, as if I were wasting my time with her. "Those two were inseparable. If Lisa confided in anyone, it would have been her."

"I messaged her. I'm just waiting for her to get back."

"She will. She's pretty active on that stuff."

Diana said she'd let me know if she recalled anything else, and we disconnected.

"Yes?" I said to Joy, who still had her hands glued to her hips. "Is there something I can do for you?"

"Who is Katie Phillips?"

"Someone I want to talk with."

"I hope she gets back to you. You didn't mess up the eggs, did you, Pop? Because if you did, that would be the end of the world."

Don't Pops sit in a recliner, smoke a pipe, and read the newspaper? And—I can barely get this out—have a dog curled up at their feet?

This Pop got busy assembling breakfast because my oldest daughter was astute—screw up breakfast, and you foul the day. Here's the rundown, and, yes, it's important: Kathleen took her eggs with no cheese or onions but coated them with a mountain of salt. Joy and I took ours with cheese and onions, and you better believe that onions were the main event. Sophia was just cheese, to the point that the eggs were optional. Hadley III, who took little interest in the kitchen, always sauntered in when eggs were frying. She was in the same camp as Joy and me.

My phone rang again while I was juggling the skillets. I didn't recognize the number. Probably a junk call.

"Jake's diner. Finest eggs the chicken ever laid."

"Jake Travis?" a woman said.

"Speaking."

"This is Katie Phillips. You messaged me yesterday about Lisa?"

I stepped away from the stove. "Thank you for getting back to me. Sorry about the chicken quip. I'm scrambling eggs for my girls. Some want cheese; some do not."

"That sounds nice. How many girls do you have?"

"Two. Three, if you count my wife."

"Is she a girl?"

"She is."

"Then you should count her. She's one of the no cheeses, am I right?"

Katie's voice sounded like sunshine after three days of rain.

"You are. Might you be a no cheese as well?"

"I am. We've learned quite a bit about each other in this short time."

"Please treat these family secrets as you would your own."

"Oh, most definitely. What can I tell you about my best friend in high school who's been dead for nearly fifty years?"

"That sounds sad."

"That is sad."

I gave her a quick summary of my reason for calling and asked if there was a time we could meet.

"You're doing this for Archie?" Her voice had become less sunshiny. Was I resurrecting painful memories?

"Yes."

"Why now?"

"He's got cancer."

"I'm sorry to hear that."

"There's more."

"Oh?"

"He got a letter stating that his and Lisa's baby was stolen. That she wasn't stillborn. She's alive."

Pause.

"Katie?"

"Wow. That's a zinger."

"Any way you can squeeze me in today?" I pleaded.

"I work downtown. I usually take lunch around one."

"Allow me to buy you lunch."

"You don't have to do that. Lisa was a good friend. If there's any better, I'm waiting for that day."

We settled on Mangroves at one. I hung up.

"Who's Lisa?" Joy said.

"Someone who died long ago."

"Who are you buying lunch for?"

"One of her friends."

"Can I come?"

"No."

"Is she cheese or no cheese?"

"No cheese. Ready for your eggs?"

"I want extra cheese on mine," Sophia said.

"I know, peanuts."

"I'm a kitty cat."

"Right. I know that, kitty cat."

I placed a plate of scrambled eggs buried in cheese in front of Sophia. "Here you go, kitty."

"Don't forget Hadley," she said. "She's a kitty, too."

"And Patty," Joy added. "Keep some for Patty."

"Yeah." Sophia jumped in. "Patty likes eggs, too."

"How do you know that?" I asked.

"She told me," Sophia said. "Kitty cats and ducks talk."

"I'm sure they do."

I placed a plate of eggs and onions on the floor. Hadley III curled her tail underneath her and nibbled at the food.

"When do we get our dog?" Sophia said.

"Sush!" Joy said.

"Look at me, girls."

They both looked at me, Sophia's fork in midair.

"Did Mommy already buy a dog?"

Joy said, "Whatever are you talking about?"

They both giggled. In Spanish. Bonita was bilingual, and our girls were absorbing a language neither Kathleen nor I comprehended. That only added reinforcement to the belief that I was just doodling my way through the days. At least I nailed the eggs.

CHAPTER 21

I arrived at Mangroves early and was camped at an outdoor table when a woman who was about the right age to be Katie Phillips approached the waitress stand. She glanced at me. I raised a finger. She raised a smile.

"Are you the man who scrambles eggs for three girls?" she said when she arrived at my table under a square umbrella.

I stood and pulled back a chair for her. "Guilty."

"Why, thank you," she said in singsong appreciation. She settled herself in the chair and didn't waste time. "So Archie is circling back." She said it as a statement, not a question.

"He is."

Age had been kind to Katie, as if it had passed over her house. She had soft brown hair with blonde highlights that reminded me of early autumn. I thought of sharing that with her, but that's as far as I got. I brought up a picture on my phone of the letter Archie had received and handed it to her. She read it while I pretended not to stare at her pink lips, which were somewhere between the girl next door and the brothel down the road. She returned my phone.

"Do you know who might have written that?" I said.

"I do not."

"Is Little Strawberry familiar to you?"

"Absolutely. That is what Lisa and Archie called their baby."

We were interrupted by a waiter in a starched black apron who took our orders. We hadn't looked at the menus yet, but Katie said she was game if I was. After he left, I asked her to tell me about Lisa.

She hesitated, as if looking for an entry point, then jumped in. "It got complicated," she said, flicking away a strand of hair that was fond of resting on her left eyebrow. "She and Archie were mad for each other, and that cut me out. I was jealous, you know? My best friend is suddenly consumed by a guy, which leaves me without my best friend. We were juniors in high school. You don't exactly go out and get a new BF. Everyone had had their friends since sixth grade. I was out in the cold. I resented that. And then after what happened to her, I was ashamed of my small feelings."

"When did you last see her?"

"The day before she delivered. She told me her mom—not a role model one would aspire to—insisted that she go to the Ziegler clinic. They never had money, and Ziegler was cheap. It was located in the rear of some motel. Parrot something. Lisa was worried about that."

"The Cardinal Inn."

"That's it. Parrot. Cardinal. Hey, for someone who loses her phone twice a day, I was close."

"Did you ever see her after she delivered?"

"I was pissed. I was left searching for a new lunch table. Not to mention that my former best friend now had a scarlet *A* on her."

"You never saw her again?" I asked, unable or unwilling to disguise my disappointment.

"See her? No. Talk to her? Yes. I had planned to see her. She'd moved in with her aunt in Bradenton. I forget her name. Lisa was always closer to her than to her own mother. Said she got a job and went to night classes to finish the school year."

I asked her what she thought of the letter Archie had received.

"Well . . ." She dipped her head. "Since your call, I've been thinking. A couple of weeks after she gave birth, or something like that—I can't be positive of the time—Lisa called me. Like I said, I knew her baby had been stillborn. Anyway, she said she didn't believe Ziegler. She claimed she heard her baby cry. She remembered seeing her, and she looked healthy. She'd been drugged for the delivery—some line about it being best for her and her child. She insisted that images and sounds were surfacing."

She reached for her Coke Zero but, instead of taking a drink, just rotated the sweating glass in her hand. I took the opportunity to take a quarter bite out of my grouper Rueben.

"When you said that on the phone, about the letter?" she said. "I had to think. I find that as I age, I have to work hard to keep my memories. Or recreate them. Then I'm afraid by recreating them, I embellish them. After that, I'm done."

"Did you believe Lisa?" I said, dabbing my mouth with a napkin.

"She did, and that's what counts, isn't it?"

"Do you think her mom would have known?"

"That's a little obscure."

"Do you think her mother plotted with Ziegler to drug her daughter, sell the baby to get cash, and then tell her daughter that her baby was stillborn?"

"Wow. I think I like obscure better. I don't think so. She wasn't the best mom, but I don't see her as being that . . . desperate?"

A trash truck rumbled down the street. A group of five children, who appeared to be around junior high age, had spent the last few minutes setting up a speaker and taking violins out of cases, leaving one open on the sidewalk for tips. They lined up. I was expecting Pachelbel or Barber, but they went straight into the theme song for James Bond.

I asked Katie what Archie and Lisa had planned to do after school.

"Archie ran down there all the time to see her. He told me later, after Lisa died—I talked to him once and then never again—that they were looking forward to their own place, here in Saint Pete. He had a job and an apartment. They were weeks away. Maybe days. I've forgotten or never knew. Not that it mattered. It was over. Just like that."

"The accident?"

She took a moment, her mind peeling back to a time scarred by tragedy, for the waypoints of our lives are great joy or great sorrow.

"According to the papers," Katie said, "Lisa was walking home from school at night. She stepped off a curb, and some guy clipped her." She flicked her eyes up to mine, for she'd been studying her glass as much as I'd been studying her hair. "He fled the scene."

I took another bite of my messy sandwich. Katie toyed with her chicken salad. I stole a glance across to Straub Park, but a runner I'd spotted earlier, her ponytail bouncing from one shoulder to another, was gone. I searched my cloth napkin for a virgin spot, wiped my mouth again, and asked Katie if there was anything else she could recall.

She swung her head. "Don't think so. Know what I learned that day?"

"That day?"

"The day I heard she died."

"Tell me."

She hesitated, then said, "'Looking up at the stars, I know quite well that for all they care, I can go to hell.' Dreary, right? I worked on the literary magazine with Lisa. We decided to put that W. H. Auden poem in. I didn't understand that poem until my best friend died. The newspaper the next day was all about the Rays and how they'd won their eighth straight game."

"Tough lesson."

We entered the doldrum of our conversation. She looked at me as if searching for which direction to go in. The Bond kids fiddled on.

"I'm not a victim here," she said with resignation. "Lisa was. It took me a spell to come around to that. Do you think her daughter is alive?"

"I don't know."

"She is."

"You know this?"

"No." She smiled at me as if we were old friends. "But I'm trying on the thought. I like it. I like it a lot."

We made aimless talk about the growth of downtown. The new high-rise condos, each successive one securing bragging rights by being ten feet higher than the previous new one. She promised to let me know if she remembered anything else. I reciprocated by telling her I'd keep her in the loop. I made a mental note to ask Archie about Lisa's aunt. She would have been the last person Lisa lived with. I was surprised he hadn't mentioned her. Maybe the chemo was taking a greater toll on him than he realized.

Two thoughts—make that three—struck me as I lumbered to my truck. Researching the past is a destinationless journey, a tunnel that leads to other tunnels, and they twist and turn into even more tunnels, world without end, amen.

Secondly, I thought of something else I'd like to paint. A canvas of women's hair.

And finally, a Rueben is a messy act to pull off in company.

I got into my truck, drove a block, maneuvered a U-turn, and returned to the restaurant. I hopped out of the truck and dropped a twenty in the open violin case as the junior high quintet performed "Bittersweet Symphony."

CHAPTER 22

I received a text from Charlene. I'd called her earlier and explained who I was looking for. She said she'd get back to me, as she wanted to check with him first to make sure it was okay for her to provide his address.

Her text contained the name and address of the man who'd been the gardener and groundskeeper of the Cardinal Inn for around fifty years. He'd started as a teenager and cut his last blade of grass at age sixty-six. He, along with Nathan Whiting, were the only people I could locate from the time that Lisa was in Ziegler's clinic. Whiting had professed ignorance. Maybe the groundskeeper had a better memory. Or less to hide.

Clive Emmons lived on Nineteenth Avenue North in Saint Petersburg, in the middle of a city that had been laid out like graph paper to accommodate the flood of Northerners who flocked to Florida after World War II. A noble jacaranda tree owned the front yard, but not a leaf marred the ground. I'd called before arriving, stating the purpose of my visit. He said he was looking forward to meeting me. His casual acceptance of my intrusion into his day struck me as odd.

I took the two steps up to the covered porch in one stride

and rapped on the door. A moment later, it opened, and a diminutive Black man with sparkly eyes stood in front of me. He was slightly bent, as if his body could no longer straighten out.

"You must be Mr. Travis," he said. His gentle, welcoming voice reminded me of the people who greet you when you enter a church.

"I am."

"You mind if we sit right out here?" he said. "It's a mighty nice day to be cooped up indoors."

I told him that would be fine with me.

"Can I get you somethin' to drink? Iced tea or lemonade, maybe?"

"Iced tea would be fine."

"You want any sugar in that?"

"I do not."

"You're not from the South originally, are you? You can always tell by the sugar in the tea where someone's from. Back in a jiff."

He sauntered into his house—he was no longer capable of a jiff—and returned holding two tall glasses of iced tea. His extended one to me. His leathered hands and forearms were disproportionally large and muscled compared to the rest of him.

"I grew up on sweet tea," he said. "Folks now don't drink it much like that, but I still do. I don't smoke. Don't touch liquor, so I figure the Lord will forgive me for a little sweetness, which is not a bad thing in this world."

I raised my glass to him. "To more sweetness in the world."

"Yes, suh." He raised his glass and took a drink. A white Honda crawled down the street, like it was looking for a specific address. Maybe a delivery car.

"I believe that Charlene explained why I wanted to see you?"

"Yes, suh. About that doctor long ago."

"Ziegler."

"Tell you something? I'm a little surprised no one ever talked to me before."

"Why is that?"

"Oh, I don't mean to be critical of folks; that's no way to be. And I'm an easy man to look over. The teenage Black gardener hunched over a bush. Pushin' a mower. Sweepin' the parking lot. To most people, I suppose I never existed. But I don't mind. I loved my work. In my small way, I made the world a neater place."

"You took care of the Cardinal Inn for fifty years?" I said.

"Fifty-three. Mr. Buford hired me when I was thirteen. My schoolin' was done by then. I needed to contribute to the family. I spent every Thursday there for over half a century, workin' for three generations of owners. Mr. Buford did more business on the weekends, and he wanted the place to look sharp."

I asked if he remembered Dr. Ziegler.

His eyes narrowed. He shifted his feet. "He does a disservice to that title. Oh, he might of had a degree, but he was no doctor, least not how you and I think."

"What happened in that motel?" I said, swinging for the fence.

He drew in his breath. His eyes wandered over the street. Three boys kicked a ball in the yard across from us.

"Bad things," he said. "At first, I jus' thought he was doing abortions that girls didn't want their parents to know about. But I realized they was too big—too pregnant—for that to be the case. I was a little ignorant of that stuff, you understand?"

"You were only there once a week," I pointed out.

"And apparently that was the day he did much of his business. I never really tole this to nobody." He took a sip of tea and placed the glass on a coaster on the table next to him.

"Did you ever see the babies leave?" I said.

Silence.

"Clive?"

"I heard you," he said with a bitterness in his voice that I sensed was directed at himself. We sat in toneless silence as he struggled with his thoughts. His eyes again got lost across the street, as if he were looking for a sign. He shifted his attention to me.

"Lemme tell you about the day that changed everything."

CHAPTER 23

"It was a Thursday, and I was back home with my wife, Lanelle," Clive continued. "She's at the store. She should be back soon. We'd jus' married and were livin' with my mama then.

"Anyway, I realized I left my trimmers at the inn. We lived on Eighteenth Avenue, not far from the motel. I decided to get them that night 'cause my job on Fridays at that time was in the opposite direction. I wanted to get to that job at the crack of dawn so I could be done early and enjoy the weekend. I worked ten hours a day, five days a week. Saturdays an' Sundays were for me.

"It was gettin' dark when I got there. A car pulled up to the back. I was walking around, lookin' for my clippers. No one saw me. I heard a woman screaming for her baby and then the doctor tell her it was stillborn. She went on insisting she heard it, and he kept tellin' her it was the drugs. Then Dr. Ziegler hustled out with a baby. He stuck it in the back seat of that car. And let me tell you, that car burned rubber leaving the lot.

"I'd seen them hand off babies before but thought nothing of it. I knew folks adopted from there, but this was somethin' different. The mother yellin' and carryin' on so. I told Lanelle what I saw. She said best to keep my mouth shut."

There was only one question that mattered, but before voicing it, I wanted to first fill in some blanks. "Have you told this to anyone before?"

"No, suh. No one asked. Besides, not sure what I'd saw or what I'd say. You understand?"

"I do."

Clive looked at me, his face etched in painful regret. "You got to realize, times was different then," he said, as if he still owed me—or himself—an explanation. "Still a lot of hate in the South, and Florida is as far south as you can get. My parents grew up with that hate. My daddy told me never to approach a white man's house by the front door. Always go around to the back. Never look a white woman in the eye. Do your job. Keep your head down. Go home.

"I don't mean to dredge up the old days. To answer your unaxed question, Charles Buford allowed terrible things to happen under his eye. But he was good to me. Good to my family. When my mama needed an operation, he paid the hospital bill and never wanted a penny of it back. That man didn't have a racist bone in his body. Least not toward me."

He paused, took a drink from his tea, and placed it back on the coaster. "Peoples is funny. All mixed up with good and bad inside 'em at the same time. I jus' couldn't come forward and point my finger at him. So yes, suh, I kept my head down. Always been afraid my silence caused a lot of harm. Guess that makes me funny, too."

I took a sip of iced tea and let an ice cube slide into my mouth. He glanced at me. "One man, though—a policeman—he did question me."

"Who was that?"

"Name's left me now. He was looking into Ziegler."

I cracked the ice cube in my mouth. "Josh Arnelli?"

Arnelli had not mentioned talking to Clive. But he admitted it was difficult to recall everyone he had spoken with.

"Might be, but I can't be sure. He was a nice fellow. Bushy eyebrows. Axed me if I saw anything suspicious. I lied. Said no. I was too loyal to Mr. Buford. I see that now."

"Did the detective ever mention that a disturbing number of the young woman were killed by errant drivers shorty after having given birth?"

"I can't say I recall that. I don't mean to be evasive; it's jus' that I don't trust my memory. You think they were related? Them deaths?"

I wasn't surprised. Arnelli, at the time he interviewed Clive, might not have seen the pattern that he admitted only appeared later.

"It's hard to say," I replied, deciding not to press him further but to stay on the subject. "You heard women crying?"

"Yes, suh, I reckon those young women heard their babies scream and knew they wasn't dead. What happened after that, I don't care to imagine. It's not like that part went on for some while, you understand? Ziegler, he jus' didn't show up one day. Then the police came. Remember, I was Thursdays only."

"Did you know Belle? The woman who helped Ziegler?"

"Saw her. She was there a lot. But I never spoke to her."

"How about her son? Nathan Whiting?"

Clive's eyes widened with fear. "He's a bad man, Mr. Jake. I saw him choke a dog to death with his bare hands. There's something wrong with him. His cornbread's not done in the middle."

"The type of man other men fear so much that they keep silent?"

Clive's face morphed into a frown, and I knew my words had hit a nerve. I followed up my unanswered question with the only question that mattered. The one I'd been holding back. "Do you know the name of the woman you heard screaming?"

The air swelled with silence. Sometimes the silence is your friend. And if you shut up and listen, it will speak with fury.

"Someone recently wrote a letter to Archie Williams," I said, keeping my voice soft. "His girlfriend was a patient of Dr. Ziegler's. Her baby was stillborn. She died shortly after. A victim of a hit-and-run."

He shuffled his feet.

"Someone who knew she called her baby Little Strawberry."

Clive shrank like an embarrassed child.

"That was you," I added softly.

"Yes, suh. It was."

"How do you know her name was Lisa? That she called her unborn child Little Strawberry."

"'Cause she tole me."

Finally.

CHAPTER 24

Had Clive buried it for so long, he was incapable of letting it out all at once? Or had he no intention of telling me any of this when we started? It didn't matter, for while his body sat on his porch, he confessed, cleansing his soul in the Jordan River, washing away his sin of silence.

He explained that he had gone inside to use the restroom. Buford allowed him to use the bathroom off his office. Clive was appreciative of that, which told me more about his feelings toward Buford and explained his hesitancy to come forward at an earlier date. He did another family motel and retail stores on Wednesdays. Neither allowed him to use their restrooms.

"I was washin' my hands, even though I knew they'd jus' get dirty again, when I heard this whimpering. Like a little animal. I peeked into a room. A young girl was layin' on a bed. She looked to be about my age. I remember thinkin' we was so different yet so alike. She seemed confused. Agitated. I could tell she was in labor.

"I axed her name and then if she was okay. Stupid, right? She said she was worried about Little Strawberry. That the doctor said the baby was in danger and he had jus' gave her some drugs to make it easier for her. I axed her about Little Strawberry. She said that was what she and Archie called the baby on account that they both had reddish hair."

He paused before he continued, focusing his eyes on mine. "I remember his name—you know, from the comic books. She was struggling to talk. Startin' to slur her words. I axed her if Archie was the daddy. She said, 'Yes, Archie Williams,' like she was mad I didn't know that. She tole me her name was Lisa. But she never said her last name. She said she and Archie planned to marry and were both excited about having a baby, but her mom didn't want her to have it. I think she was losing her ability to concentrate, rattling on and all. It took great effort to talk. I admired her for that. It was like she knew she was in danger and she was trying to . . . Lord, all she got was me." Clive wiped his eyes with the back of his hand. "All she got was me."

"You didn't do anything wrong, Clive."

"I didn't do nothin' right, either," he spat out.

Years ago, I'd assassinated a cardinal of the Catholic Church in Kensington Gardens. He wasn't a real cardinal, but I didn't know it at the time. A week—or is it a day?—has not passed without him popping into my head. Here's my point: The sins we think we commit are often far worse than those we do commit.

"Don't be harsh on yourself," I said. "It does no good."

Listen to me, Clive. I was a tick away from hurtling myself out of a London hotel, but I didn't, and now I make cheesy eggs.

"Do you hear me, Clive?"

His eyes lingered on his glass of tea. Something familiar. Something good. He glanced up at me. "I hear you."

"What else did she say?"

A blower fired up somewhere in the neighborhood.

"Not a word. I think it was gettin' too hard for her to talk. Anyway, I heard a door shut. I scampered out of there. I jus' missed being seen by Belle. At least, I thought she didn't see me."

Something about his statement ignited a question, but it slipped out of my mind. "This was the day you left your clippers, correct?"

"Yes, suh."

"And it was Lisa you heard?"

"Yes, suh."

"The letter?" I said. "Why now, Clive?"

"You believe in dreams?"

"Tell me about yours."

"Lisa came to me. 'Bout two weeks ago. She thanked me for calling her. Then she tole me it was time. She said, 'Do you—'"

"Calling who? Did you call someone?"

"She tole me in the clinic that if anything happened, to call her aunt. Said her name was Allison Gannon. I remembered it by thinking it was one letter off from cannon. I found the number. I called, but not because anything happened to her. I called Lisa to tell her that her baby was alive. I tole her that and—"

"You talked to Lisa after she gave birth?"

"Yes, suh."

"What was her response?" I asked.

"I don't know. I said, 'Your baby is alive.' Nothin' else."

"The letter. Why now, Clive?" I asked for the second time.

"I'm gettin' there," he said, and I felt bad for pushing him. "The dream I was tellin' you about? I was sittin' on a bench at Crescent Park. It's the one facing east. I like that bench. It's got a pretty view. Lisa just showed up and plopped down beside me. She said, 'Do you remember me?' I answered, 'Yes, you're Lisa." She said it was time I tole what happen. That her baby was taken, and Archie needed to know. I knew, in my dream, exactly what she was talking about.

"Then she said she had to go. That I was waking up, and our

time together would be over. That gives me the chills right now. She stood and walked away, and I remember, in my dream, never feeling so alone in my life as when she left me. I found this Archie Williams fellow and wrote that letter the next day. Figured if he was the wrong Archie, I did all I could do. When you called? I knew I had the right Archie."

"The day you saw Lisa," I said, backpedaling, "was she the only patient of Ziegler's there at that time?"

"Yes, suh. Far as I could tell."

"And no other babies were on the property that could have belonged to someone else and not to Lisa?"

"No. Clinic wasn't that big. No more than a couple rooms, really."

"Do you know what became of her baby?"

"I do not."

Of course. That would have been too easy. I prowled my mind for the question that had slipped out earlier, and it slipped back in. "You said you thought no one noticed you. Did they?"

He gave a nod, a slow double-dipping of his head.

"Clive?"

"I hear you, Mr. Jake." He paused before coming back in. "Nathan, Belle's boy, paid me a visit. It was a Sunday, and I was home alone. My mama always cooked dinner for folks who couldn't get out and delivered it to their homes on Sunday. I was pettin' my dog, Rascal. Nathan said his mother said I was snoopin' around that day, and I needed to keep my mouth shut. He tole me not to never mention what I saw that day. I tole him I didn't see anything. Didn't know what he was talkin' about. He said to keep it that way."

He let his breath out. "The dog I tole you he strangled to death? That was my Rascal. He was pettin' Rascal, and he jus' put both his hands around the dog's neck and choked it to death. I buried Rascal in the backyard 'fore my mama got home. I tole her a car hit him. I was too embarrassed to tell her what happened. How weak I was. How I just sat there. I never said a word to nobody till now, and I'll tell you somethin' else: In my dream, Lisa was dressed like I saw her in that bed, her hair a mess and her clothes soaked with sweat, and when I woke, I was sweatin', and I think it was her heat on me. I know it was. I'm glad you came today, Mr. Jake. At least now I'm ready."

"Ready for what?"

"For Lisa to come back. I want to tell her I did what she axed me to do. I'm afraid she's stuck someplace and will always be wondering."

PART II

INFANT SLEEPER, NEVER USED

CHAPTER 25

Lisa.

She was no longer just a girl in a high school yearbook. No longer the insufferable memory of a sick man. I, too, now saw her lying on a bed. Afraid. Confused. Hot. Sweating. Knowing something wasn't right yet unable to control the events that were shaping her life.

I stopped by the Panera on Fourth Street and bought fresh bagels. When I climbed back into the truck, the odor of bagels moved in with me. I hit Detective Rambler's number as I pulled out of the parking lot.

"What do you got?" he answered.

Two sesame seed, two everything, and two asiago, but I didn't think that was what he was referring to. And a pecan roll, but that was already half-gone.

"Can you run a history on a Nathan Whiting?" I asked him.

"Who's Nathan White?"

"Whiting. He hung around the Cardinal Inn when Ziegler was dealing babies."

"You talk to Arnelli?"

"I did. He's convinced there were crimes being committed but never had enough to follow. I could use an FDLE report."

The Florida Department of Law Enforcement, FDLE, provides reports on known criminals and investigations. Florida's Sunshine Law allows citizens to access those reports, but often, certain items are deleted or redacted. It was best to get the unscrubbed report rather than a document you think is complete but may be missing pertinent facts.

Rambler said, "I'll see what I can find, but don't hold your breath. Unless they opened an investigation, nothing will be there. They don't report suspicion. What are you fishing for?"

I was about to take the ramp to the interstate when I had a better idea. I braked to change lanes and swerved behind a car that had been treating the speed limit as the word of God.

"Whiting's mother was Ziegler's assistant," I explained. "I met Whiting. He claims he doesn't remember anything."

"But?"

"We all remember something."

"Please tell me there's more."

"I just left a man who was the gardener at the time. He claims to have heard Lisa's baby cry on his way out the back door. Whiting choked the man's dog to death to shut him up. Right in front of him."

"Just now?"

"Time of the crime."

"You want me to pull a file on a man who choked a dog forty years ago? I'll bump it ahead of last week's double homicide."

"I just told you a baby was alive, and her mother was informed she was dead," I said, not trying to hide the frustration in my voice.

"Tap the brake pedal. Anything else?"

"An unknown number of the women caught in Ziegler's

web died within a year after giving birth. Hit-and-run. Different cars."

Pause.

"This from Arnelli?" Rambler asked.

"Straight from the fringes of his conscience. I'm giving you a serial killer who was never investigated."

The line was silent.

"Still there?" I said.

"You think dog strangler was involved?" he asked. "I need more than that to reopen or open for the first time."

"I'll get more," I promised him.

"Do that," he instructed me.

I disconnected with Rambler and called Arnelli to see if he had talked with any of Ziegler's or Belle's neighbors. I was considerate in my questioning. I didn't want to come across as accusing him of not fulfilling his responsibilities. Not only would that shut him down, but I saw no evidence he had done anything wrong or in any manner ignored obvious signs.

Arnelli said he didn't recall questioning neighbors but offered that Ziegler had another office on Second Avenue North that was part of a larger practice. Everything there seemed to be legitimate. He had interviewed some of Ziegler's patients, and he received glowing reviews. Arnelli's theory was that Ziegler used his practice to identify young women who would "benefit" from his other services, which he ran out of his Cardinal Inn clinic.

I shared with him that I'd found the gardener, and he remembered talking with Arnelli. Arnelli said he wasn't surprised that he didn't recall questioning Clive. People remember talking to a homicide detective because it's likely the only time in their lives they will interact with one. By comparison, the detective, over a career, will interview hundreds of people, if not pushing a thousand.

My better idea.

I decided to canvass Ziegler's old neighborhood. That was one reason I called Arnelli, as I wanted to see if he'd gleaned anything from a similar effort decades ago. My endeavor would have been in vain had it not been that, like Clive Emmons years ago, I needed to use a restroom.

CHAPTER 26

Of the coming of the Lord

He'd hustled to his car after the man paid him a visit. He caught up with him at the first traffic light on Gulf Boulevard. Five minutes later, the man pulled into a scrawny restaurant across from a gas station. He hit the pumps. Topped off his tank. Checked the tires. Bought snacks. He observed the man, who seemed at ease talking with the bartender who served him. After the man left, he went to the joint, took a seat at the bar, and struck up a conversation with the bartender. *The guy who was just here? I met him somewhere. Real nice fellow. You don't happen to know his name, do you? That's right. He told me he lives around here, but I forget where. Right again! Drag getting old, right? Ha ha ha.* It wasn't hard after that to find his home. The difficult part was not to draw attention to himself.

He was waiting for him when he pulled out of his neighborhood that morning. Followed him downtown. Observed that he had lunch with some chick. *What a fuckeroo. A hot wife and he still cheats. What's with those kids playing violin?*

And then the man was at Clive Emmons's house.

Clive?

The hell?

He pondered how the man knew to go to the home were the gardener lived. *He must be getting close. No shit, Sherlock. But why? Who had he talked to?*

It had been bad luck, having the yard guy scheduled for Thursdays. He'd overheard Belle tell Doc that they needed to change days. Having a pair of eyes roaming the property the day they did their business was not wise. Doc had shrugged it off. Not his motel. Not his call. Besides, what would we tell Buford? He was suspicious but didn't want to know, and no way did they want to open that box. Both parties understood their relationship. Don't ask questions. Keep your head down. Mind your own business. Keep the money pouring in. Besides, Doc had pointed out, Buford had taken a liking to the kid. Best let it slide.

He'd found the little snipe hanging around the bushes outside the entrance to the clinic. Spending too much time on a flawlessly trimmed hibiscus. But then the whole thing unraveled fast. Buford died. Right there in his office. Doc closed up shop. Dropped off the map. It wasn't long afterward that a detective came knocking. He had moved on by then, unloading vegetable trucks at a Publix warehouse. Christ, he'd never seen so many bananas.

Doc, did he have an uncanny sense or not? Man was as close to a father as I'd ever have. Well, except for that. Nothing fatherly about that. Here we go. That day in the park again. How that started all the ways I'm screwed up. Wake up, dickhead; who gives a shit? Doc sure as hell didn't. Fuckwhistle never even said goodbye.

He watched as the man bounced down the front steps of Clive's porch. *He always walk like that?* He pondered what to do with what he'd just witnessed. He couldn't risk what Clive might be saying. He decided not to follow the man. He needed to skedaddle home and gather his stuff. Relocate his operation before resuming his surveillance. He was certain the man didn't know he was being followed. He never used the same car twice.

Just like the old days.

CHAPTER 27

Dr. Wayne Ziegler had resided in a craftsman-style house on Seventh Avenue North in what was now referred to as the historic district. It didn't start out like that, and I wondered at what point it had crossed the border.

I brought the truck to a stop under a live oak that commanded the street, its confetti leaves filling in the curb. The neighborhood was peaceful. A woman pushing a stroller. The ubiquitous delivery van. A man, hidden under a wide-brimmed hat and wearing long sleeves, backed a mower off the ramp of a flatbed trailer attached to a pickup truck.

I knocked and knocked and knocked but was about twenty years too late. Ziegler had last lived there forty-some years ago. It was his last known residence before he slipped out to the second floor flat on Waddell Street in Key West and then into air. I did find one person who had resided there for over forty years. She lived one street removed from Ziegler and had never heard of the man.

"You might want to try Georgy," my longtime resident advised me. She looked like Grandma Moses—thin hair, glasses, and a Vermonty-looking checkered shirt. "She's on the corner of Second Street North and Sixth Avenue North. Gray house."

I wasn't sure I was up for that. I needed to use a restroom. That's what I got for chugging water every morning, followed by half a pot of coffee and then a reservoir of iced tea.

"Has she lived here a long time as well?"

"Heavens, no," Vermonty said as if I should know better. "She's young like you. She runs the historic society for the neighborhood."

"I wasn't aware there was such a thing."

"There's not, really. We just like calling it that. Georgy settled in about ten years ago. We call her the Genealogy Queen. She's into history and all that stuff. I am, too, especially when someone else does the work. If anyone knows anything, it would be her."

I thanked her and headed off to the corner of Second and Sixth to see if the Genealogy Queen was home. I was half hoping she wasn't because—well, you know why.

I PUNCHED A DOORBELL with a sticker under it that read PEACE TO ALL WHO ENTER. A woman with short blonde hair framing a smiling face opened the door.

"Hi. May I help you?" she sang, each word landing on a different note.

I introduced myself and explained what had brought me to her door. How Emma—that was Vermonty's real name—had suggested I see her.

"As in the Ziegler babies?"

"Yes, ma'am."

"I know of him. One of the more interesting characters we've had. Very different from the occasional mobster who roamed the alleys in the 1920s and '30s. Step on in. I don't think I have anything specific on him, but let's take a look."

She floated into her house and tossed her face over her left shoulder. "I'm Georgy, by the way."

"As in 'Georgy Girl'?"

She turned her head again and flashed a peach smile. "I wish. I love that song. My mom was obsessed with a Toto song 'Georgy Porgy.'"

"I'm not familiar with it."

"Listen to it once and pity me for the rest of your life."

"That bad?"

"Worse."

"But 'Africa' is a classic."

"Go figure, right?"

"What got you interested in local neighborhood history?"

"I like the common people in history," she said as we entered her living room. "Have a seat."

A pair of white couches faced each other, separated by a long wood table. A large picture window looked over the front yard, and white bookcases stuffed with neatly arranged books stood on the opposite wall. Table surfaces and walls were decorated with photographs. Many of them were black and white. All were framed identically. I sat on the couch with my back to the picture window. A fly, pinging off the glass, buzzed behind me.

"You can have Archduke Ferdinand," she continued, "the Queen of Sheba, bonnie Prince Charlie, and Anne Boleyn." She'd been pulling books out of the bookcase and stuffing them back in. "None of them have any greater claim on humanity than a peasant in a field. Here we go."

She pulled out a photo album and placed it on the table. She took a seat next to me. "These are pictures and news articles from the time Ziegler was here. I've been digitizing this stuff, but let me tell you, that's a job and a half."

I inquired how she gathered her information.

"I started a club to capture and preserve the people of this area. We collect stories, photos, clippings, anything people squirreled away. Folks are eager to not just clean out their closets but to learn that something they saved for so long will be organized and preserved."

I started leafing through the book. It was pages of pictures. Most had a tagline describing who was in the picture and the year it was taken. The Shusters moved down from Pennsylvania in 1926. They lived on Seventh Avenue Northeast for twenty-six years. The Bradenburgs owned a Chrysler dealership on Central, circa 1937. The Boyd family in the 1970s and '80s were sailing champs at the Saint Petersburg Yacht Club. All four children boasted ribbons.

"There's a lot of effort here," I said, complimenting her.

"You're telling me. I'm sorry. Can I get you something to drink?"

Well, that was the last thing I needed.

"I'm fine."

"How about some iced tea or lemonade?"

She didn't wait for an answer but jumped up and returned a minute later with two long skinny glasses. "Fresh-squeezed lemonade," she said. "That's the only way we drank it in Biloxi."

I thanked her and took a sip of lemonade that puckered my lips and, unfortunately, went straight to my bladder.

"Anything there?" she asked.

"Not yet."

"Do you have a picture of Ziegler? That might help."

I took out my phone, and as I did, she scooted next to me on the couch. I showed her a picture.

"Um," she said. "He doesn't ring a bell. Let's see."

We turned the pages looking for a picture of Ziegler and scanned yellowed newspaper clippings hunting for his name. Georgy carried a hint of late-season jasmine. I wondered if she shared her house, her life with someone.

"He must have kept a low profile," Georgy said. "Let's try another time period."

She stood, went to the bookcase, fidgeted with some books, selected one, and settled next to me again. We started and finished the second book without ever spotting a picture of Wayne Ziegler. I drained my lemonade without realizing it. Fool.

"I'm sorry," Georgy said. "These two are my best shots. I can't say I'm surprised, though. Those with secrets often stay behind closed doors."

As I stood to leave, I asked if I could use her bathroom. I could be in a downtown restaurant in fifteen minutes, but sometimes we don't have fifteen minutes. I unconsciously adjusted my belt buckle to line up with the buttons on my shirt. Stupid habit. I vowed to end it right there. And I did, until one last time.

"Absolutely," she said. "Last door on your right as you head out."

I entered the half bathroom, did my business, and was washing my hands when I caught the reflection of a series of photographs in the mirror. I turned around and examined them.

There were three and they appeared to have been taken on the same day. A neighborhood picnic in a local park? I leaned in and examined the largest of the three. It was a group shot. A "one, two, three, smile" photograph. He was there. In the back. Standing in front of him was a boy. Shorter. Large ears. I examined the other two photos. They weren't staged but were slice-of-life shots. The first was no dice. I scrutinized the third. And there they were. Standing under a tree. Ziegler had his arm around the youth with the big ears, and did they not seem just a wee bit cozy?

Nathan Whiting had not changed much over the years.

Never knew the man.

CHAPTER 28

He is trampling out the vintage

He always knew he'd do another one. It was only a question of who. When. Never why. To ask why would be to question his very existence.

He was sitting at Harry's Beach Bar. Last stool on the end. He always claimed that stool. Less chance of anyone yakking it up. *Hey, where are you from? How long you here for? Is this a great place, or what?* Christ, did it ever occur to the dimwits that some people actually lived here? He'd gone home, packed a suitcase, and then decided to hit Harry's before heading out to his country hideaway. He didn't know when or if he'd be back.

He'd been lucky in the past. He knew this. When you are young and fortunate enough to have luck as a tailwind, it's easy to swell with self-congratulatory praise. Throw in a couple of decades, the thousand headlines of those less fortunate than you, and you give luck the credit it's due.

The third girl—or was it the fourth? Anyway, he'd barely clipped her. Stupid twit had spotted him at the last moment and jumped away. *Can't blame her, right?* He thought he was going to have to back up, run over her again, but her head had hit the curb, and lordy, you should have seen the blood. He'd sped off. She died four days later, never having regained consciousness, which was good, seeing as how she'd given him a deviant stare, their eyes locked together.

Then there was Lisa somebody. Doc said she had to go fast. She was adamant that her baby was alive and was making quite a fuss about it. A persistent little filly. He didn't like fast jobs. He was a planner. A plotter. But in the end, she was nothing more than another thump on the fender. *Another bump in the road. Yuk. Yuk.* Trickiest part of her was stealing the car. He'd grabbed one at a Walgreens when a woman left it running. Problem was, he got caught between two cars at a red light exiting the parking lot. He could see the woman staring quizzically as she tried to figure out where her car was. Each crime depended on a successful preamble crime. That's when he realized how lucky he'd been. Cops weren't bright, but they weren't dumb. Sooner or later, they'd add two plus two. Might even get four. Thank God they didn't pay much attention to stolen car reports. He'd always picked older cars. Preferably in lower-income neighborhoods. Think the boys in blue went to the mat for those?

He'd done the final job and then, poof, Doc just up and quit. Vanished without a whisper. Doc. He was a bright guy. Knew when to pull out. He'd never heard from the man again. That's the way to do it, dude. That's how to roll.

Still, would it have hurt him to have said goodbye?

He took a long pull on his beer and stared at the Gulf of Mexico. All men lose their thoughts when gazing over water, and although he was an exception in many instances, this was not one of them. He struggled to bring them back, for he had business to attend to.

Guy walked right across my property. Said he's looking for some man's daughter. Then gave up too easy. I trail him and he finds Clive.

Who else will he find? How deep might he dig? Doc always said to shut them down before they got too loud. No need to reinvent the wheel here. This fucknoodle has a woman in his life. Looks like a pair of girls as well. Like I don't have experience in that area? How cool would that be? I'll—

"This seat taken?"

"Huh?"

"This seat? Is it taken?"

"No."

A man pulled back the stool next to him. "I'm a Hoosier myself. Where're you from?"

CHAPTER 29

I departed Georgy's house and took the I-375 ramp to 275 South. Twenty-five minutes after seeing photographs of Ziegler and Whiting side by side, I was again in front of Nathan Whiting's house. Whiting had denied knowing Ziegler, saying that although his mother worked for him, he didn't know the man. Yet he clearly knew Ziegler and spoke to him.

No one answered the front door. I trudged around to the back. His boat was on the lift, but there was no sign of him. I took the opportunity to peer in a back window. No dirty dishes on the counter. I circumvented to the front of the house. A middle-aged woman stood in the adjoining yard watering white and periwinkle vincas.

"Excuse me," I said. "Have you seen Nathan?"

She adjusted her hose to cover the flowers on her left. The petals danced and dodged the water. "Saw him pull out when I pulled in from Publix. About an hour ago. The little weasel's been skittish last couple of days. In and out. Comin' and a-goin'. Why are you looking for him, if you don't mind me asking?"

I told her we knew some of the same people years ago, and I was hoping he could help me find them.

"That why you dropped by the other day?"

My flower lady didn't miss much.

"It was. Does he take off often?"

"No. He spends most his time fiddling on his boat. That and selling stuff."

"Selling stuff?"

"He rummages through trash at night. He always has people dropping by his house and leaving with odd stuff. Old furniture. Garden tools. Suitcases. Barstools. Stuff like that."

I asked if she talked to him much.

"See that hibiscus bush here?" She jerked her head to the side while keeping the hose on the flowers. "I can hardly walk around my house anymore. I asked him a zillion times to cut it. I gave up. To answer your question, no, I don't talk to him. At all. He's not right."

"How so?"

"I know, how so. You really a friend of his? Not that I'm judgmental or anything, but I can't imagine him having friends."

"You've known him long?"

"Been neighbors for going on fifteen years, and no, I don't know him. No one does. We all steer clear of him, on account of Alice Ann's dog."

"What happened to Alice Ann's dog?"

She flipped her hose up to a yellow home with a single garage door on the other side of the street. "That's her over there. She had a dog that was fond of doing his business in Nathan's front yard. Charlie. Cute little thing. He was always complaining about it. One day, Charlie was just gone. The world's worst neighbor was out front whistling that day. He never whistled. That man doesn't have a note in his heart. Never could prove anything, though. So, not to be contentious, but we both know you're no friend of his."

"Never said I was."

She turned the nozzle off. "You're right. You didn't. Do I really want to know why you want to talk to him?"

"Probably not."

"Are you weasel shit like him?"

"I'll leave that to you. I'm looking for a man's lost daughter and thought he might be of assistance."

"That sounds legit, only because I don't think you could come up with that on the fly."

I handed her my card, wondering if I'd just been insulted. "If he or anyone else pops up."

"Okey dokey." She pocketed the card and turned the nozzle back on. "But I wouldn't be waiting around the phone if I was you. When he left today, he was lugging a suitcase bigger than him. You know, a carry-on."

CHAPTER 30

Albert Einstein said that time and distance are one and the same. That thought massaged my mind as my truck climbed the Tierra Verde Bridge. Archie had called and asked if I would drop by and apprise him of my progress. I was eager to question him about Lisa's aunt whom Katie had mentioned. As I crested the bridge, I snuck a glance to my right, trying to catch a glimpse of my house across the bay. I did, and it always amazed me how small it seemed. From a distance, everything shrinks. Miles. Minutes. Years. People. That's what triggered Einstein, though I think he was referring to a larger scope. But was he?

Rambler called as I started my descent.

"Ralphie piss the floor again?" I answered. I wasn't sure our last conversation ended on the best note and wanted to make amends.

"Your buddy Nathan Whiting was a person of interest," he said.

"In what manner?"

"Murders."

"Did I hear an *s*?"

"You did."

A tightness gripped me. I'd sensed this was where the tunnel was heading. What I might have to tell Archie. That was not a conversation I wanted to have.

"Arnelli said they never had enough to go after him," I said.

"Most of this was after Arnelli retired."

"Tell me."

"It's in a file."

"I'd like to see it."

"I'd like you to see it."

That line caught me by surprise. Rambler rarely called on me for help. Our relationship ran the other way.

"Can we arrange that now?" I said. I'd rather talk to Archie after I met with Rambler and had a chance to review the file he mentioned.

"What's that beachfront place? The one right on the water?"

"Paradise Grille?"

"See you in twenty," he said.

I entered the Tierra Verde roundabout, did a 360, and headed back to the beach. I punched Archie's number, told him something had come up, and lobbied to reschedule. He was cooperative, though his voice dripped with disappointment. This time, instead of glancing to my right to try to spot my house, I glanced to my left, but it was not to be found.

DETECTIVE RAMBLER STROLLED ACROSS the pavement, a sunbaked marshal in a spaghetti western. He took a seat on the bench across from me. We were shaded by an outmatched umbrella that fought gallantly against the sun.

No sooner had he sat down than he popped up. "Screw it. I'm grabbing a beer. You?"

"Allow me," I said.

I went to the counter and came back with two beers. I

handed him one and took a gulp of mine. It was cold but not cold enough. I dipped my head at a folder he'd dropped on the table. "That's our man, Whiting?" I said.

"It is. Where do we stand?"

We.

I filled him in on my visit with Georgy, the photographs, and my most recent trip to Whiting's house.

"Fifty percent of all violent crimes are never solved," he said after a long pull on his beer. "Murder. Rape. Bludgeoned bodies. That armpit of humanity who commits those crimes lives among us. We pass them every day. Unnoticed. On the streets. In the stores." He dipped his head at the folder. "We never even got close to charging Whiting with anything."

When he didn't follow up with that, I said, "But?"

He gazed at me. "If he ever were to be charged, it wouldn't be for one murder."

"How many?"

He shrugged as if the number was insignificant.

Everything shrinks.

"Five? Ten?" he said. "Baker's dozen? Take your pick."

My eyes wandered out over the azure waters of the Gulf. A young girl splashed in the waves as her companion took pictures. A woman bent over the sand. She plucked up a shell and placed it in a basket she was carrying. Two paddleboarders stroked their way north, their arms gleaming in the sun, and farther out, where the water draws a line with the sky, a boat raced in from the Gulf toward Pass-a-Grille Channel. I knew that on that boat, music was blaring, and people were drinking and laughing as the sun and wind lashed their faces.

Rambler said, "Ziegler never left enough of a trail to warrant a formal investigation. He likely performed abortions before Roe-Wade. He adopted a new business model when abortions became legal. Some women claimed they heard their babies cry while he insisted they were stillborn. You got all this from Arnelli, right? And he told you that some of the young mothers were victims of hit-and-runs."

"He did."

"Arnelli called after he met with you. Told me to look at the file again. That when he was talking to you, it was coming back to him. That he thought they had more than he alluded to when he spoke with you."

"And?"

"The more we know, the more we don't know. We don't know how many babies Ziegler delivered. We do know that number is at least a hundred and eighty. We don't know how many illegal abortions, nor do we care. We don't know how many women came to him for an abortion, and he talked them into going to term in order to arrange an adoption. We do know that many couples were thrilled to hear he had a baby for them. We don't know how many of those black-market babies belonged to mothers who were told their babies were stillborn. Many of those women who soon died."

"About that last part," I said.

He took a drink of his beer and continued. "You met Heather Kirkland, right? Arnelli said he told you about her."

"I did."

"Arnelli remembered, after he met with you at Doc Fords, that there was another woman. A Melanie Crawford." He dipped his head at the folder. "She's in there. Ziegler delivered her baby but told her it was stillborn." He placed his elbows on the table and continued. "Crawford claimed that Ziegler put her under. Like a laughing gas. And that she heard her baby cry, and it sounded healthy. She snooped around afterward. Talking to people at the Cardinal Inn. 'Have you seen my baby? Have you heard my baby?'"

I found myself wishing Rambler wasn't there. That the case wasn't taking the dark turn it was taking.

"When did it happen?" I asked.

He gave an ugly frown. A hump of the shoulder. "Four weeks, maybe?"

"How?"

"Hit-and-run outside a Seven-Eleven. Arnelli asked me to search hit-and-run fatalities in Ziegler's later years. We found nine. We think Crawford was the first. The connections weren't apparent, you understand? Not enough Ziegler mothers had stepped forth." He punched out his breath and added, "A cop feels bad when something goes on under his nose. Hindsight's a bitch, but life doesn't unfold like that."

I asked him what the normal number was of young women who were victims of hit-and-runs over the same time period that Ziegler operated his clinic.

"A rare to non-occurring event."

"Anything to put it in perspective?"

He polished off his beer. "Funny you ask. I ran the numbers. In the last forty-five years, three women of similar age have been victims of hit-and-runs. It's worse than it sounds. The population has more than doubled over that time."

We were quiet for a moment, digesting the implications of his statement. A man and a woman approached the far end of the picnic table.

"Are these taken?" the man said to me.

"All yours."

"Thanks." He and the woman camped out there.

I shifted my attention to Rambler. "You mentioned that Arnelli was retired when the department looked deeper into this. What did the detective who—?"

"Forget it. The dick who took over was edging out of his career. He wasn't interested in another headache. Who's this person you're searching for again?"

"Archie Williams's daughter. Her mother, Lisa Trowbridge, was a Ziegler patient."

"That's right." He bobbed his head a few times. "And Lisa?"

I thought I had told him, but maybe not. "Victim of a hit-and-run. Not long after being told her baby was stillborn."

"I take it you haven't shared this with him?"

"I have not."

"What are you going to tell him?"

I had no answer to that.

CHAPTER 31

The sun was half buried in the Gulf by the time I pulled into Archie and Bobbie Lee's driveway. I didn't want to worry Archie by suggesting that Lisa was murdered after her baby was stolen. What would that even sound like? *I discovered there's a high probability that Lisa was deliberately mowed down to keep her silent. Yes, that means you have a daughter. No, I can't find her.* If, in the end, the only thing I did for Archie was to conclude that Lisa was murdered and that his daughter couldn't be found, wouldn't he have been better off never to have engaged me?

I hit the doorbell, setting off the Westminster chimes inside the house. The door swung open.

"Don't you love it?" Bobbie Lee said. Her perky voice lifted my spirits. She really was a winner. "Every time someone comes to the house, I think it's time for tea and biscuits." She curtsied. "Why, Mr. Darcy, please do come in." I tipped my imaginary top hat as I stepped inside. "Follow me. Archie and I are out back drinking in the sunset."

Bobbie Lee led me through the kitchen—no, I didn't stare at the island—and straight out the back door. Before we got within earshot of Archie, she said, "He's a little winded. He had a good day, just overdid it a bit."

We joined Archie around a firepit, the tendrils jostling for attention in the air. He started to rise, and I told him to stay seated.

"What's your pleasure?" Bobbie Lee said.

"A sip of everything," I said.

"Oh my God. I know exactly what you mean."

Archie chuckled. "It is a shame that we must choose."

"Bourbon on the rocks," I said.

"Two fingers coming up," Bobbie Lee said. She swirled around to a bar cart.

"How's the hunt coming?" Archie said.

Super. Your high school lover was murdered, and I have no clue who or where your daughter is. What's the latest news from the cancer front?

"Moving along," I said. I filled him in on what I knew. That I'd visited with Charlene. His pair of ex-wives. Lisa's friend Katie Phillips. Josh Arnelli, the retired detective who kindly agreed to meet and share what he had from that time. I reviewed Nathan Whiting, the son of Belle, who was Ziegler's right-hand assistant. I left out my meeting with Georgy. And Clive. I didn't mention I knew who had sent him the letter proclaiming Little Strawberry's existence. I skirted around all references to hit-and-runs.

"You've been busy," he said. "I appreciate that. You said Ziegler started as an abortion doc? Then he switched gears?"

"Apparently," I said, tempering my response, for there was little you could say about Ziegler with certainty. "He was discreet, as one would expect. That makes it difficult to reconstruct his life years later." I wanted to clear up some things he told me earlier and test his memory. "Did you say Lisa's mother recommended that she go to Ziegler?"

I thought he'd told me as much, but I wasn't sure. Or was it Katie Phillips who had mentioned it?

"She did."

"And after her pregnancy, she moved in with her mother's sister?"

"Within a week after she gave birth, she moved in with her aunt in Bradenton. We thought she would be more help in raising the baby. Even without the baby, Lisa was tired of living with her mom. They both agreed it would be better if Lisa lived with her aunt."

"I should talk with her aunt."

"I didn't give you her name?"

"No."

"Bonehead. I'm not myself right now. Her name is Allison Gannon, though I've not spoken to her since those days."

As I hadn't divulged my meeting with Clive Emmons, I couldn't share with him that I already knew her name. "Katie Phillips mentioned the aunt but couldn't recall—"

Archie interrupted me. "I couldn't remember her name when you were over for dinner. That's why I didn't mention her at the time. I was too embarrassed."

"Arch," Bobbie Lee said.

"I know," he replied. He glanced at me. "Next time something or someone comes up that I don't remember, I'll be more open."

What would that sound like? *There's someone you need to talk with, if only I could recall their name.*

"Don't worry," I said. Archie would only handicap my efforts if he was more concerned about the appearance of his mental acuity than about finding his daughter.

"It's all good," Bobbie Lee said, picking up the undercurrent of the conversation. "Jake has her name." She shifted her attention to me. "Talk to her. Lisa was closer to Allison than to her own mother."

I opted to continue with Bobbie Lee instead of Archie. Archie had obviously shared everything with her. "You said Lisa was induced?"

"She was," Bobbie Lee said. "She was in her thirty-fifth or so week. Ziegler said the baby had to come early, and that's why he drugged her."

"He would have needed to add the amnesia drug," I said. "It's not necessary in order to induce a woman to use a drug that nearly puts her under. Plus, he was not an anesthesiologist."

"We realize that," Bobbie Lee said testily. "But what sixteen-year-old girl will argue with a doctor?"

"And Ziegler told her it was a stillborn?"

"And here we are."

I took a healthy sip of bourbon that burned my throat. Bobbie Lee massaged her drink, her mint-colored fingernails rotating the glass. She seemed at ease filling in for her husband. I sensed a genuine interest in finding Archie's daughter for him. For them.

"What can you tell me about Lisa's last day?" I said, shifting my attention back to Archie.

"She called me," Archie said. "From her aunt's house in Bradenton. We were supposed to meet that evening."

"Did you ever meet her aunt?"

"A few times, before all this happened. Not afterward. She'd answer the phone, we'd chat, then she'd put Lisa on. Lisa always got along well with her aunt. I remember getting the impression that her aunt was on our side. She supported us, and that meant something."

"When was—?"

"She was genuine, too. Her aunt. Funny, how facts and details age but impressions remain clear. Ageless."

I asked him when was the last time he had talked with Lisa's aunt. As the tail end of the question left my lips, I wished I hadn't asked it, for I knew the answer. The context of the phone call.

"I can't answer that," Archie said.

"I understand. Let's back up. When did Lisa become suspicious that her baby was alive?" I knew the answer from my conversation with Clive, but did Archie?

"We were on the phone one evening. She said that Ziegler had put her under. Claimed he did it for her safety. He came back in the room and said the baby was stillborn. But she swears she heard it cry. Said it sounded fine to her."

"Maybe it was wishful thinking," I said, challenging his memory. "Her mind playing tricks on her."

"We discussed that. She insisted it was real. Said the whole birthing experience was coming back to her, frame by frame. Like I said, we talked every day, and I went down to see her every other day. Her last day—" He cleared his throat.

"It's okay, babe," Bobbie Lee said. Her adoring eyes never left her husband's face.

Archie continued. "Her last day, we made plans to meet in Bradenton that evening after her night classes. At a McDonald's." He took a breath, stood and walked into the house.

"This is hard for him," Bobbie Lee said. "He's an emotional man. No apologies."

"What's the latest word from his doctors?"

"Mildly encouraging."

"What does that even mean?"

She chuckled. "I know, right? He'll beat this. I know he will."

Archie returned to his seat. He handed me a yellowed folded paper napkin. "Open it," he instructed me.

I did. In pen were the words *But never doubt I love.*

"'Doubt thou the stars are fire,'" Archie said. "'Doubt that the sun doth move, doubt truth to be a liar, but never doubt I love.' It was from a poem she liked."

"Lear."

"Excuse me?"

"Shakespeare."

He eyed me for a moment before he continued. "The last time we saw each other, she jotted that down and handed it to me."

Bobbie Lee had been gazing at her husband. She shifted her eyes to me. "On the last night, Archie went to meet her at the McDonald's," she said. "It was their usual meeting place. He waited an hour and then called Lisa's aunt."

My mind, increasingly aware that my two girls would be grown women someday and far removed from the protective shield of childhood, erected a wall. It disallowed me imagining the words that Lisa's aunt spoke to a young man, consumed by love, sitting alone in a McDonald's.

Bobbie Lee continued in a soft voice. "She told Archie there had been a terrible accident. That Lisa had been struck by a car. It was winter. Dark. Whoever hit her had not stopped."

Archie took over the narrative from Bobbie Lee. "I sat there until they closed. Staring out a window. Eleven o'clock. I stood. I walked out the door a different man from the one who had walked in. My success in burying that evening has a direct correlation to my success in business. Abigail and Lester will never understand that. No one does."

"I do," Bobbie Lee said, reaching over and touching her husband. "And I think Lester might as well."

"I know, honey."

"And your little girl, wherever she is, had a good life," Bobbie Lee said. "*Is* having a good life. I never knew my birth parents, and I had a great childhood and loving parents."

"You were adopted?" I said to Bobbie Lee.

"I was," she replied in an upbeat voice. "A private adoption. I've never felt that urge to find my birth mother or father. Some people do, and I respect that. But not me. My mother was a loving woman. My father was a wonderful and generous man. But I do understand that my birth mother might want to meet me. Nor would I mind it. I heard she was young and just couldn't bear the responsibility. I always wanted kids myself, but that ship has sailed."

"Are your parents alive?"

"Unfortunately, they both died years ago."

"I'm sorry to hear that."

"Funny, now that they're gone, I find myself wondering more about my biological mother. Weird, right? It's like we all have this need to know there's someone living who is part of us. The whole experience allows me to understand Archie's quest to find his daughter, to search with him."

She stood and walked over to her husband. She knelt in front of him and clasped his hands in hers. "Just like me, your little girl had loving parents. She's happy. We're going to find her. You can tell her about her mother. How special she was and how she loved her so very much. Jake will find her."

Bobbie Lee shot me a sideways glance that, if I'm not mistaken, translated to *get your ass in gear.*

CHAPTER 32

It was late by the time I wheeled into my driveway. The girls were asleep. I dropped a Jo Stafford album on the floor model 1963 Magnavox. She'd been on my mind since the first Ronstadt tune I'd heard at Archie's home. I adjusted the volume and joined Kathleen on the screened porch, where the solitary candle jiggled in the dense darkness.

I kissed the top of her head. "Where's Morgan?"

"Just missed him. How was the dragon slaying today?"

She does that. Always asks about my day before I have a chance to inquire about hers.

"You first," I said.

"Sophia said something to me in Spanish that I didn't understand."

"Guess that whole two-language thing backfired on us," I admitted.

Kathleen gave an uncharacteristic shrug. "Win some, lose some. My day: I taught my class on Eudora Welty—I told Todd I wasn't offering it next year; it's boring the lights out of me—helped Joy on her dolphin project, and told Sophia we can never have a dog because her daddy hates them."

Todd is the department chair. Every year at the Christmas party, he drinks too much and slurps over Kathleen.

"You did no such thing."

"I certainly did. I'm bone tired of Southern short stories. *The Optimist's Daughter* has become *The Teacher's Drudgery.*"

Quick, isn't she?

"What did you really tell her about a dog?"

"That good things come to those who are patient."

"Please do not indoctrinate my children with that."

"Your turn."

I recapped my day. Told her about Clive. The letter.

"You found who wrote the letter to Archie," she said.

"I did."

"But didn't tell him that?"

"Correct."

"Why?"

"I'll get to that."

"And Bobbie Lee was adopted?"

"She was."

"Like our girls. So at least Archie has that. Wherever his little girl ended up, she, like Bobbie Lee and, hopefully, our two, will look back with only fond memories. That should ease his burden."

Kathleen and I had discussed what being adopted might mean to our girls once they were older. Many adopted children are fine not knowing their biological parents. Others make it a life mission to hunt them down. That can be hard on the adoptive parents. They would confess to understanding the drive, the need to know about birth parents. But still, to love a child unconditionally yet have them obsessed with someone who gave them up could be tough. The birth mothers of both our girls were young and didn't want their babies. They were happy to hand them off. Would a woman knock on our door ten, twenty years from now and demand to see her child, legal document be damned? In the case of Lisa, though, her baby, if alive, was stolen from her. But the baby never knew that. It was unlikely the adopting parents knew that either. At least, I hoped they didn't know. In any event, Lisa would never knock on anyone's door.

"When the girls want to know about their birth mothers, we need to share everything with them," Kathleen said. "And we need to tell them both at the same time."

It was the eleven-thousandth time Kathleen had brought up the subject of how and when we would inform the girls they were adopted. I was disturbed by her preoccupation with the subject. She was equally bothered by my breezy attitude.

"They'll be fine." Like I said, breezy.

"You keep saying that. How can you be so sure? So optimistic?"

"It's the natural state of a shallow mind. There's another, more pressing issue than stolen babies," I added.

"Is this the 'I'll get to that' part?"

"It is. Many of the birth mothers in Ziegler's later years were killed."

"Years later or—?"

"Within months after giving birth."

I explained what I knew. As I spoke, I wondered about Lisa Trowbridge's death. It would have been in Bradenton. Was it even included with the others? Were there more outside the local jurisdiction?

"I see," Kathleen said when I finished. "We have a peripeteia. Are the police going to reopen those cases?"

"Currently there's not enough to warrant the effort," I admitted. "Rambler wants me to carry the ball."

"You do owe him. If you find something, it would be a sense of closure for those still alive. And for those who remember." She stood. "I'm beat. I'm going to bed to read."

That surprised me. She usually stayed up later than me. "Welty?" I said.

"Not a prayer. I've discovered grocery store checkout lane magazines."

"Talk about a peripeteia."

"Who knew I had an interest in thirty-four decorating ideas, twelve recipes, eight new diet ideas, three tips for better sex, and the latest Hollywood couple to discover parenting."

"One of those sounds promising."

She kissed the top of my head. "I'll *dog*-ear those pages for you."

She left to pursue her newfound passion. I went to the study and sequestered myself in front of my computer with Rambler's file beside me. I made a list of the victims the police had identified. All were struck by different cars. All the cars were stolen. That's not correct. All the cars they were able to trace were stolen. Many of the vehicles were never identified. As I suspected, Lisa was not part of that list.

I organized the list by time. By location. By age. Searching for a pattern. All had family contact information, including the name of the officer who delivered the news to their parents.

Witnesses to Lisa's death said a white car gunned her down as she crossed a street. One witness said the car had been waiting at the curb and started from a parked position. Another stated that he saw the car careening down the street at a fast speed before losing control and striking Lisa. There was no mention of it being a stolen vehicle. They might not have known that at the time, if ever. Neither witness lifted any information from the plates. After the initial article on Lisa's death, there was nothing else. She was a high school student who, walking out of night classes, got run down by a car and was never heard from again.

I sent a text to Rambler asking him to contact the

Bradenton police and request their records, assuming they had any.

I compiled information on five of the victims. Phone numbers and addresses. I had little reason to believe I could locate a family member, as time had created too much distance. But what if the killer was still out there? One of Rambler's ghosts wandering the streets?

Hadley III came in. She looked more awake than I felt.

"How's the hunt?"

"Meow."

"Tell me about it."

"Meow."

She jumped on my lap. I scratched her behind the ear. We had a moment.

"What do you think about getting a dog?"

"Meow."

"Tell me about it."

It was 1:09 a.m. I was holding a conversation with a cat. I shut my computer, went to bed, and ruminated on how to keep my girls forever young. But that wasn't my last thought. For as my conscience faded, the final remnants of the day were the autumn fields of a woman's hair and the dry jasmine perfume of another. The smallest hiccups of the heart blot out everything else.

CHAPTER 33

Where the grapes of wrath are stored

He swung open the metal door to the pole barn, then stepped inside. He had made certain to drop by at least twice a year to check on the cars. And the pictures. They'd be what? In their fifties and sixties now? Looking in the mirror and despairing over the lines, the sagging skin, youth slipped out the back door when they weren't paying attention. The way he saw it, he did the little slut-twats a favor, immortalizing them in those years when innocently strolling down the street stirred unbidden lust in men.

He got in a car. A '73 blue Datsun 240z. A sporty little number. He'd dubbed it Dream Destroyer One. He did not consider himself a murderer. Never took another's life. He destroyed dreams. He'd never been allowed to dream, so why should others? He settled behind the wheel. No picture in this one. He didn't start posting pictures until after the second—*or was it Dream Destroyer Three?*

His ad hoc method of completing his assignments had left him with a random car collection. He desired a method to identify and link each car with its allotted task. He used Belle's camera to take pictures of the girls before Doc drugged them. Told them it was like a before-and-after picture, except he never took an after. They all smiled, though he couldn't help but notice even the dense ones seemed a little annoyed by a nerdy guy with a camera at the foot of their bed. After the first two—three, whatever—he'd tripped on the idea of taping the picture of the girl to the corresponding car. Problem solved.

He climbed into another car. *What's with the happy face?* He had never smiled at a camera. No one had ever smiled at him, and he didn't know how to do it or why. His mother—he was clueless as to who she was—had ditched him at birth. His feminine bone structure and large ears ensured that his contemporaries in school shunned him, except when they ridiculed him. See the lonely boy on the playground? See the student the teachers avoid because of his sullen attitude and limited academic potential? See the freak sitting by himself at lunch every day?

At choir, they sang "The Battle Hymn of the Republic." He thought he had a good voice, wailed for glory and freedom, until the girl next to him—some blonde number who scowled at him at every opportunity and who was no doubt royally peeved about her assigned spot—said he was tone deaf. *Do the world a favor, freak, and don't sing. Seriously, just shut up.* After that, he lip-synched Julia Ward Howe's words. Could recite them backward. Sideways. Upside down. He filed them in his brain to call upon in a manner and time he deemed appropriate. Certainly, his life would have a rallying cry to stir the soul.

Through twelve years of public education, there was only one question he ever wanted answered: *Why did she have me if she didn't want me?* From algebra to English, from linear equations to Harold Pinter, the answer was not to be found. He caused a little ruckus to see if the world would notice. It did not.

A bolt of inspiration jolted him.

How neat would it be to use the car that killed—who the hell was he looking for?—Lisa, that's her. How neat would it be to use that car to teach him a lesson? I mean, the idiot mentioned her name. Must be some reason he's digging for her, but none good for me. Think that would wake them up. Hello! It's me! Still punching the clock.

That brought a chuckle as he remembered a conversation with a high school guidance counselor whose face reminded him of turtle skin. Sitting in a cramped, windowless office with bright posters on cinder block walls. Birds soaring over mountains. A whale breaching. A flower in full bloom. A photograph of a salmon jumping upstream. Underneath it, BELIEVE YOU CAN AND YOU'RE HALFWAY THERE. Then the question from the ancient woman who glared at him with poorly disguised contempt from across a metal desk. It was his first day back after being expelled for a week for setting off a sulfur bomb in the girls' lavatory—the little ruckus. *I'm confused*, she admitted, though he could tell that she considered him beneath her station in life. *Your test scores are exceptionally high, but your grades don't reflect your abilities. And your actions. Well, young man, you can see where they landed you.* Then she popped the big gasser. *What career do you envision for yourself, Nathan?*

He found Lisa's car.

Well, loggerhead face, I was thinking . . .

CHAPTER 34

A low tide provided ideal running conditions on the beach the following morning. Early risers collected shells and scanned magic wands over the sand. At the jetty, where tides and currents warred with each other and the jagged rocks held fast against the foaming sea, stood a new sign. It had not been there yesterday. It read BEWARE OF EXTREME DANGER.

I turned and headed home along Pass-a-Grille Channel. I sprinted the last half mile, my lungs burning in pain. After a five-minute cooldown, I lowered the punching bag and pummeled it until my arms and shoulders were deadweight. Then I kicked the snot out of it. Like the rocks at the jetty repelling the sea, my efforts made no impression on the bag. I went around to the bay side of the house and, facing the rising sun, did three yoga poses I'd recently added to my morning routine. The last was warrior three, my arms spread forward and out, expecting to take flight. Florida sunrises are rarely challenged, and this morning was no exception. The few straggling clouds that floated in the lower eastern horizon vanished as the sun beamed rays of confirmation on water and land.

I showered under the outdoor showerhead on the side of the house, dried, dressed, and headed to the kitchen to fix a breakfast of scrambled eggs, smoked trout, onions, and bell peppers. No cheese. I'd managed to convince the girls that cheese would be disrespectful to the trout. Morgan had caught the fish yesterday and given us the fillets. Joy complained that she wanted French toast. I promised her that French toast was next up on the menu. Sophia said she wanted Spanish toast. I said no problem. Kathleen corralled the girls into her car and carted them to a library reading time. She would go to the college from there. Bonita would pick them up at eleven.

I poured a mug of coffee and hightailed it into my study. I took out the notes I'd made the previous night. Before I made my first call, Rambler rang.

"What do you got?" I said.

"You know I'm a cop, right?"

"Think so."

"My phone is never on silent."

"My bad. What did you find?"

"I'm not done stewing."

"Take your time."

"One a.m."

"Justice never sleeps."

"But I do," he pointed out.

"Did you find anything?"

"Lisa Trowbridge was never linked to the others," he said. "It was outside our jurisdiction. No one saw the connection. I'll send the Bradenton report, but there's not much. Conflicting witness reports. No tag. Generic car descriptions."

"The coverage of her death at the time didn't mention a stolen car."

"They never made the car," he said, confirming what I'd already decided.

"I'm going to contact some of the next of kin—at least, the ones I can find."

"And we're taking a hard look at reopening the case. Or, to be more precise, starting a new one concerning a previously unidentified series of related murders. You studied the file, right?"

I told him I had.

"Did you pick up that several witnesses across different killings described the driver as a young man?"

"I did."

"Why don't you stop by Whiting's place?" he said. "See if you can ruffle him. If he sees a badge, he's liable to run."

"Already did. Neighbor said he took off, suitcase in hand."

"Find the bastard."

He punched off.

I found a number for Allison Gannon, Lisa's aunt, and left a voicemail expressing the purpose of my call. Though I was tired of hurling myself at dead-end leads, I manufactured enthusiasm and started in on the rest of my list.

Nineteen-year-old Bree Winfield had been walking across a street in downtown Saint Petersburg when a car swerved around a corner, clipped her, and fled the scene. Bree was DOA at Saint Anthony's hospital. No suspects. My middle-of-the-night article did not mention that she'd just given birth. None of the hit-and-run articles had. That heartbreaking coincidence surfaced later.

Bree had been a patient of Dr. Ziegler. She was not married. I could find no information on her family life, other than her parents' address and phone number. Records showed that the family still owned the house, which was not the case with any of the others. That made Bree Winfield's family my best lead. No one answered the number. I left a voicemail that I was investigating the death of their daughter and to please give me a call.

The rest of the phone numbers no longer belonged to the

victims' families. The reality was cold. Who has the same phone number for forty years? Fifty?

I leaned back in the chair and blew out a breath I didn't know I was holding. I stared at the address for Bree Winfield's house. Time to put my ass in gear.

CHAPTER 35

Twenty-seven minutes later, I swung into a cracked concrete drive on East Fifty-Fourth Street. The single-block house had a brown palm frond on the roof. A disfigured prickly pear cactus staked out the center of the front yard, daring anything to encroach upon its territory. Once upon a time, Bree Winfield had lived here. She went to high school down the road. A car ended her life during her senior year. Middle of the day. A small, empty brown paper bag, along with two classroom books, and been found next to her body. Her mother had explained that the bag was for her lunch. She brought the empty one home every day so that it could be reused.

I hiked up to the door and rapped it with my knuckles. The door swung open.

"Hello," an elderly woman said in a hollow voice. She wore a cream dress with yellow flowers on it. Her white hair puffed out on both sides of her head. Virginia Winfield's daughter had died when she was seventeen. That put her mother somewhere in her early eighties.

I introduced myself and rushed out why I was there.

"You left a message?" she asked.

"I did."

"I must have been out back. Not that it matters. I don't know how to use that answering machine. My neighbor set it up for me years ago. No one ever calls on that line anymore. Why didn't you call my cell?"

I explained that I didn't have her cell number.

"No. I guess you wouldn't."

"I'd appreciate a few minutes of your time, Ms. Winfield."

"You can call me Betty. I haven't talked to anyone about Bree in a long time. Come on in. I'd love to tell you about her. She loves this hot weather, but I can do without it."

I started to follow her into the house but abruptly slowed my gait so as not to plow into her. Betty was steady on her feet but strictly low gear. We settled in the somberly furnished front living room. I sunk into a couch and thought I might hit the floor. Betty sat in a recliner that faced a TV. A cluttered table abutted the chair.

"I think of Bree with every breath," she said. "My husband passed six years ago this November. At least they're together now. But he was awful mean to her when she got pregnant. Know what killed him?"

Was I supposed to guess? "I do not."

"Knowing that when she died, they weren't on the best of terms. That took a little of him every night until one morning there wasn't enough of him left to wake up."

I asked her how Bree came to be under the care of Dr. Ziegler, opting not to follow her into the history of her deceased husband. It didn't work.

"It was like a door or window was open, and every day, part of him slipped out. I told him that Bree isn't mad at him. But he didn't pay no attention."

Betty's insistence on referring to her deceased daughter in the present tense made me consider that a part of her had slipped out those windows as well. I repeated my question concerning Ziegler.

"He was recommended to us at church," she said. "By Pastor Hibbard. That was before we learned he took all the church money. Bree and I both liked him—Dr. Ziegler, not Pastor Hibbard. I know he had some controversy later on, but we had no problem with him. Delightful man, really."

Her comment was not a surprise. I'd read that those who dealt with Ziegler found him a charming and caring person.

"We didn't have no money," she continued. "No insurance. Butch—that was my husband—was between jobs. Dr. Ziegler had a nice little clinic he ran out of the back of a motel. Cardinal Inn—that's the name."

I asked her if Bree had wanted to keep the baby.

"Heavens, yes. I told her not to worry. That I would help her take care of it. We were both so excited for the future. Talked about it all the time. All the things we would do with the baby. All the good times waiting for us."

"Where was the father?"

"Oh, he was a fine boy. But he wasn't for her. I mean, they might have made it, but . . ." She trailed off. Her eyes got lost out the window. "Well, they never got the chance."

I asked her to tell me about her daughter's experience with Dr. Ziegler.

"He had an assistant. Name's left me. She was all business, but the doctor was warm. But Bree's little boy was stillborn. That broke her heart. She would have made a wonderful mother."

"How long after that did she die?"

"Who?"

"Bree."

"Oh, she's not dead. She's just not here."

"I understand. How long after she gave birth did she leave?"

"Two months? No, no. Not even that long. She'll be back, though."

"That had to be hard. Losing the baby and your daughter not coming home."

Her jaw quivered. "It is," she said with effort. "But I got to be here for her, understand? I can't take the road that Butch did."

"I'm sure Bree's proud of you. Was she fully conscious during the delivery?"

"I took her to the clinic when she started having contractions. Dr. Ziegler told me later that he had to get the baby out fast, for both her and the baby's safety. He had to put Bree under."

I phrased my next comment carefully. "Did Bree have any recollection immediately afterward?"

"What do you mean?"

"When the anesthesia was wearing off."

She bit her lower lip. The door of a mailbox clanked behind me.

"She told me she heard her baby. He sounded real healthy to her."

"How did she know the sex? Did Ziegler tell her?"

"Yes. But then she claimed later that she remembered seeing him. That he was kicking and all."

"What did you think of that?"

"I told her that Dr. Ziegler said it was stillborn. That it was her mind playing tricks on her."

"Did she persist in believing she heard her baby?"

"There's no unconvincing Bree when she sets her mind on something. She said she heard Dr. Ziegler and his assistant mumbling something about getting him out of there. But you got to understand that she was drugged. I told her that. The mind can do terrible things to you in that state. Don't you think so?"

It is by the grace of our delusions that we advance from one day to the next. I had no desire to crumble Betty's world, though I sensed she had doubts.

"I do," I said. "Did she ever approach Dr. Ziegler after she gave birth and express what she heard?"

"He told her what I just said. That those drugs can mess you up."

"Did she bring it up on more than one occasion?"

She didn't respond. The air was thick in silence. A clock ticked somewhere in the house.

"Why these questions about her giving birth? What are you suggesting?"

Lines of worry creased her face. I tented my hands in front of me. I didn't know what to say and wished I wasn't there.

"There were some other hit-and-run victims during that time," I said in a gentle voice, as if that would soften the words. "I'm just trying to see if they're related. Did Bree—"

"Are you with any law enforcement?"

"No, ma'am. I'm being retained by the family of another victim." I returned to my earlier question, already regretting my use of the word *victim*. "Did Bree share her memories with Dr. Ziegler on more than one occasion?"

"Yes." The firmness of her reply surprised me. "About a week before she went away, she went there again, to the clinic. Dr. Ziegler was busy, but she talked to Dr. Ziegler's assistant. The name I don't recall."

"Belle."

"Was that it? I really don't remember. She told Bree that her baby was stillborn and that hallucinations were a common side effect of the drug. But Bree told me that night that she thought the woman was lying to her. She was a gone a week later. Walking home from school."

"Did she ever mention her crying baby to anyone other than Dr. Ziegler and his assistant, Belle?"

"Not that I know of. She did say there was another fella there the day she saw Belle. Just sort of hanging around."

"Did she say who?"

"She didn't know him."

"Did she describe him in any manner?"

"Younger guy, about her age, with a mustache and Dumbo ears. I remember her saying that. Bree has a good sense of humor. Now I have a question for you."

She paused.

Tick. Tick. Tick.

"Yes?"

"Do you think it was the drugs?"

Betty Winfield wasn't as far gone as I thought she was. Do I lie?

"No."

Tick. Tick. Tick.

"And that doctor gave my grandbaby up for adoption?"

"I don't know if we'll ever learn the truth."

Tick. Tick. Tick.

"And she was murdered?"

I remained silent, unable to formulate an answer. Her head slumped. She kneaded her hands together.

"There's something I want to show you," she said, raising her eyes to meet mine.

I trailed her down a hall and into a nursery. A crib. A rocking chair. A dresser. A dustless bookshelf. A record was propped next to a record player. *Winnie the Pooh and the Blustery Day* with Sterling Holloway.

"Bree and I had the nursery all ready. I saw the future every day. Caring for the baby. Baby's first Christmas. First birthday. When she went away, my future died. But I got to keep it nice. Keep it ready. Don't you think?"

I nodded. "It looks nice."

"I miss her smile," she continued. "I miss my husband

coming through the door at five thirty. I miss watching TV with someone. I miss having a newspaper at my doorstep every morning, and I miss John Denver's voice, but most of all, I miss my little girl. I never knew miss could fill every minute and hurt so bad."

She went to a dresser, opened it, and pulled out an infant sleeper. She handed it to me. I had no choice but to take it. It was decorated with dogs. Cats. Ducks and squirrels.

"What do you do with an infant sleeper, never used?"

CHAPTER 36

He has loosed the fateful lightning

Of course, it didn't start. It had been sitting there for nearly half a century. He considered using one he'd tuned up and had taken to trail the man in the black truck. Mr. Hot Shit. No, he would use that car. He was an artist. He had a body of work to preserve. An oeuvre. He would do it right. Take his time. This, after all, was to be the finale.

He moved into the two-bedroom 1930s bungalow on his country property. He'd purchased it years ago, not just for its pole barn, but when the world ended—and, hello, it was just around the corner—he wanted a quiet place from which to observe the fireworks. Far from the madding crowd of humanity that he never understood. From the uncaring faces, not a single one of which had ever shown interest in him. The only time the world took notice of him was when he smoked the girls' room. Lesson learned.

Belle would insist that he was always strange. Withdrawn. Her interest in rearing a child stemmed from obligation, not from any maternal instinct or desire. In the end, he was more accomplice than son.

He thought of returning to his house. *Might want to get the box out of the garage.* But he assumed that the man was on to him. That his house was hot. Besides, the whole thing would be done in a week, and he'd be back on his boat, tying fishing line.

Dream on, scrotum brain. You ain't never seeing that place again.

He admitted that the past was catching up to him faster than he was running from it. That his house was toast. His boat. He'd made peace with that. Had already started formulating an alternative plan. He checked his watch. Time to vamoose. Got some surveillance to do. He got in a car and headed down his long and winding driveway. *Let's see what Hot Shit is up to.*

CHAPTER 37

Allison Gannon, Lisa Trowbridge's aunt, returned my call and stated that Archie had called her as well. She provided her address in Bradenton and added that she was looking forward to my visit.

As I gunned the truck up the Sunshine Skyway, I stole a glance at the water below me and the boats scarring its silvery surface. It's hard to look at a boat and not pine to be on it. Conversely, I've never been on a boat, glanced up at the bridge, and wished I was in a car. Concrete highways are great, but they're one-dimensional compared to the unshielded winds of laneless seas.

Twenty minutes later, I pulled into Allison's drive. A man in the double garage was hunched over a red 1965 Mustang. He looked up when I climbed out of the truck. I introduced myself and explained that Allison was expecting me.

He thrust out his hand, and we shook. "Adam Linker. I'm a neighbor. Allison lets me use her garage for my projects. Seeing as how my own garage is full of yesterday's projects." Linker had rosy cheeks, a biblical beard, and a booming voice. He was more teddy bear than man. “Allison said you’d be stopping by. Terrible story about your niece, Lisa, all those years ago.”

“She was Allison’s niece.”

“That’s right,” he replied in a kind voice. “She said to send you out back. That’s where she paints.”

A paver-brick walk led to the backyard, where a large woman stood behind an easel, paintbrush in hand. A pair of glasses clung tenuously to the edge of her lumpy nose. She peered over those glasses.

“Tell me what you think,” she said. “Be honest. I’m too old for bullshit.”

She stepped away from her painting. I walked behind her, expecting to see something from the catalog of Florida amateur oil paintings. An ibis. Maybe a pelican or two. Sunsets on the beach and waves upon the shore. Instead, it was of a rainbow-colored clown holding a bouquet of dead black flowers. What is it with all the clowns? The only word that seized my mind was *creepy*.

“It’s nice,” I rushed out.

“You don’t think it’s too creepy?”

“Not at all. Why the dead black flowers?”

“It goes with the title. I come up with a title first and then paint it. This one is called *Funeral for a Clown*. I assume you’re Mr. Travis?”

“Jake.”

She wiped her hands on a cloth. “I’ve been painting since forever. My sister was good at it as well. Our mother used to tell us the gift of the brush ran in our hands. Have a seat.”

I sat in a wicker chair that creaked with my weight. She chose a green cushioned loveseat next to a dry fountain. The air was fresh and felt good compared to Betty Winfield’s house, which had that stale and lifeless odor of the old. I didn’t tell you about it because it seemed an unkind thing to point out, but now you know.

"I was surprised to hear from Archie yesterday," she said. "Talk about a shout-out from the past. Know what I remember him for? 'Is Lisa there?' I got to the point that when the phone rang, I just yelled at Lisa to pick it up. She moved in right after she lost the baby. Beth—that was her mom, my sister—stayed up in Saint Pete. The two of them needed a break from each other. I was planning on Lisa and the baby moving in, but only Lisa came. That was . . . tough. You know what happened?"

"I do."

Unlike Katie Phillips, whom age had skipped, the years had taken up residence in Allison. But that in no manner affected her demeanor or confidence.

"Sad," she said. "Tragic, really. I lost my only child and husband five years later. It was a rough spell. My husband was walking in the woods, carrying our baby. He tripped on a branch and went down. Hard. Our little boy was eleven weeks. He broke his neck and died. My husband was destroyed with guilt. About a year later, I surprised him and came home early to fix lasagna. He surprised me by killing himself that night. He left a note saying not to cry, that he wanted to be with Brennen, and that our baby boy would never be alone again."

"I'm so sorry," I said, wondering how the conversation had gone so dark so fast. I recalled Betty Winfield's story about her husband. Do fathers get out of this gig alive?

She laughed, which surprised me. "I left out the best part," she said. "He added that the lasagna was great. That brings a smile to this day. Sorry to bomb you with all that. For some reason, I have a strong desire to get it out when meeting people, and I'm prone to delivering it like the weather report. It's a cleansing and allows me to go on. Now, how may I help you?"

As I had with Archie, I asked her to recap Lisa's final days.

"I'm not sure I trust my memory. But, for what it's worth, Lisa planned to meet Archie at McDonald's after night school. She told me she had some good news for him. I knew Archie, of course. If ever two people were in love, it was them. My dumb sister said they were too young to know love, but that's only because Beth had never found love and was jealous when others did. She couldn't stand that her daughter was happier than her. I was ten years younger than Beth. No offense to her memory, but I was a nicer person."

"Did Lisa ever mention that she heard her baby cry?"

She wiped a finger under her nose. "You ever have any memories that you know to be true, but you turn them away because you don't want them to be true?" She scrunched her face. "Did I say that right?"

"You did. And I know what you mean."

"Yes. She told me she heard her baby cry. Lisa said her memory was coming back. I suggested it was her mind playing tricks on her. But she didn't buy it. She was convinced that her baby was alive."

"What did she say about Dr. Ziegler?"

"She called him."

I sat forward in the chair.

"She called Ziegler? When?"

"Three to four days before she died."

I asked her what they discussed.

"She accused him of lying to her. That her baby wasn't still-born. That she heard it cry. She was pretty adamant. I give her credit. Remember, she was just coming up on seventeen."

"Did she tell you how Ziegler responded?"

"He explained it was a common side effect of the drug. That he was sorry, but her baby was stillborn."

"What did he do with the infant's body?"

"He destroyed it. Produced a death certificate."

"Do you have it?"

"Last known possession was with my sister, who he mailed it to. I assume it's long gone."

I wasn't surprised that Ziegler had provided fake death

certificates. He would likely have produced fake birth certificates for the adopting parents.

"She told me she was going to find her baby. She decided to call someone else."

"Who?"

"I don't know. Someone associated with the clinic that Dr. Ziegler ran."

"Do you believe that Lisa's death was related to her calls to Dr. Ziegler's clinic?"

She didn't answer.

"Allison?"

"Not at first. At first, I was overcome with grief. But later, when news of what Ziegler had done leaked out, I wondered. The timing, you know? Her calling Ziegler. But the police said it was a random hit-and-run. They never found the guy."

I circled back to her earlier comment. "Can you remember anything about the second person she called?"

"Not off the top of my head."

"How about the bottom?"

Funny guy, right?

She smiled. "Never was much there."

"Perhaps the person's job," I implored her. "His assistant was a lady named Belle. Did Lisa call her?"

"No. She said she couldn't trust her, seeing how close she was to Dr. Ziegler. But I remember thinking it was someone who hung around there. Maybe not an employee."

"Did she contact the motel to see if they knew? The owner was a man named Charles Buford."

She shook her head. "No. She said it was someone her own age. I was home when she made the call, but I was in the other room, and she got up and closed the door. I remember her asking him how that mustache was coming along. I was standing in the kitchen. Funny how your mind holds on to the most inconsequential detail."

"You mentioned earlier that she had good news for Archie. What was it?"

"She'd gotten a phone call claiming her baby was alive, but she wanted to tell Archie first. I assumed it was that, though I told her it was probably a prank. Someone looking for money."

"Any indication who called her?"

"No. But he must have known Lisa, right? How else would he have known she was here?"

I told her there was a young man, the groundskeeper, who had befriended Lisa and who Lisa had confided in. That he was the person who made the call.

"You know this?"

"He told me."

"That makes so much sense," Allision said. "That's bothered me for years. What else did he tell you?"

"Lisa's baby was not stillborn."

"Wow. You said that about as casually as I recited my somber tale. So Archie has a real chance of finding his daughter."

"He has a daughter. Finding her is another issue."

"I see," she said, bouncing her head up and down as if mentally digesting the implications of my confirmation.

The conversation stumbled on until I thanked her for her time, and we parted with the usual empty promise to keep each other apprised.

"Pleasure meeting you," Adam said in his resonating voice as I passed him. "Good luck finding your niece." I didn't correct him.

At the crest of the Sunshine Skyway, I noted a gray sedan jostling behind me. But then it passed me, though I passed it a little later. Some people never learn to drive at a constant speed. I settled into the flow of traffic, steering the truck with the fingers of my left hand.

Maybe it was Betty Winfield mentioning John Denver

earlier; for whatever reason, I put on Lana Del Rey's cover of "Take Me Home, Country Roads." I listened to it repeatedly until the traffic faded, and there was nothing left of the world except her soulful voice lamenting the road home, but that wasn't where I was headed.

CHAPTER 38

Of his terrible swift sword

He sat in his car on a residential street in Bradenton and grudgingly admired the man in the black truck. *One focused son of a bitch, I'll give him that. Scuttering around and talking to people.* But who? And why? He had taken extra precautions this time. Not only a different car, but he wore large sunglasses. Shaved off his mustache. Lonely, squirrely little mass killer that he was, he had grown fond of his life. He had no intention of kissing it goodbye. He might have been blessed by lady luck a time or two in the past, but he wasn't going to leave it in her hands this time.

The man walked out of the house. *Who lives there? A Ziegler baby? What dots is this turdface connecting?* He tried to remember what the articles on the hit-and-runs had said. He had clipped them out of the newspapers and placed them in the box but had not revisited the holy scripture in decades. If questioned, he would say he was fascinated by the murders and felt terrible for the girls. There was no crime in keeping old newspaper articles, was there, officer?

He knew that circumstantial evidence would challenge his claim. He also knew that circumstantial musing would not be enough to open fifty-year-old murder cases. That would be DNA's job, and there was nothing to connect him to his victims. He had never even so much as touched one of them.

He followed the man back over the Sunshine Skyway. *Christ, it's high. Is that wind?* He took a couple of deep breaths, counted to ten, counted to ten again, and the moment passed. He decided to stop trailing the man. Despite his efforts to be invisible, if he followed him continually, it would only be a matter of time before the man became suspicious. He knew that obscurity was his friend.

Yeah, I remember now. I did a job in Bradenton. Dimples. Stupid girl had actually confided in me that she thought her baby was still alive. Oopsie. Wrong person to call. Was that the Lisa job? Shit.

The man in the truck peeled off I-275 onto Pinellas Bayway. He sped by. He'd been developing his own agenda as the miles slid by underneath him. There was one person left from that time. One person who could talk, possibly point a finger at him. Who might lead to Lisa. *Fool. He's miles ahead of you. You got to end this now.*

With both hands on the wheel, his Rays baseball cap low over his face, he navigated to his new destination. On the way there, he stopped at a sporting goods store. He bought a face mask of the kind that fishermen use to protect themselves from the sun.

CHAPTER 39

Nathan Whiting's house was on the way to Clive Emmons's, which is why I went there first.

I didn't expect Nathan to be home, and I was right. I knocked on his neighbor's door. *No, I haven't seen him since we last talked. No, there's no way he could have come back without me knowing it. His grass needs cutting. What do you think that does to my property value?*

I thanked her and ribboned my way through surface roads to Clive Emmons's house. My mind played out a sequence of events as I gunned it from one traffic light to another. Lisa calls Ziegler. She claims she heard her baby. He tells her she was hallucinating, which was natural. She remains convinced that her baby is alive. She makes a second call, searching for validation—this one to Nathan, a boy about her age. But he only confirms what Ziegler said. She gets depressed. Starts to doubt herself. Wonders if she really is hallucinating. Ziegler goes to Whiting. *I got a job for you. I know, she called me as well.*

Her phone rings. Your baby is alive, Clive says. I saw it. I heard it. She's excited. She calls Archie. Let's meet. I got great news. What does she think of Ziegler at that point? Does she realize she's tripped over something bad? Does she have fear? Or does her joy drown her instincts, which would be shouting that something was very, very wrong, and she should contact law enforcement?

Lisa and Archie never meet. She's a fatal victim of an unsolved hit-and-run that evening. Someone acted fast. Did Lisa, as she spotted the speeding car, think it was an accident? Or did she realize with horror that she was being silenced for discovering the truth?

I parked in the driveway, took the front porch steps in one stride, and punched the doorbell. I wanted to see if Clive had more to add to his story. Maybe there was something he forgot to mention or withheld. Behind me, a car blasted down the street, its exhaust system refitted to create as much disturbance as possible.

I hit the doorbell again and knocked on the door.

It swung open.

"Hello?" I said, poking my head into the front room. "Clive? It's Jake. Anyone home?"

A screen door slammed shut in the kitchen.

"Clive? Hello?"

I hustled through the front room and into the kitchen. Clive Emmons lay in a pool of blood, his eyes wide open, his mouth contorted in a struggle for air. I rushed to his side, fighting the urge to dash out the back and chase whoever had just bolted. Clive had been stabbed multiple times in the upper torso. His hands were cut and bloodied, the result of fighting his attacker.

"Stay with me, Clive," I urged him. I called 911 while applying pressure to his wounds. His arms and hands jerked in spasmodic movement. His eyes were solid on mine. Then they closed.

"Stay here, Clive. The ambulance is coming. Stay with me. Open your eyes. Clive. Clive."

I checked his pulse. None. I administered CPR. My mouth on his. My hands pumping his chest.

"Honey, I'm home." A woman's voice rang out from the front room. "I had to park in the street. There's a truck—"

A woman, who I assumed was Lanelle Emmons, entered the kitchen. She screamed and threw herself on me. Her fingers clawed my eyes. She bit my ear, yanked my hair, and punched my defenseless head.

Push hard. Let the chest spring back. Stayin' alive. Stayin' alive.

CHAPTER 40

Detective Rambler stepped through the back door that had slammed shut when I'd first come in the house. I sat in a metal chair in the kitchen with ice cubes wrapped in a dishrag pressed to my left eye. Lanelle's fingers had found their mark. A Band-Aid was on my right ear. Her teeth had been as accurate as her fingers.

"One neighbor saw a masked man running clumsily through the yard," Rambler said. "Another caught a glimpse of a car burning rubber. We'll know more, or not, after we canvass the neighborhood."

I'd called Rambler after I convinced Lanelle that I was there to help Clive, not hurt him. She finally realized that, despite her feral attack on me, my mouth was on her husband's lips, my air going into his lungs. When the ambulance arrived, she'd climbed in after they loaded Clive. He'd lost a lot of blood, and there was no way of knowing what damage his internal organs had sustained.

Rambler dragged back a chair from the laminate-topped table. "Let me see it," he said.

I lowered the washcloth.

"Consider yourself lucky that Mrs. Emmons didn't have a crochet needle in her purse," he said with admiration.

"Or think of the knives," I said, dipping my head toward a knife block on the counter. His eye followed my head.

"Or the knives," he said. He pushed his chair back farther from the table and crossed his legs. He reached into his pocket, took out a sleeve of gum, unwrapped it, and stuck it in his mouth. He gnawed on it for a moment. "You know the ancient Greeks chewed gum?"

"I missed that."

I thought he was going to say more, but apparently that was today's trivia. His rested his droopy eyes on mine. His eyebrows furrowed as if he were contemplating mysteries that had vexed the gum-chewing Greeks.

"From the top," he said.

"I knocked on the door, and—"

"Oh no," he said, wagging a finger at me. "I said the top. Why did you come here?"

I explained what had brought me to Clive Emmons's house. That this was my second visit. That I'd just met with Lisa's aunt. That Clive told me in my initial visit that he had called Lisa and told her that her baby was alive and that Lisa's aunt verified that Lisa had gotten a call with "good news." That we needed to entertain the thought that the serial killer was still open for business.

Rambler worked his gum around in his mouth. "Do you think Clive might have notified other birth mothers as well?"

"That was one of the reasons I dropped by. I wanted to see if he had anything to add to our last conversation."

"The killer knows you're digging up bones," he pointed out.

"I know."

"How?"

"I don't know."

He grunted. "You checking for tails?"

"Am now."

"Day late."

I got up and placed the washcloth in the sink. I told him about my meeting with Virginia "Betty" Winfield. How her daughter's experience with Ziegler and her death were similar to Lisa's.

"I checked with Arnelli," Rambler said. "He was homicide and had no reason to pursue stolen car reports. It never occurred to them, or it occurred too late, that the hit-and-runs were premeditated and therefore were homicides. You know much about reports on stolen vehicles?"

I admitted that I did not. Rambler explained that the FBI had a National Crime Information Center, the NCIC, that kept records for up to four years after they were entered into the system. But when Ziegler was operating, they kept the files for only ninety days.

"By the book," he continued, "they were supposed to keep them indefinitely. But files back then were housed in steel cabinets, not on silicon chips. For the sake of logistics, a homicide file would go to a steel vault, a stolen car to an aluminum trash can." He paused before adding, "As far as we can tell, not a single vehicle used to kill a mother was ever recovered."

I processed that and said, "And if we took a sample of stolen cars from that time?"

"No hard statistics, but over eighty percent are eventually located. Serial killers have habits. Rituals. They often preserve something from each of their victims. A ribbon. A lock of hair. A photograph. What's the chance of those cars disappearing and never being found? I don't know, but likely far less than our killer keeping the cars."

"That would take some space. Can you get a search warrant for Whiting's house?"

"Think the cars are in his bedroom?"

"Maybe we find a clue as to where they are."

"You got anything to convince a judge?"

"Nothing."

"That answers your question."

He stood and walked over to the sink. He opened the cabinet underneath it and spit his gum into a wastebasket. He missed. He bent over, picked it up, and flicked it into the can.

"It will take a month of Sundays," he said, "to get this cold case up and running to a point where we could petition for a search warrant. That's if the department even decides to reopen. And based on the lack of evidence coupled with how long ago it was, that's a long shot."

"My thoughts as well."

"Whatever you find is inadmissible."

"I'll keep you posted."

"I'll claim we never talked."

CHAPTER 41

His truth is marching on

H*oly shitskee, was that close or what? All the more reason it was the right decision. Was he dead? How the hell would I know? I never killed anyone, remember?*

When he'd heard the front door open, he'd bolted out of Clive's house and jumped in his car. He crushed the pedal but then eased back and cruised out of the neighborhood at a leisurely pace, straight to his sanctuary in the interior wasteland of Florida. Although the rising tide of urban sprawl had transformed much of the barren coastal land, his barn was still in Sticksville.

He stopped at his gate with double No Trespassing signs. He got out of the car and unlocked the padlock. He pushed the gate open, drove through, hopped out, and locked the gate behind him. He crawled down the long dirt driveway and up to his compound. It was shielded from the road by wild, thick native growth. A barbed wired fence encircled the property.

He parked in front of the house, walked to the pole barn, unlocked the padlock, and swung open the heavy door. He stepped into his shrine. Eleven cars. The instruments of his life's work, glowing with impeccable cleanliness. Years ago, he'd briefly floated the idea of selling them. That would throw the hounds off his scent, should they ever get a whiff of him. Or would it leave breadcrumbs back to him? Still, it had been fun to envision the conversations.

Yes, the picture comes with the car. Who? A girlfriend I had at the time. She's long gone. She was fun, though. We hit it off, that's for sure.

He did what he did every time he entered his pole barn. He selected a car and eased himself in. He lowered his pants and masturbated, his eyes never breaking from the photograph taped to the dash. On this day, the lucky vehicle was a rust-colored 1977 Honda Accord. He'd been thrilled to steal it. The Accord made its debut in 1976 and was already being heralded as a game changer. That job had been in Bradenton. Where he had just followed the man.

Sweet Jezebel, I could stick my tongue in those dimples. For some reason, she's behind this whole thing.

"What do you think, old girl?" he said, cleaning up his mess. "Think you're game for one more trip?"

He became a man with a mission. New tires. Plugs. Gas. Didn't take as much work as he thought. You got to hand it to the Japanese. In the '70s and '80s, they were decades ahead of Detroit. When he was finished, he took it for a test drive, gunning it and getting a feel for it. Timing, after all, was critical.

Satisfied that the machine was up to its task and would not disappoint him, he puttered it back into the pole barn and cut the engine. He went in his house and sat at the kitchen table. He looked up the address of the big-ass Gulf-front house the man had gone to. Archie Williams. Never heard of him. Some businessman. Was he one of Ziegler's babies? No, he was too old. He couldn't fathom a connection, why the man had gone there. He brought up his phone and swiped through pictures he'd taken of the man's family. Some Hispanic woman was always hauling the two young girls somewhere. To a library. A museum. Holding hands.

No one ever held my hand.

He slapped his face. *Where was this sentimental BS coming from?* He'd noticed it creeping up over the past few years. Feeling sorry for himself.

He stood and went to the sink. He took a drink of tap water. He sat down. He stood up. He paced and then, unable to stand the walls that always confined him, went outside. He hiked the property. His head split. Ever since the man had approached him when he was in the boat, his head had felt as if an axe was implanted in it. There was something calm, assured about the man. Such people irritated him. Made him mad. *They think they're so much better than me.*

He went back into the kitchen. He again looked at the pictures he'd taken of the Hispanic woman and the two girls. Several of the mother. He'd followed her to some college.

Eenie, meenie, miny, moe.

You can't destroy the dreams of a dead person.

CHAPTER 42

Time, Marcus Aurelius observed, is a violent river of events, swept away no sooner than they are seen. If the swept-away silent lives of those young women were ever to be heard, it had to be me. I didn't look for this battle. It found me.

Nathan Whiting had lied to me on every front. He knew Dr. Ziegler. That didn't make him guilty of anything but raised issues as to why he would lie. The obvious reason was that he was party to, or knew of, Ziegler's and his mother's actions. That they drugged young women, pawned their babies, and told the heartbroken mothers that their babies were stillborn. And if a mother questioned the narrative? Kill her.

I needed a break. If the cars, the instruments of death, were preserved, would they still have remnants of blood, bone, and possibly DNA? I debated whether to hit Whiting's house at night or during the day, assuming he wasn't home. Both had attractive elements as well as drawbacks. I choose the day, not wishing to waste the minutes. I kept a diligent eye on the rearview mirror at all times. But it wasn't Whiting's driveway I parked in nor his doorbell I rang.

His neighbor opened her door.

"Hi, there," she said. "It's you. Still looking for weirdo?"

"I am."

"What happened to your face?"

"A woman attacked me while I was giving CPR to her husband."

"She must have wanted him dead pretty bad."

"She didn't attack him."

"Oh, I see. Does any of that have anything to do with why you're here?"

"Might. Have you seen Whiting?"

"Negative."

"I want to get into his house."

"Why?"

"It's possible that he killed multiple women over fifty years ago."

She punched the air with her fist. "I *knew* it. You figure he left clues?"

"I don't know. But I do know there's no way I can get in without you noticing it. I'm asking for your silence."

"You fixin' to break in?"

"I am."

"Tonight?"

"Right now."

"I'm going in with you."

"I don't think that's—"

"Nonnegotiable. How do we get in without drawing attention to ourselves?"

"That big hibiscus bush you hate so much? I'm—"

"I don't hate it. It would just be nice if the twerp trimmed it every ten years."

"It blocks a window. Likely a bathroom. I'm going to smash it, enter, and open the rear door for you."

"Just like that?"

"Just like that. By the way, I'm Jake."

"Suzy with a *z*. Let's do this, Jake."

Five minutes later, I opened the rear door to Nathan Whiting's house and let Suzy in.

"Where do we start, Jake?"

"You get the kitchen."

"Aye-aye."

There were no cameras or signs of a security system. Curtains and shades blanketed the windows. I searched Whiting's bedroom first and then went to the spare bedroom. It appeared to be unused. Suzy reported that there was nothing of interest in the kitchen. "Ham and cheese in the fridge," she said. "Man must have lived on it. Some nice fish fillets in the freezer. I'm hitting the front room. You?"

"Nothing yet."

"Roger that."

I wandered out to the single-car garage. It was littered with fishing gear, empty trash cans, and an assortment of furniture I assumed he'd collected on trash day and not yet sold. There were two boxes stacked on top of each other that, judging by the dust and grime on them, had not been disturbed for some time. I opened the top one. Old shirts. Towels. Some kitchenware.

I placed it aside and opened the bottom box. More of the same but with a collection of self-help books tossed in. I rummaged around, looking to see if there was anything else. There was a folder and an envelope with the word *deed* scrawled on it. It was likely to his home. I put the envelope in my pocket, although I wasn't sure why. I examined the other contents of the folder. Yellowed newspaper clippings. I carefully unfolded one.

It was a news article from the *Saint Petersburg Times* about the death of a woman in a hit-and-run. I checked the date. Smack dab in the middle of when Ziegler transitioned his business to selling babies.

The second clipping I examined held an article about another hit-and-run.

And so it went.

I knew what I had, but I also knew what I didn't have. The manner in which I had obtained it, as Rambler had advised, made it inadmissible in court. But, more importantly, there was no law against possessing old newspaper articles. A good defense attorney would point out that Mr. Whiting was crest-fallen about the number of young women being run over by cars. He kept them as a reminder to do good in the world.

"How you doing, Jake-o?"

Suzy startled me with her comment. I'd just found a small object in the bottom of the box. I stuck it in my pocket. "Good. You?"

She walked up to me. "Found this," she said, showing me a framed picture. It was of Whiting and Ziegler. It appeared to have been taken the same day as the pictures I saw at Georgy's house. "This is the dweeb when he was younger. He's standing pretty close to that man."

"That's Dr. Ziegler," I informed her.

"Think they were lovers?"

"No way of telling."

"Put my dollar on it." She peered over my shoulder. "Whatja got here?"

"Newspaper clippings."

"About those Ziegler babies?"

Had I ever told her that Whiting was linked to the Ziegler babies?

"Why do you think Nathan was related to the Ziegler babies, and what do you know about them?"

"Nothing."

"Suzy."

"Really," she said pleading innocence, "nothing everyone else doesn't know."

"Whiting ever talk to you about it?"

"God, no. But the neighborhood scuttle was that he was involved."

"I'm going to take this box," I said. "If he shows up, call me."

"I think that boat has sailed. That leaves me cutting his grass. Hey, you want any of the fish fillets?"

"I'll pass."

"Yeah, me, too. At first, I thought I'd help myself to some, but it seems a little weird."

I patched up the window I'd broken with cardboard and duct tape. I put the folder of newspaper clippings in the back seat of the truck. When I climbed into the driver's seat, I remembered I'd placed two things in my pocket. One was the property deed. I stuck it in the center console, wondering why he kept the deed to his property in with the Ziegler memorabilia. The other item was the object I'd found when Suzy had entered the room and startled me. I also placed it in the center console.

It was a dog tag. It read CHARLIE.

CHAPTER 43

Clive was listed in stable condition the next morning. I wanted to talk to his wife, Lanelle, and assumed she would be with her husband at the hospital. I told Kathleen where I was headed. She asked how the chase was going. I asked her how her classes were. She inquired what my next move was. I countered by asking what the girls were doing that day. And so it went. Lobbing questions back and forth. Each day, we turn our backs and go our separate ways, the days dragging until the night, and I see her again.

Ten minutes after I left the house, I called her.

"You forget something?" she answered.

"Give the word and we put the girls on Morgan's boat and sail away."

"Do people do that?"

"Do we care what people do?"

"We do not. Little hard, though, with a dog, a cat, and a sometimes duck."

"Did you buy a dog?"

"Oh babe. You can't buy love."

"You did, didn't you? You're just waiting for this thing to blow over."

"I would never consider such a life-altering decision without your consent."

"No, you wouldn't. You'd just do it."

"I take offense at your implication, sir."

"You know I'm ballistic for you, right?"

"Not the most romantic word."

"Apeshit?"

"Going the wrong way there, bud. I'll take a rain check on the boat. Find the human disease who killed those girls. And the answer's yes."

"Which questions?"

"The only two that mattered."

She hung up.

And I thought she struggled with math.

LANELLE WAS NOT AT the hospital when I dropped by to see Clive. "She went home to shower and change," a nurse told me. "She spent the night with Mr. Emmons. He's doing fine, but he's sleeping now."

I trudged to the parking garage and headed to Clive and Lanelle's home, hoping I didn't pass her on her return trip to the hospital.

"Oh my gosh," Lanelle said when she answered my knock on her door. Her hand shot up to her mouth. "Did I do that?"

"It doesn't hurt."

She giggled. "It looks like it should. Whew, you have one red, white, and bruised eye."

I told her I'd just come from the hospital and was unable to talk with Clive, as he was sleeping.

"I spent the night there. Just came home to grab a shower and change clothes. My Clive was lucky. A whole lot of blood but nothing serious. He was yappin' this morning like a schoolgirl coming home from her first date. I reckon he plumb wore himself out. Come on in, Mr. Jake. You and I always gonna have a good story to tell."

I followed her into the living room, where the morning sun shafted through the east windows and cast a welcoming glow on the floor.

"Can I get you a coffee or anything?"

I told her I was fine.

"You can't believe how sorry I am."

"Don't worry about it."

"Nice of you to say that. The doctor said the knife just missed his vital organs. You got here in the nick of time. The Lord was looking over us, that's for sure."

"Did he say anything about the man who attacked him?"

"The Lord or Clive?"

"Either."

"I was just foolin' with you," she said with a sly smile. "Clive said he had a hood like a ski mask on. But he knew it was that Whiting man. Could see it in his eyes. Clive told me he told you about him."

"He did. Did Whiting say anything to Clive?"

"No. You sure I can't be gettin' you something? A coffee?"

"Only if you're having one."

She stood. "I am. Anything in it?"

"Heavens, no."

She laughed. "I hear you. Two heavens nos coming up."

Lanelle returned and handed me a Sunken Gardens mug.

"Thank you," I said.

"No," Lanelle said with a smile. "Thank *you*."

"You might want to take that back."

"Why's that?"

I told her it was likely me who had led Whiting to her door.

"Clive and I figured as much," Lanelle said. "Honestly?

'Bout time Clive put this thing to rest. You just"—she winced a smile—"forced the issue a bit. Clive wants me to show you something. He told me after your visit that he didn't tell you everything. He knows it's now or never. I'm thinking fighting a knife might have something to do with that."

She rose and went to a bookcase with twin doors at the bottom. She squatted down, opened one, shuffled some things around, and closed it. She opened the second one, rearranged a few items, pulled out a folder, and grabbed the bookcase with one hand while getting up.

"My knees don't take too kindly to bending no more. Here you go." She handed me a slim yellowed folder. "You go ahead and take a look."

I opened the folder. Inside were two sheets of paper. Each had a list of women's names, dates, and dollar figures.

"Clive said to tell you he's sorry he didn't share this with you earlier. He said it was too much for him to process during your first visit. He has conflicted feelings about the Cardinal Inn, old man Buford being so kind to him and his mother. He and I differ on that."

"What am I looking at?"

"If I'm not mistaken, Mr. Jake, that is exactly what all this ruckus is about."

CHAPTER 44

I studied the faded papers in my hand. Maybe a dozen names. Was I looking at the victims? Adoptions?

"You know Clive was only there on Thursdays, right?" Lanelle said. "He told me that, over time, listening and picking up on conversations, Thursday was the only day the doctor did his devil work. You're looking at the Thursday girls."

I asked her how Clive got the names.

She took a patient sip of her coffee. "By the time Clive started taking care of the property, Ziegler was in his later years. There'd been rumors." She dipped her head at the paper in my hand. "You can thank his mama for that. Although she liked Mr. Buford and all he did for her, she said she could smell the devil in Dr. Ziegler. Probably thought she was doing Buford a favor come judgment day. She told Clive to write down the names of those young woman. Said she was gonna pray for them. That woman was always tight with God. Too tight for my taste, but it got you that list. How about I heat this coffee up a bit?"

"Allow me," I said.

I stood, and she handed me her cup. I refilled both our

coffees in the kitchen, careful not to step on the bloodstained part of the floor. I handed her mug back to her. It was from the Museum of the American Arts and Crafts Movement. I'd noticed that much of the furniture in the house was from that period. I complimented her on it.

"That would be Clive's mother. Too tight with God or not, that woman had good taste and was a bargain hunter extraordinaire."

I reclaimed my seat and picked up the list I'd placed on a side table. Next to each woman's name was a date. I found the date that Lisa's baby was born. Next to it was—

"Mr. Jake?"

I glanced up. "Yes?"

"I said Clive got paid once a month. Buford would have him come in the office and pay him in cash. The safe was on the floor. It was a combination safe, and Buford never got it right the first time. You know Ziegler ran his clinic out the back, right?"

I told her I did.

"Clive said Buford kept files on his desk. No computers. One was labeled *Motel* and the other was *Ziegler Clinic*. He peeked in that folder one day when Buford was fiddling with the combination, and there it was. Names of the women who had checked into the clinic's guest room. For some reason we will never know, Buford recorded them as hotel guests."

"Did Clive copy them?"

"He wrote them down while Buford cursed at the safe. Scribbled as fast as he could. He added the dates later. You notice they're a little neater. But he got caught one day. Buford popped up, saying he felt a pain. He saw Clive with the open file and asked what he was doing."

"How did Clive squirm out of that?"

"Didn't need to. Burford grabbed his chest and hit the floor deader than a nail. Clive was lucky."

I recalled Charlene telling me that her grandfather dropped dead on the job. *Died standing in his office.*

"Did Clive continue to copy names after Buford died?"

"No. Not long after Buford hit the floor, Ziegler hit the road."

I scrutinized the page. Some names had *transaction fee* next to them. I asked Lanelle about it.

"Clive thinks those were the folks who bought the baby."

I asked her how Clive knew who bought which baby.

"Clive said he was working one day, cleaning up around the back of the motel. He was minding his business when a car pulled up. A woman and man got out and went inside. Clive said no more than five minutes later, they came out carrying a baby that fit in both hands.

"The lady got in the back seat with the baby, and they drove away. Clive went in the office a little later to get his pay. Through the door, he heard a girl screaming and Dr. Ziegler telling her he was sorry, but her baby was stillborn. It wasn't just his mama wanting a prayer list. Clive made that list 'cause he knew what was going on there was wrong. He thought it best to keep track. In case it could do some good someday."

"But how did he know who bought the babies?" I asked for the second time, for if she'd answered my question, I'd missed it.

"I'm a-gettin' there. That was a bit trickier. Remember I told you Buford registered the pregnant girls as motel guests? Clive said the names were in a separate ledger, right next to the one that had the pregnant women's names in it. He assumed those were the folks getting the baby. He figured Ziegler was splitting the pie with Buford."

"Pretty aggressive for a teenage gardener," I said.

"I hear you. I think Clive's mama was urging him more than he lets on."

"Two lists," I said. "One with the names of the pregnant

women and the other with the names of who adopted the children."

"That's correct. Though ask Clive three times how he got the list and he might give you four answers. Forty years ago, remember."

"Did Clive ever see other babies being passed off?"

"Yes, sir. Two, three times? Maybe more."

We were silent for a moment.

I asked her if Clive had ever showed the list to anyone.

"Who would he show it to? The police? Think they would have taken some scrawny Black boy seriously? I know times have changed, but mind you, they had a lot of changin' to do. He kept it, thinking the day would come. He was right. You are the man who brought that day."

"Clive told me he knew Lisa Trowbridge by name. Did he ever talk to any others?"

"Not that I know of." Lanelle took a sip of her coffee and dipped her head at the folder. "It rested in peace for nearly fifty years until you knocked on our door. And after you, came the attack on Clive. You've been asking a lot of questions; now I got one for you."

"Yes?"

"What are you going to do to protect my Clive?"

CHAPTER 45

I have seen him in the watch fires

Despite the slit for the eyes in the fishing mask, he knew Clive had recognized him. He called the hospital, but Melinda, the humorless woman who answered, had refused to release information beyond his condition. Stable. Needed to be family or have some power of health care shit he never heard of. He called back, hoping to get a different person, but it was drab Melinda again. He hung up.

You want to talk about power over health? Huh, Melinda? You want to dance with me?

Maybe it was time to pull a Ziegler. But nothing compared to the deep satisfaction, the rapturous fulfillment of getting away with it. Sitting at home while someone else's world imploded. Knowing the immense effect. The power he possessed. He wanted to experience that smug feeling one last glorious time.

Johnny Carson was gone, though. Checked out years ago. May 22, 1992. *A date that will live in infamy.* He knew there was someone else sitting in that chair, but sitting in the king's chair didn't make you the king. The world spins, and prominence fades. *Think of it. I clipped a few girls, and there's still plenty of them running around, aren't there?*

He contemplated his options, though he'd pretty much settled on one. Still, he wanted to make sure it was the best. That a runner-up hadn't gained attraction.

First up. Cut and run.

Nah, too dull.

Or.

Kill the man.

Certainly not walk on my property again, but that's not the goal here. Destroy the dream, not the man. Let him live in hell on earth.

Or.

Knock off his wife.

Just doesn't send me. Besides, betcha the girls hurt him more.

That settled it. He would cut down the man's two girls, destroying the man's dreams.

Hubba-hubba.

CHAPTER 46

I strolled onto the screened porch that evening as if the sole destination of the day was that moment. Home is where your feet leave, but not your heart. My heart rests on the salt-water bay, glistened by the sun at day and melodied by the moon at night.

I'd just come in from Sophia's room. A recent addition allowed the girls to each have their own room. She wasn't fond of sitting still in the bed, preferring to climb on me. Over me. Burrow under me. When I'd left her, her feet were on her pillow and her head at the end of the bed. I'd only been able to read one book to her. Kathleen had been in Joy's room reading *The Baby-Sitters Little Sister*. "An oldie but goodie," Kathleen called it. We alternated every other week. Next week, I'd read to Joy, and Kathleen would get the honor of wrestling with Sophia.

Kathleen, while scratching Hadley III behind her ears, chronicled her day. She'd only had one class, Major American Novels, which was new for her. She'd been given the choice of teaching American novels or modern British poetry. She'd chosen wisely. Kathleen thinks she likes poetry, but, as she constantly rediscovers, her feelings stem more from obligation than from genuine appreciation. After class, she'd gone over to see Bobbie Lee. I sensed a budding friendship there.

"Archie's not doing well," she said. She untied her hair and fluffed it out over her shoulders. "He usually rebounds from his chemo in a few days, but that didn't happen this time. The doctors told her not to read too much into it. She asked how you're coming along."

"What did you tell her?"

"That you had several promising leads."

"She fall for that?"

"She urged me to urge you."

"That's a lot of urging."

"It is. He desperately wants to see his daughter. She desperately wants him to be happy."

"Bobbie Lee isn't jealous?" I said, for it was something that had been nagging me. "Her husband battling death and his mind simultaneously entranced by the woman of his youth?"

"We discussed that. Not at all. She has a wonderful balance of romanticism and practicality. She fully understands and supports Archie's quest."

"He claims he's still in love with Lisa," I reminded her. "A woman who died nearly fifty years ago. Can that be?"

"Can what be?"

"Can he love her?"

"Is it written that youthful love must disintegrate?" Kathleen said. "That passion, once so consuming, be placed in a box, only to be peered at with mild curiosity decades later? Passion means to suffer. To endure. I find his position wholly acceptable."

I choose not to question the matter further, for she seemed well entrenched in her beliefs. We were silent for a moment. Morgan was night fishing, and his absence felt strange.

"She insists that doesn't impede their relationship," Kathleen said, speaking as if her thoughts had unconsciously vocalized. "Archie knows Lisa is gone. He understands it was only by Lisa's death that he met Bobbie Lee. He found late love because he lost early love."

I reached for my glass of bourbon as Kathleen's last comment bounced around in my head. Instead of taking a sip, I held the glass, strangely disinterested in bringing it to my lips.

"Do you?" Kathleen said. "Have any leads, promising or otherwise?"

"I do."

"Well, hot dog. Let's hear them."

I filled her in on my day.

"Clive is going to make it?" she said when I'd finished, picking up on the most important thing.

"He is."

"And Lanelle gave you a list of names?"

"She did."

"Talk about burying the lede. Does this list have the name of the couple who took Lisa's baby?"

"It does. Mr. and Mrs. John Smith."

She hesitated. "I see. And I assume there were other Mr. and Mrs. Smiths?"

"You assume correctly."

"I'm sorry, babe."

I didn't tell you about that because my disappointment was overwhelming. While sitting with Lanelle, I'd scrutinized the pages. Before I got to Lisa's date, I realized I was seeing a lot of *Mr. and Mrs. Smith*. I didn't ask Lanelle about that. I don't know why. I'm sure she saw the futile names.

"But not every name is Smith," Kathleen pointed out in a wishful voice.

"I'm guessing they mixed it up. Might have had a few legitimate adoptions sprinkled in."

"Which just makes it harder," she said. "You really only got through one book with Sophia?"

"It wasn't easy."

"Oh, I'm not being critical. Do you think she has restless leg syndrome?"

"I think she just prefers sitting on someone instead of next to them."

Kathleen stood, sending Hadley III flying. She flopped on my lap.

"Wonder where she got that from?" she said.

I raided my mind for a reply, but why spoil the moment? Linda Ronstadt's song "Long Long Time," which I'd heard in Archie's house, had been repeating itself in my head all day. And now, against that soundtrack, something about Archie's expedition to the past seemed terribly misguided, almost circular. But my errant thoughts, exhausted from the field of battle, refused to organize.

Kathleen retired to bed to grade papers, which she admitted was not as much fun as learning twelve tips on how to organize your closet. I went to our study, gave a shot of water to a white and pink orchid we'd picked up at the Saturday Market a month ago, and pulled out the folder I'd taken from Whiting's garage.

It contained articles and clippings about the Ziegler babies. I arranged them chronologically. They appeared to start at least halfway through Ziegler's satanic tenure. At the bottom of the box, the last thing I pulled out was a birth certificate. Nathan's.

His mother was listed as Molly Ribhorn of Leesburg, Florida. Father unknown. Another document showed he'd been adopted when he was one year old. No mention of what happened to his mother. His adoptive parents were George and Cynthia Whiting.

George Whiting had been a fireman for the Leesburg Fire Department when he was let go amid sexual misconduct behavior. His sister, Melissa Blankenship, maintained that her brother was innocent. Several clicks later, and I had a picture of Melissa She was a nurse at the Leesburg Hospital. *Belle*. Whiting's adoptive parents must have pawned their child off onto George's sister. I recalled Charlene's comment about Whiting. *Funny, I don't recall that being Belle's last name.*

I created two folders on my computer. One was about the clinic, and the second covered the hit-and-runs. The folder on the clinic was much larger, for when the news broke about what Ziegler had been up to, DNA testing had started. Unfortunately, more people—adults looking for parents, next of kin searching for unknown family—were disappointed than were successful. There weren't many happy endings. Many of those involved in the search shared similar comments. They felt compelled to look, even knowing the odds were against them. Some gave up. Some are searching to this day.

The hit-and-runs were so similar it was hard not to believe the police hadn't put them together. Easy to see now, for I was perched on the high hill of hindsight. The news reports read the same. *Police are asking if anyone saw anything to contact them. Witnesses claimed to have seen a speeding car. A man with a mustache. Maybe not. It was hard to see.* Almost all the incidents were at night.

I finally arrived at the time when Detective Arnelli appeared.

> It has long been suspected that Dr. Ziegler performed abortions at the clinic prior to *Roe v. Wade*. After the Supreme Court ruling resulted in legal abortion, according to sources, he still operated the clinic out of the back of the Cardinal Inn where he'd been for years. Sources speculated that he sold

```
babies out the back door while telling
their mothers that their children had
died. According to Detective Josh
Arnelli of the Saint Petersburg Police
Department, there might be a link
between the mothers of the Ziegler
babies and an unusual spike in the hit-
and-run deaths of young women. Arnelli
declined to elaborate and refused to
give details of the investigation, other
than to admit that the whereabouts of
Dr. Ziegler were unknown. Police were
asking anyone with helpful information
to please contact Crime Watchers.
```

I recalled Arnelli's words. We let the press know we had suspicions in hopes of getting a tip. He'd been reluctant to admit they realized a possible connection between Ziegler and the hit-and-runs.

Nathan Whiting had saved an article on each of the women who were killed. Serial killers are trophy hunters. They mark their success. They like visual or tangible reminders of their conquests. Psychologists suggest that such items symbolize conquest of the victim. Others opine that those souvenirs, also referred to as trophies, serve to ignite, to relive the thrill of their deed. There were endless studies linking sexual frustration and early childhood abandonment in serial killers.

The killers who never get caught had a knack for shutting down their impulse before doing something sloppy. From Jack the Ripper in London to the Zodiac Killer in San Francisco, the identities of many mass murderers have evaded extensive manhunts.

I was certain that Nathan Whiting had killed the young

mothers who complained they had heard their babies cry. But I had not an iota of proof.

There was an old Polaroid camera in the bottom of the box, the type that developed the picture immediately after you took it. I started for it but stopped. I went into the kitchen and got a pair of rubber gloves from under the sink and a large ziplock bag. I put the gloves on and placed the camera in the bag. Maybe it could be of use to Rambler.

My ability to focus drifted away. I brought up the picture of Lisa Trowbridge on my phone that Archie had insisted I have. Like a dog on a hunt, Archie wanted to motivate me. I resented being manipulated but could not fault his method.

Lisa had a slight tilt, a sorority pose, to her head. She beamed a confident smile. A wholesome and eager face. I took of sip of my drink, but the ice had melted and diluted it beyond recognition. I went to bed. When my head hit the pillow, our conversation on the screened porch was waiting for me. Something Kathleen had said before questioning if youthful love must disintegrate. Her discourse on passion. I fell asleep.

FOUR ELEVEN A.M. I'D been dreaming. A woman—I didn't know her but felt indescribably close to her—had gazed longingly into my eyes. "You can't be romantic and practical," she said, her voice conveying great pity for me. "You must choose."

CHAPTER 47

Of a hundred circling camps

Make your plan. Execute your plan. He'd highlighted that in a self-help book he'd picked up in those middling years when he'd felt the seeds of ambition and self-respect. He'd watered them a little, and then, to his great relief, they wilted away.

Nothing had panned out. Warehouse worker. Short-order cook. Fishing guide. That sucked big-time. Four hours on a boat with no break from the talking heads. Pure hell. After that, he logged twenty-three miserable years standing behind the counters of various convenience stores selling cigarettes and lottery tickets to people who hadn't enough money to cover their rent. *And they thought I was a loser.* He'd calculated that his maximum exposure to any one person was rarely over one minute. That he could handle. But it was a struggle.

The day his first social security check hit his bank account, he didn't bother to call in. He fed himself from what he pulled out of the water. He had judicially saved his paychecks and tucked away a little bit of money every month for four mind-numbing decades. He traversed the neighborhood streets at four a.m. on trash day. Amazing the good stuff people threw away. He sold it online. Tax-free money. He was oddly gifted at managing his paltry savings.

What career do you envision for yourself?

He had purchased the pole barn, the cottage, and the fifteen acres they sat on decades ago, picking them up at a sheriff's auction. Taxes were peanuts. No AC. Not much need for heat. He'd bought the property to keep his trophies in one location. Under one roof where he could caress them. Prior to the pole barn, they were scattered in different storage facilities. That was not only expensive but also unsatisfying. The moment he collected them, could view them with a sweep of his eyes, touch one after another with a trace of his finger, he knew he'd made the right decision.

The decades flipped by. Remorse never came knocking.

Then the man walked across his lawn. That evening, he developed a headache. And they kept rolling in. Kick-ass head pounders, not your run-of-the-mill pop-a-pill-and-lie-down variety. No, these came on like A-bombs, blowing a mushroom cloud through the top of his head.

Next up, cue the nightmares. He'd had a doozy a few nights ago. The crunch of bone. The sound of flesh smacking the hood of a car. A scream. A thud. He'd forced himself to awaken from the lucid dream. Calmed himself by remembering the reward. The thrill of speeding away. Then, later those nights, a beer in front of the TV, his heartbeat back to normal. Watching Johnny Carson. Ed McMahon. *High-yooo*. He never understood what they were laughing at. *Was there a joke there?* Gotta dig Doc Severinsen, though. That cat wore some cool threads.

He needed to clean his house out in the event Clive pulled a Lazarus number and popped his eyes open. Had to get the stuff out of the garage. Get his box. There was no smoking gun there, but close enough.

Hell, I don't even remember what I put in there. The deed to the farm's not there, is it?

He pulled into his driveway at 3:13 a.m. He wore dark clothes. He let himself in the front door. He went to the refrigerator. No need to waste food. He filled four plastic grocery bags. He went to the garage. He froze. The missing box. His face exploded with sweat. He thrashed around, scattering tools and two outdoor chairs he'd picked up from the curb a week before. He'd been thrilled to find them. Not only in good shape, but they matched.

The man. It had to be him. Could tell by the way he walked he wouldn't hesitate to bust a window to get what he was after. But how did he know, or was he just lucky?

He ran his hand over his forehead. He took a deep breath. His breathing slowed.

Focus. If he doesn't know, he'll figure it out. If Clive lives, even easier. I need to do my last act and then get the hell out of Dodge.

His back-of-the-envelope escape plan had always been to cash out and sail away. He knew that, in all likelihood, that was now off the table. He'd have to write the place off. To sell it would be to leave breadcrumbs to his door. He was oddly serene about that. His head no longer hurt. His mind was focused and clear. He saw the next few days laid out before him and, beyond that, the bright, endless field of gold that had forever been just beyond his fingers, that no other human being had touched.

Glory, glory, hallelujah. His truth is marching on.

CHAPTER 48

Jenna Cappabianca, whom Heather Kirkland had described as the person doing the "heavy lifting" in exposing Ziegler, texted me early the next morning. She was back from her cruise and would be happy to meet anytime. Anywhere.

Jenna and her deceased husband, Mack, had adopted a Ziegler baby over forty years ago. Jenna had always been suspicious of the manner in which fate had intervened and granted them their most fervent desire. The couple was unable to have children and had been repeatedly passed up for adoptions. Mack ran a fishing charter and was often on the water thirty days straight. His income was seasonal. More suitable candidates were positioned before them. Ironically, Mack later opened a fish house that became a crowd favorite.

They'd told their son, Kyle, that he was adopted. Kyle grew up with loving and supportive parents, but he desired to know his birth mother.

Jenna and Kyle's break had come eleven years ago. A woman, Lori Elmhost, said she'd given birth at Ziegler's clinic, but her baby was stillborn. Lori's stay at the Cardinal Inn was within a week of Kyle's birth date. She lived close to the Cappabiancas at the time. Jenna remembered Ziegler telling her that her baby was coming from a "local" woman. Despite hearing that Lori's child had died, Jenna had knocked on her door.

Jenna convinced her to submit to DNA testing. Jenna Cappabianca won the lottery. Lori Elmhost was Kyle's biological mother. Kyle's birth certificate was bogus. The death certificate Dr. Ziegler had presented to Lori Elmhost for her little boy was equally fraudulent.

But Jenna wasn't done. A genealogy enthusiast, she crusaded to unite more Ziegler babies with their parents. Posting on social media, Jenna compiled a list of women who had either given birth at the Ziegler clinic or adopted from there. It took long, grueling hours of endless leads, culminating with DNA testing that, more often than not, did not bring closure. Those seeking the truth were driven by Jenna's rare success. The results, however, were discouraging. Luck had played a prominent role in Jenna's story.

I was excited to meet her, although, I reminded myself, she had warned me it was slow going. I also wanted to meet Lori Elmhost, Kyle's biological mother. Why wasn't she the victim of a hit-and-run? We agreed to meet at 11:00 a.m. at a coffee shop on Second Street North. I got there early. A woman who was about what I assumed to be Jenna's age walked in. We made eye contact. She tilted her head and pointed a finger at the counter.

"You must be Jake," she said when she approached me after getting a drink. A computer bag was draped over her shoulder. I stood and introduced myself. We exchanged pleasantries, and I asked how her cruise was.

"Same old same. Hop off the boat. Hit the tourists' places, grab a drink at some famous beach bar you'll forget before the end of the year, buy street art that you'll question as soon as you get home, and hop back on the boat."

"Not your first cruise."

"Or my last. I had a blast."

She had a smooth alto voice. Dangling earrings just missed the top of her collar.

"So," she said, leveling her eyes on mine, "you're looking into the Ziegler babies. Tell me why again?"

I'd been vague when we messaged each other. I'd also learned more since then. I told her everything.

"I wish I ran into you years ago," she said when I'd finished. "Nathan Whiting? Belle's son? I never even thought to look into him. That's just wild. And the gardener—what's his name?"

"Clive Emmons."

"I'm glad he's okay. And you think Ziegler had a hand in killing young mothers who realized he'd stolen their babies?"

"I do."

"That's terrible. Jeez, I feel like getting back on the ship."

"Did Lori ever mention to you that she heard her baby cry?" I asked.

"No. She was put under because Dr. Ziegler considered her to be at risk. When she woke, she was told her baby had died." Her hand shot up to her mouth. "Oh my gosh. What are you suggesting? That it's only because she didn't hear her baby cry that she's alive?"

"It's possible."

"I just can't imagine," she said, staring at the table. She raised her head. "You're looking for this man's daughter, right? That would be Lisa Trowbridge's baby."

"Correct."

"To be honest with you, my drive to unravel the Ziegler mess has diminished over the years. It's unrewarding work. The occasional jackpot, sweet as it is, doesn't compensate for the heartbreaking failures. I found Lori, Kyle's birth mother. That's what I set out to do, and I'm proud of that. Happy for my son."

I asked what records she had that might be of assistance to me. I gave her the date Lisa Trowbridge was in the clinic.

"Let's take a look," she said. She opened her bag, took out a laptop, set it on the table, and flipped it open. "I like looking at the big screen. Research burns your eyes. All you do is cross-reference until you can't see straight. Give me that date again."

I did.

"Well," she said, studying her screen. "You might be one of the lucky ones. Elizabeth and Howard Popham adopted Lisa Trowbridge's baby. I mean, I think they did based on what we've pulled together."

Great. I find the Pophams and wrap this puppy up.

I asked how she got the name. Clive's list had only *Mr. and Mrs. Smith* listed next to Lisa's name.

She humped her right shoulder. "Luck? Coincidence? They stepped forward when all this hit. They'd always thought the manner in which they received their baby was a little suspicious. Arrive at night. A quick handoff. Little information on the birth mother. They claimed the whole process was a bit shady."

"But they took the child."

"You have to understand. Not only were these people desperate to have a child but Ziegler also practiced at a reputable clinic downtown. Anyway, they contacted me. Gave me the date of their adoption. Said a lot of people learned of Ziegler by word of mouth. Your Lisa was the only woman during that period. I didn't know the exact date she was there, but the police had cobbled together a rough list of names and dates."

I didn't recall Arnelli telling me about a list of names. Had he forgotten?

Jenna's hands flew over her keyboard. "Here we go." She peered up at me. "You're looking for a girl, right?"

"Yes. Ziegler told Lisa she had a girl who was stillborn. The death certificate says girl."

"Oh, I'm so sorry. The Pophams adopted a boy, and his birth date is—let's see—about thirty days off." She'd been staring at her computer. She glanced up at me. "This is what I hate about this. I can't tell you how many times I get close, only to fail. It's disheartening."

"Would he do that?" I said, not willing to give up. I'd been so close.

"Do what?"

"Fake the gender. Alter the date of birth?"

She twisted her face. "I suppose. Now you see why I stopped doing this."

I switched tracks and asked her about Lori Elmhost. She said she'd be glad to give her a call and see if I could stop by. But as we spoke, I had little enthusiasm for meeting Lori. I was beat. Every road was a dead end. Every person another "I'm sorry. It was long ago."

Our conversation drifted on, but nothing of substance surfaced. We were on the sidewalk, preparing to part ways, when Jenna said, "You know what's really peculiar about this whole thing? The eerie similarities between my son, Kyle, and his birth mother. I mean, Lori never spent a second with him, yet he smiles like her. Cocks his head like hers, and I hear his voice, his intonations, in her voice. It's almost as if they could have run into each other one day and known. Anyway, good luck with your hunt."

LORI ELMHOST, IN A painful exchange I have no desire to reconstruct, said that knowing her son was alive with loving parents and that she'd been robbed of motherhood was almost more painful than believing he was dead. She was ashamed of those feelings.

Lori had no memory of giving birth. She never heard her baby cry. I deflected her questions concerning my interest in her state of consciousness after delivery. Didn't tell her that the drug doing its job had saved her life. I thanked her and left as soon as I could.

I climbed into my hot truck. I was empty. Frozen and unwilling to commit thought or muscle to even the simplest of tasks. The Tahitians have a word, *fiu.* It translates poorly, but it's a feeling of lost hope and ennui. Of meaninglessness. A world drained of purpose. I needed to reboot.

I headed to the pink hotel.

CHAPTER 49

The hotel was built in the 1920s by an Irishman from Virginia, was named after a character in a play by a French dramatist that was turned into an English opera, and is set in a town named for its Russian counterpart. It had also been completely shuttered for six months, and part of it for a year, following twin hurricanes. My salty piece of land had not been targeted for over one hundred years. Then we got two hurricanes within thirteen days. Programmed to make constellations out of stars, we seek comfort in patterns, refusing to accept randomness in the world.

"Another lap?"

"Why not?"

The bartender, a new man I didn't know and who had no interest in knowing me, swapped out my empty beer mug. A woman passed behind me trailing hints of perfume and sunscreen. Children squealed in the pool and a man strummed a guitar as he sang about someone he once loved and maybe still did. The salt-infused wind from the Gulf of Mexico was thick with the busted streets and wrecked dreams of distant lands. I took in a sommelier breath, the fragrances of my life inflaming my lungs.

In the pool, a young girl jumped into her father's arms, scampered out, and did it again. I thought of the young women I believed Nathan Whiting had mowed down. I wondered if, at one time in their lives, they had a father to catch them when they jumped. Outstretched arms always ready for them. That thought spurred Revelation visions of what I would do to any man who harmed my girls.

I felt disloyal to Archie, for my motivation was fueled more by finding Lisa's killer than her daughter. Was I prioritizing that which I had a reasonable chance of achieving over that which I did not? The woman next to me started humming along to "A Whiter Shade of Pale," which the guitar player had started singing. She occasionally broke out of her hum and sang a few words. She had a good voice. I would think of her and that song again. When someone's face—well, you'll see.

I called Garrett. He was my childhood friend. The man I stood shoulder to shoulder with for five years in the army and the brother I never had. He picked up after one ring.

"Talk to me."

He was also a man of few words.

"I tripped over some scumbag who mowed down a dozen young mothers over forty years ago. I met him, and he tailed me. He tried to kill a man who knew him at the time, but I was lucky and interceded. He's not done, and I can't find him."

Garrett grunted. "I land at two-ten," he said after a pause. Then he hung up.

I signed the chit, left half my second beer, slid off the stool, and walked through the sun-bathed courtyard of the hotel. I climbed into my truck and rested my bare right arm on the center console. It burned. I remembered that I'd placed what I assumed was the deed to Nathan Whiting's property in it. I should have looked at it earlier. I opened the console and fished it out. It was for a different address, not his Treasure Island home. I brought up the location on my phone and checked the county auditor's website to see if Whiting still owned it. He did.

As Kathleen would say, "Hot dog."

CHAPTER 50

I can read His righteous sentence

He checked his watch. Ten-fifty. Plenty of time. He wondered if they'd come out the same way they exited yesterday. They'd skipped out like they'd just discovered fairies were real. *What the hell could possibly be so interesting in there?* He'd gone in after they left. He wanted to see if there was some sort of schedule. He couldn't be trailing them out of their neighborhood every day.

"May I help you?" a matronly woman behind a desk had asked when he presented himself. He considered the desk.

Old, but good shape. Easily get a couple hundred for it.

"Sir?"

"Yes. My grandchildren are visiting, and I would love to bring them to a reading time. What do you offer?"

"What ages are they?"

I'm not sure. Is two days from dead an age?

"Four and eight," he'd thrown out.

"Hmm. That would be different classes."

But I saw them go in and out together.

"Is there any program, in the morning—say, around ten-ish —where they could be together? I hate to separate them."

"We do have a general reading class open to all ages. Many of the younger children are fine listening to longer stories. I think it's good to get them involved at an early age. We're breeding a whole generation with short attention spans."

"I couldn't agree more. When is that?"

"Wednesdays and Fridays. Ten to eleven. I think it's so nice that children have such loving and nurturing grandparents."

"Yes. Well, we're a dying breed."

He had turned to leave.

"Do you want some information?"

"On what?"

"The program."

He'd smiled at her. He saw people on TV do that. "Of course," he said in a pleasant voice that shocked him. "That would be swell. You know, while I've got you here, my oldest made friends with a girl who comes here. Her nanny, a Hispanic woman, brings her and her sister. I don't know their name. You don't happen to know if they attend that program, do you?"

"That would be Bonita and the Travis girls. You know, we also have a special class on Thursdays. It's late in the afternoon to accommodate working parents. It's also open to all ages."

"Thursday? As in tomorrow?"

"Yes. At five o'clock. It's reading and discussion. It allows the children to express their thoughts. It's become quite popular. It's good for the children to respect the opinions of others. The Travis girls rarely miss it."

"My daughters will like that."

"I thought they were your grandchildren."

"You know how it is. You consider them your own."

"That is *so* nice."

Now he sat in his car.

Now he waited for them.

He looked at the picture of Lisa Trowbridge on the dashboard. "We're dancing today, sugarplum. We are dancing today."

He ran his finger over the faded photograph. It was all he ever knew about touching a girl.

CHAPTER 51

There are few options when crossing Tampa Bay from Saint Petersburg. None were convenient to where I was going, which was straight east. I went south, preferring the Sunshine Skyway to the dysfunctional Tampa traffic grid. When I hit the I-75 interchange, I banked north and then east until I outran civilization on a straight, coilless road.

I clocked another half mile after the address on Whiting's deed so that I could scope out the area. There was nothing to scope. Also, on my first pass, there had been a car behind me, and I was unable to get a good look.

This time, the country swath of asphalt was deserted. I parked the truck on the shoulder and crossed the pavement. The gate was locked. A pair of No Trespassing signs anchored both ends. No surveillance cameras. That didn't surprise me. Nothing at his home indicated he utilized electronic surveillance. The satellite map of the area showed a decent-size pole barn on the property as well as a small house. Records indicated the property had been last purchased thirty-seven years ago. Was it empty? Did it hold dilapidated farm equipment? The police had never found a single car that could be tied to the hit-and-runs. Had Whiting kept his instruments of death?

The gate connected to a chain-linked fence with a string of rusty barbed wire running across the top. I followed it for fifteen feet or so in each direction. There were no breaks. That was unfortunate. I went back to the gate. The narrow drive took a hard curve on the other side and disappeared. Selloum palms, with their broad leaves, stood six to seven feet tall, creating a green wall. Purple blazing star wildflowers struggled for sun, and cabbage palms stuck up through the tangled undergrowth. I debated trying to shimmy up a tree and jumping the barbed wire. But it was the middle of the day. I'd rather return at night. With wire cutters.

MORGAN AND GARRETT WERE waiting for me on the back porch when I arrived home. I explained where I'd been and what I'd seen. That satellite pictures showed two structures on the property, one clearly larger than the other.

"The cars were never recovered?" Garrett said.

"Correct," I replied. "But records are spotty. Or nonexistent."

"How long a drive?" Morgan asked.

"An hour."

We decided to leave and kill time at a diner about two miles from the property. That was the best way to eliminate potential traffic delays if we wanted to hit Whiting's place at dusk. Garrett and I would approach the structures while Morgan stayed in the truck. In the event that Nathan or anybody entered the gate, he would notify us.

As we headed out, I tried to keep my mind from racing ahead, from hypothesizing about what we might find. For all I knew, Nathan Whiting was into organic gardening, and the pole barn was full of rusted farm equipment.

I called Kathleen. She didn't pick up. I texted her. I thought of calling Bonita to let her know as well. She had the girls at the library for a late afternoon reading session. Most of the reading classes were in the morning, but one day a week, the library held a reading class in the afternoon.

That was today. Thursday.

CHAPTER 52

By the dim and flaring lamps

"What do you think, honey?" he said to the photograph on the dashboard. "Hey, I'm talking to you, dimple face. You remember me, don't you? That's right. I could see it in your eyes right before smack city. We had our moment."

The first job had been born of extreme caution. He and Ziegler were having a postcoital conversation. Ziegler had offered him twenty bucks to suck him off. Then the doc popped this: How'd you like to make real money? Told him that one of the girls fought the drug like a damn Amazon warrior. She whined that she heard her baby. That it—he, she, whatever—was not dead. Demanded an explanation. Just showed up at the clinic.

Ziegler: We can't have that, can we?

Whiting: No, we can't. *We? Why do I care?*

Ziegler: It's for the best. They have no clue the favor I'm doing them. And you should see the folks who adopt them. Luckiest day in their lives, not to mention it's the best thing that could ever happen to the baby. Being raised by a stable, mature couple. Not some teenage slut. You see?

Whiting: Sure.

Ziegler: From now on, I'm giving you and Belle both a hundred dollars for the part you each contribute to.

Whiting: What's my part?

Ziegler: Security.

Whiting: Security?

Ziegler: She threatened to go to the police. We can't have that, can we? Think of all the future parents we'd disappoint. All the babies denied a proper and natural family.

Whiting: What do you want me to do?

Ziegler: Whatever it is, don't tell me.

What career do you envision for yourself?

Whiting: Four hundred.

Ziegler: For both of you?

Whiting: For me. Keep Belle out of it.

Ziegler: Two hundred.

Whiting: Four.

Ziegler: Deal.

He took his new role seriously. Devised a plan with two rules. First rule: Don't get caught. Second rule: Thou should have no other rules than the first rule.

He figured the key to the first rule was no fingerprints. He'd seen a cop show or two, and it was always the fingerprints that did the perp in. Later, when revisiting this youthful decision, he was grateful he'd stuck to his thesis. Who could have foreseen DNA? Made fingerprints child's play.

He'd only stolen a car for the first job because he'd just bought his first set of wheels, a baby blue 1970 Ford Fairlane 500 with an optional V-8. He knew it would be hot after the job. He'd been walking past a Chevron station when a car pulled up. A man dashed out the door and into the restroom on the side of the station. When he came out, his car was gone.

He had no idea there'd be a second job. A fifth. A tenth. Hey, Doc, why not give them a little stronger drug? Ziegler explained that if he gave more, he risked the patient's life. Whiting wasn't so sure about that. In fact, he thought Dr. Ziegler might not know what the hell he was doing. But the money was accompanied by something totally unexpected. Something far more fulfilling.

I'm good at this.

And afterward? Sitting there with Johnny and the gang. Hearing them laugh at jokes he didn't understand.

Guess what, world? I don't need your jokes. I am God, the destroyer of dreams.

He glanced at his watch. He placed his gooey Baby Ruth back in its wrapper. The front door of the library opened. He tossed the candy bar on the floor on the passenger side. He was parked at the end of the lot with an unobstructed runway to the front door.

People started streaming out. Children holding the hands of adults. He squirmed in his seat. Felt a hollowness in his chest.

The stream turned to a trickle.

Nope. Not them.

Naw.

There she was. The nanny. The two girls. All holding hands. *Jesus Fucking Christ, what is it with this hand thing?*

Steady now.

Steady.

He crept forward. Three more steps and they would be in the parking lot.

Two.

One.

He stomped on the gas pedal.

He hath loosed the fateful lighting of His terrible swift sword.

CHAPTER 53

His truth is marching on

The woman said something to the younger girl, who was fidgeting and turning back toward the library. The woman looked up. Her eyes locked on Nathan's. The younger girl broke away and sprinted back to the library. *What to do?* He hesitated. Eased up on the gas. *No! Two out of three ain't bad.* The woman, ignoring the younger girl and without taking her eyes off the car, took a massive step back, jerking the older girl with her. He veered to the right to intercept the woman and the older girl whose hand she still held. The front tires hit the curb. The car jolted over it. The woman took another leap back and swept up the girl with one arm. *Christ, she's fast. Strong.* He was faintly aware of the younger girl dashing back inside the library. Faintly aware of sweat trickling down his forehead. Faintly aware of the whole thing going to shit.

At the last split second, he spotted the mailbox. A big fucker planted in cement with two concrete posts guarding it.

Abort. Abort.

He braked hard and cut the wheel to the left, barely missing the fortress mailbox. He clipped a white Mercedes SUV and screeched toward the exit. In the rearview mirror, he saw the woman. She'd let go of the older girl's hand and was running after him. Screaming at him in Spanish.

What the f? Crazy bitch.

He pulled out into the street and eased into the flow of traffic. He dialed up a radio station. A climactic calm settled over him. He'd failed. No biggie. Could have been worse. *Time for plan B. Swing by the country home and then adios, world. This is Dream Killer One checking out. Be jubilant, my feet!*

Nathan Whiting knew his "Battle Hymn of the Republic."

CHAPTER 54

I was chewing a buttered roll in the diner and complaining to Morgan and Garrett that it was stale when Kathleen called and informed me that our daughters had nearly been run down in the library parking lot over an hour ago. Kathleen had been conducting office hours, and Bonita had been unable to reach her.

She explained that Sophia, as that pistol was prone to do, had broken away from Bonita. She wanted to go back into the library and get a second free bookmark. Bonita, while holding Joy's hand and starting to turn around to retrieve Sophia, had spotted the car. Everyone was fine. The girls weren't aware of the severity of the situation.

Now you know why Bonita has voting privileges.

Would Whiting have returned to his property? Might he be there now?

"Did she get a description?" I asked Kathleen, though I didn't need one.

"Older man," Kathleen said.

"Mustache?"

"Didn't say. But he wore a Rays baseball cap. And the car

was old. Bonita doesn't know cars. But she thought it was seventies or eighties."

"Did she add anything else?"

"She told me to tell you that she saw death in the driver's eyes, and he saw anger in hers. That she knew what he wanted to do, and he had no chance against her. As soon as she knew both girls were safe, she gave chase. She also—"

"On foot?"

"On foot. She also told me to tell you to do a better job protecting her babies."

That might have been Kathleen.

"We're heading out to his place now."

"Jake?"

She paused, forcing me to come in. "Yeah?"

"End this."

Ten minutes later, with the truck parked a quarter mile away, Morgan, Garrett, and I hiked back to the property. If Nathan wasn't there, we didn't want to spook him by planting an empty truck at his entrance. Night was closing fast, aided by anxious clouds darkening the western horizon.

We didn't know if Whiting was on his property but assumed he was for planning purposes. Garrett would circumvent the grounds and approach the house from the rear. I had the front door. Morgan had lookout. We snipped the fence in an area that was not visible from the road.

Garrett ventured to the left, and I picked my way down the long driveway, staying a few feet off to the side. It was rough going, navigating around cabbage palms and an unexpected field of prickly pear cactus. I wondered if Garrett had encountered the same, but I didn't think so. Satellite photos of the property indicated it was more scrub land, with most of the growth around the road frontage and on both sides of the drive.

The drive ended at the house. A car was parked between the

house and a pole barn. Whiting's. I recognized it from the day I first went to his home. The smell of gas hung in the air. Must need a tune-up. A toolshed stood off from the pole barn. Discarded pots littered the ground. A hose was rolled up on a reel.

A light glowed from inside the house. I texted Garrett. He replied that he was in position behind the house. I calculated how long it would take to storm the front door. It was still a good distance to the house. If I dashed to the car, that would cut the distance by two-thirds. Keeping low, I sprinted to the car and huddled up against it. The pole barn was now behind me and about a hundred feet away. I texted Garrett again.

Storm front door, count of ten on next text.

He texted back.

Your count.

I texted him.

Ten . . .

I counted back. Nine, eight . . .

At three, I vaulted up and charged the door. I kicked it in. That didn't go well. My foot went through the door, but it didn't open. I wrestled my foot out and tried the doorknob. It was unlocked. I swung the door open. Garrett was waiting inside with his gun drawn. A radio was on. Toyotas on sale this weekend. Free hot dogs. Garrett cased another room.

"Empty," he said.

"His car's out front," I said. "Pole barn?"

"Or outside waiting to ambush us. If he's on the property, he knows we're here."

I called Morgan to make sure that all was quiet in the front. He replied that there'd been no activity.

"Tell me about the front of the barn," Garrett said.

"Two big doors. Sliders. Closed. One pedestrian door. The back?"

"Double doors, but no pedestrian. You take the front,"

Garrett said. "See if the door's unlocked first. Would have saved a few seconds just now and kept the noise down."

"I was expecting—"

"If no answer, try the sliders. I'll do the same on the other end. I smell gas."

"I think it's his car," I said. "I smelled it coming in." But as I spoke, I realized that when I'd crouched down next to Whiting's car, the smell was no greater than it had been farther away.

"No," Garrett said. "That's not it."

Our eyes locked. What if Whiting was getting ready to torch his house and flush us out right into the barrel of his gun. Was he that good?

He was a mass murderer who'd gone undetected for nearly half a century. Tailed you and you didn't have a clue.

"We need to get out of here," I said.

"Not the doors. There's a window in the bedroom."

Garrett had turned and was halfway in the bedroom as he spoke the last words. He kicked the glass out and vaulted through the window. My head followed his heels just as a giant swoosh of flame engulfed the house.

CHAPTER 55

Our God is marching on

He had left the library and hightailed it straight to his farm.

Did age do this to me? Was I just lucky with the baker's dozen?

His insouciant attitude toward his failure deserted him on the trip back to his hideaway. *Never should have done it in broad daylight. But they're not out at night. Then figure out a different approach, stupid cocksucker. And three at once?* That, he now saw, was the Achilles' heel of his plan. The split second the youngest girl bolted, he'd realized he was in trouble town. Too much space. Too distracting. The slight hesitation, the indecision, had cost him.

He wished he'd opted for the Houdini plan and vanished. Doc hadn't hung around for some meaningless grand finale, had he? *Should never have scratched that itch.* His failure doubled his resolve to leave no trace. When he returned to his property, he'd gone inside, turned on the radio, and packed a single bag. He went to the pole barn.

Can't put them in a suitcase, can I?

He had five five-gallon cans of gas. The pole barn and house were wood. One gallon would do the trick. But he didn't want to do a trick. He wanted to do hell. He soaked his house and then laid a trail to the pole barn. Inside the barn, he'd emptied the cans around the perimeter and crisscrossed the dirt floor. Doused the cars. Bathed everything. He knew the fire wouldn't destroy the cars, but he wasn't worried about that. Even if they were traced to stolen vehicles from fifty years ago—which he doubted would occur—there was nothing to link them to the deaths of the women.

Searching for a positive spin, he considered that missing the girls in the library parking lot might have been for the best. After all, he'd been having second thoughts about never realizing the money from his property. What if the man chasing him had no conclusive proof? Why toss away all those years? All that bread? He decided he'd head west for a while. Let things cool off. Then he'd reintegrate himself into his old life little by little, with one foot out the door should there be any hint of trouble.

Really, shitbrain? What else are you going to talk yourself into?

He had a more pressing issue: what do to with the pictures. The fire would certainly destroy them. He was torn as to whether that was good or bad. To lose all physical connection to the past would be hard. That would be like losing part of himself. As if nothing remained of his life. Cherished items help create your identity. They trigger an emotional response. Provide a sense of continuity and connection to the past. He'd read that somewhere, though why and when escaped him.

He decided to leave the photographs taped to the dashes of their respective cars. RIP. The car he had used to kill Lisa Trowbridge and in his botched library job was the last one to receive the gas shower. He had just finished with it when a noise from outside startled him. He pulled back the front door just enough to gain vision. He saw the man. His foot was stuck in the front door of his house.

How'd he find me? Ah shit. Goddamn deed was in the box. Look at him. Standing there like a one-legged ostrich.

The man extracted his foot from the door, turned the knob, and entered his house.

Oh boy, do I have a surprise for you.

He started to leave the barn, pivoted, and went back in. He opened a cabinet and took out a gun and a set of car keys. Though his car was out front by the house, he had another set of wheels in the rear of the property where there was another gate, obscured from the road. He had recently purchased the car using a fake driver's license to register the temporary tag. He figured that would keep the fuzz off his tail.

He left the barn and crept close to the house. He wanted the flames to get there as quickly as possible. He struck a match. Dropped it on the ground. A trail of fire sprinted across the barren earth. Its quickness and dedication astonished him. He'd dosed that side of the house, the windward side, with five gallons.

He was barely clear himself when the house erupted into flames. A Black man vaulted through a window. *Who the fuck is he?* Nathan Whiting turned and galloped back to the barn, giddy with excitement.

High-yooo! Going to have a hot time tonight!

CHAPTER 56

"That your man?" Garrett said when I sprang to my feet.

Whiting was scampering away from us and toward the pole barn. He had the awkward, unsmooth gait of a person who struggled to run.

I sprinted after him. I wanted to take Whiting down and then enter the pole barn to see if the cars were there. Whiting was halfway between the house and the barn when he dropped behind his car. I instinctively slowed and crouched. Garrett split off to my right so as to come up behind Whiting.

Whiting stood and fired twice in my direction. Garrett returned fire. I sprinted toward the pole barn, hit the ground, rolled, got up, took two giant steps, and threw myself around the corner of the barn. Shots rang out from behind me, and it was only then that I noticed the flame. It slithered like a demented snake, approaching the pole barn from the house. Whiting must have laid a trail of gasoline over his property with the intent of burning everything. The barn was weathered wood. You could torch it with a cigarette lighter. Behind me, the house roared with fire.

More gunshots. Whiting was no longer a factor. His luck

had run out on a dark, fiery hot Florida night, forty years after he'd killed God knows how many young women. He'd ended up in a gunfight with the one man in Florida you did not want to engage with. Garrett had been a sniper in the army during a stretch of years that was rapidly uncoupling from our present lives. Garrett wouldn't shoot to kill, though. The dead share no secrets.

I wasn't wild about entering Dante's pole barn. I hustled over to where the flame was now only a few feet from the barn. I kicked dirt on it. Dragged my foot over the path where the flame was heading. But the ground was too hard, the fire too determined, my efforts too paltry. The flame hit the pole barn and climbed the building.

I ran around to the other side, away from the fire. I grabbed the handle of one of the sliding doors and swung it open. Ten cars? Twelve? All older models. I was looking at Nathan Whiting's trophy room. The fire faced me from the opposite end. I glanced up. Wood beams. The whole place was a tinderbox. I ran to the nearest car and opened the driver's door. Inside, taped to the dash, was a faded picture of a young woman. I reached for it and stuck it in my pocket. I started for another car as a river of fire crossed the dirt floor and breached the walls.

Would the gas tanks explode? Did I want to hang around and find out? They're dead. Let them go.

It wouldn't be long before the roof stared to burn, and the fire, starved for oxygen, would make it difficult to breathe. I started to run to the open door but stopped just as abruptly, my legs refusing to obey my brain.

Feel the companion of the dead.

In an act of defenseless and volcanic stupidity, I spun and ran toward the flames, the dead women howling me forth. I had to find Lisa. Let her know that Archie still had the McDonald's napkin she's scribbled on forty-five years ago.

I sprinted from car to car. I swung open the driver's door, reached in, snatched the picture, and dashed to the next car. The flames, angered by my defiance, doubled their intensity. Whiting must have thrown gas on the cars, for the ones close to where the fire had entered the pole barn were soon covered with liquid flames, though the fire did not seem as enthusiastic about metal as it did about wood. I recalculated my route and rushed to the cars on that side of the building.

I opened a door, coughed, grabbed a photo, and hustled to the next car and the next. Five pictures. Seven. I hacked out every breath. I yanked my shirttail out of my pants and covered my mouth and nose with it. Two more pictures. *How many did he kill?* The heat was relentless and still no Lisa.

Years ago, I'd watched a man named Stephen Cole walk out of a burning house holding two young children in his arms. He emerged from the flames as if he were impervious to them and they held no power over his immortal body. I'd rarely spoken of the event, for I did not believe what I had seen. Had my eyes deceived me? Or was my recollection accurate, and I refused to acknowledge that the supernatural exists in our world?

I only mention it now because I did not expect such a miracle to bail me out. Lisa or not, that barn would not be my casket.

Two cars left.

I opened the door. I ripped the picture off the dash. Not Lisa. That meant, if she were here, she was in the car closest to the door and engulfed in flames.

Without thought, I bull-rushed the flames. I opened the door. My hand was singed. I reached in and snatched her. My back started to burn, and then it was wet. Morgan stood at the entrance of the pole barn, hose in hand, spraying water in my direction. Garrett was beside me.

"Time to haul ass," he said.

PART III

DOOMED AT BOTH ENDS OF LOVE

CHAPTER 57

Do I give Archie the photograph? I was conflicted, convincing myself of one course of action and then seamlessly flipping to the other.

It was two days later, and Kathleen and I were again motoring over the Tierra Verde Bridge to visit Archie and Bobbie Lee. I had a bandage on my forehead, pockmarked burns scattered over my body, and a picture in my pocket. Not to belabor the point, but wouldn't Archie have been better off if he had never engaged me? Never mentioned his quest to his old college roommate, Yankee Conard?

I'd been rehearsing what to tell him. That wasn't going well. No sooner did I start than I'd jump to the end, and it was always the same. *Lisa was brutally plowed down the night she was to meet you at McDonald's. No clue who or where your daughter is. Glad I could be of assistance to you.*

Morgan, upon hearing gunshots, had abandoned his post and come running. At first, they couldn't find me. Garrett said he feared I'd been shot and searched for me outside the pole barn, knowing only a fool would enter a burning building.

Then, remembering that he knew a fool, Garrett drenched himself in water from a spigot on the toolshed. Morgan ran a hose from the shed, stretched it as far as he could, and showered us both.

Both men exercised the admirable traits of reason and caution.

Rambler had all the pictures, except one. He also had the camera I'd found in Whiting's box and placed in a plastic bag. He talked with the local sheriff, who had more than a few questions for Garrett, Morgan, and me. We explained who Nathan Whiting was and what we had found on his property. By not returning fire, Garrett had lured Whiting out from behind the car he'd used as cover. He then shot at his legs. Once Whiting went down, Garrett tied his hands behind his back and came after me. We called for an ambulance. When they hoisted Whiting onto the gurney, I walked over to him.

"How many?" I asked him.

"Not talking," he said.

Rambler had since notified me that Whiting was in stable condition and refusing to speak.

"What did you tell Archie about Whiting?" Kathleen asked.

"That he was refusing to talk."

"Does he even know who Whiting is?"

"I told him I'd explain more in person, but he was an accomplice of Ziegler. I'll need to explain Whiting's role. That we found Whiting's cars. That we don't know how many women he killed, but each car had a picture in it, and one of those pictures was of Lisa."

We were quiet for a moment. Kathleen stared out the side window. The fingers of her left hand drummed the center console. "I don't know about that," she said, her head still turned away.

"What part?"

She looked at me. "All parts. Telling him that Whiting killed those girls and likely killed Lisa. And then giving him her picture."

"What's the alternative? Withhold it forever?"

"I don't know."

"I can't hide behind that."

"You can sit on it for a day or two."

"That will make the story different?"

"It will buy time."

"For what?"

"Don't be difficult."

"Don't be vague."

"I don't know, okay?" she said with frustration. "Maybe you find his daughter and deliver the bad news with good news."

"Maybe I win the lottery."

"What's with you?"

"I'm tired of chasing down the past. Too many pieces are missing. It's futile."

"You always urge me to exceed my limitations," she said. "To go beyond what I think I can do."

"When have I ever said that?"

"Last night in your sleep."

"He'll find out, K. When the story breaks. Not just about Whiting but about the cars. There'll be an official investigation into the deaths of those young women."

"How much time does that leave us?"

"Not my call."

We were silent for a few beats. A pickup pulling a boat passed us in the other direction. The boat flew an aberration of the American flag. The car behind the boat was smaller than the boat's outboard engines.

"Show it to him," Kathleen said. "No hesitation."

"I thought you just—"

"I changed my mind. He has the right. You have the obligation. Keep it simple."

"Wanna pull over and have sex under the mangroves?"

"This is serious. You need to focus."

"Just sounds like more fun."

"Not every day is a hoot," Kathleen reprimanded me. "Bobbie Lee said it's just tearing him up, knowing that he has a daughter. She doesn't know what he fears most—that he'll run out of time before he finds her or that he beats the cancer and spends the rest of his life searching for her."

"I've met people who have been searching for years. Decades. It wears them down. It's no way to live. My advice to him will be to forget looking for her."

"You'll say no such thing."

Was I ready to walk away? Had I taken it to my limit? Exceeded my limit? When was the last time I went fishing? Spent my time the way I—

"Jake?"

"What?"

"Keep looking. One more mile. Promise me?"

"I—"

"Promise me."

"Fine. For you. Not for him."

"I'll take that," she said. "So where does that leave us?"

"I'll play it by ear," I said as we entered the roundabout. "I'll tell him I've still got a couple of loose ends but nothing promising. He'll read between the lines."

And what he'd read was bullshit, but I didn't share that with Kathleen, who likely knew as much.

Kathleen flipped down the visor, took a brush out of the glove box, and ran it through her hair. She put the brush back and snapped the visor in place. "I don't mean to ride you. Just make sure that when you stop searching for Lisa's daughter, you're in a place that when you look back years from now, you know you took it as far as you could and then, exhausted, a few steps further. No regrets."

That woman. She might be my north, my south. My thread and my needle. My wooden bridge over rushing waters. My brass horn mornings, my cello sunsets. But she was wrong.

No one escapes this gig without regrets.

CHAPTER 58

"My favorite couple," Bobbie Lee bubbled when she greeted us at her front door. She and Kathleen hugged. I got a punch in the arm. "Hey, cowboy. I heard you shot it out with some dirtbag who helped Dr. Quack years ago."

"My partner was involved in the gunfight."

"Partner? Who might that be?"

"An old friend."

"Do I want to know?"

I spread my hands.

"What is it you said you do for Yankee Conrad again?"

"He's a fixer," Archie said, approaching us from the kitchen. "Yankee recruited him for special projects; he just won't admit it."

Was that an insult?

"What happened to your forehead?" Bobbie Lee asked.

"I banged it on the lift climbing out of my boat."

"Hmm. Must have been a hot day. It looks like a burn."

"Curling iron?"

"Are you going to be evasive all night?"

"Maybe. Maybe not."

Another punch. She was feisty tonight. "You're no fun. Let's go out back. I fixed a kick-ass charcuterie board, and you can tell us all about this Whiting fellow and what's behind your evasive behavior."

Archie and I trailed Kathleen and Bobbie Lee through the house. "Any progress in finding my daughter?" he said with an undertone of impatience in his voice.

"It's slow going," I said.

"But you're still going, right?"

"I am."

Archie didn't respond. He was a natural bullshit detector.

The four or us relocated to their backyard fronting the water. Olympian clouds bulged high over the Gulf of Mexico. Flashes of lightning cobwebbed the sky. I've said it before, but it bears repeating. Lightning in celestial clouds conjures images of the ancient Greek and Roman gods, discarded by the race that created them, battling for relevancy. I wonder if someday the world's current religions will join them. Zeus and Jesus. Jupiter and Mohammad. Mercury and Moroni. Athena and the Mother Mary. History's fairy tales cast together in the wastebasket of man's imagination.

Archie tended bar. Kathleen and Bobbie Lee opted for white wine. Archie and I settled on bourbon on the rocks.

"Bobbie Lee," Kathleen exclaimed, looking over a live-edge board decorated with cheese, meat, fruit, and bread. "It's artistic. I hate to disturb it."

"Thank you," Bobbie Lee said. "I enjoy doing it."

"I have no problem," I said. I reached in and loaded a plate with strawberries, two types of cheese, and a coal-black piece of chocolate.

Halfway through a strawberry, Archie said, "Don't keep me waiting."

"Archie," Bobbie Lee said. "Let the man swallow."

"That could be all night."

After a deliberate chew to remind Archie I wasn't his marionette, I launched into what I'd discovered. I omitted the photographs in the cars. It was a game-time decision. I told him about Clive calling Lisa. That he was the man who wrote the letter to Archie saying that Little Strawberry was alive. Archie interrupted to ask how Clive got his address. That point clarified, Archie urged me to continue.

"Let him come up for air, honey," Bobbie Lee said.

"I'm fine," I assured her.

"You've been eyeing that summer sausage."

I took a toothpick, speared a piece of sausage, and stuck it in my mouth. "I met with a detective who investigated the Ziegler case," I said. "There were multiple hit-and-runs that might have been connected to Ziegler's ex-patients."

"Speak English," Archie demanded.

"Some of the mothers whose children were stillborn were murdered in hit-and-runs that were never solved."

If you asked me why I blurted that out, I couldn't tell you.

"Go on," Archie instructed in a steely voice. I felt Kathleen's eyes on me.

I dumped it all. My meeting with Lisa's aunt, Allision. The tragic tale of other women who had claimed they heard their babies, even though Ziegler said they were stillborn. The unexplainable hit-and-runs. How Whiting had gunned for my children. The scene at the barn. The burning cars.

"He went after your children?" Archie asked. He gained some lost respect saying that. Putting the here and now over what I'd just dropped on him.

"He did."

"I'm sorry. You didn't sign up for that."

"Are they okay?" Bobbie Lee asked Kathleen.

"Thankfully, yes," Kathleen said. She'd been pretty chill about the whole incident, which worried me. "They didn't realize what was happening. Or at least that there was intent.

Bonita, our nanny, saved them. She would have thrown herself in front of that car to protect them."

We were quiet for a moment, and then, out of that abyss, Archie said, "She was murdered."

"That appears to be the case."

He stood and walked away.

Bobbie Lee popped up. "That's how you burned your forehead," she said as if she were angry with the world. She hustled after her husband.

CHAPTER 59

"Guess you decided to tell him," Kathleen said.

"Guess so."

"I'll give you credit for two things. Telling him was the right thing to do."

"And the second?"

"Sex on the beach would have been more fun."

"Don't know about that. Have you tried the sausage?"

"Oh buster. That's going to cost you. How long do we give them?"

"Until the sausage runs out?"

"I keep forgetting how simple you are."

"I've done nothing to mislead you."

"No, you have not."

Archie and Bobbie Lee returned. Archie looked determined. Bobbie Lee looked like a party balloon the day after.

"This Whiting fellow is refusing to talk?" Archie said.

"He is. But the crime units will scour his house and what's left of the cars. They'll find something."

Bobbie Lee said, "Are the police going to investigate the other murders?"

"They are," I said. "But—"

"Whiting won't talk," Archie cut in. "The women are dead. He never touched a victim, and it was all fifty years ago." He knifed me a look. "Do I have that right? You've done a fine job of avoiding the obvious. I—"

"Archie," Bobbie Lee said.

He raised his hand. "I was just going to say I appreciate your tact. But let the facts fall. I'm sure you agree that Lisa's death confirms that our daughter is alive."

"It does tend to—"

"Our mission no longer runs on the fumes of hope. Where do we stand?"

How about I pass the baton to someone else?

I tilted forward, clasped my hands together, and rested my forearms on my knees. I counted to three before I spoke.

"I've met with Abigail. Your former wives, Lauren and Theresa. Katie Phillips, Lisa's best friend in high school. A woman named Heather Kirkland, who is the go-to person in investigating the sins of Wayne Ziegler. Charlene, the granddaughter of Charles Buford, who owned the Cardinal Inn when Lisa was there. Arnelli, the retired cop. Clive Emmons and his wife, Lanelle. Whiting, before he fled. Betty Winfield—her daughter, Bree, was a victim."

"I commend your effort," Archie said in a conciliatory tone that didn't fool me.

"Aunt Allison," I continued, for I wasn't done patting myself on the back. "A woman named Georgy. She lives in Old Northeast, where Ziegler lived years ago. She's into local history, and it was at her house that I first connected Whiting to Ziegler. Whiting, when I met him, denied ever speaking to Ziegler. And Jenna Cappabianca, who adopted from Ziegler and led me to a false lead on who might have adopted Little Strawberry. I thought it was wrapped up then. I thought wrong."

I leaned back, worried that my tone had come across as a

tad hostile. Upon hearing my litany of names, I thought of the adage that if you find yourself in a hole, it's time to stop digging. Do I share that with Archie?

April. The pole dancer. I'd forgotten about her. And I lied to you earlier, telling you that Rambler had all the pictures except one. I had Bree's picture as well. I don't know why I kept it. I thought I wanted to give it to Betty Winfield, but I was rethinking that.

"We're grateful for what you've done," Bobbie Lee said.

Right, but is Archie?

"He's not done," Kathleen piped in.

Yes, I am.

"I am not," I said.

"I always knew it was a long shot," Archie said.

"I plan to revisit some people," I said, a limp statement that I doubted fooled Mr. Bullshit Detector. "Many of them hadn't thought of Ziegler in years. It's possible they've recalled further details since I first questioned them."

"Chin up, Archie," Kathleen chimed in. "Jake always finds his man. Or, in this case, his woman."

"Why did you talk with Abigail?" Archie said.

His question caught me off guard, for we had not been discussing her. "I wanted to make sure she wouldn't hinder my search."

"What makes you think she would do that?"

"Because if successful, my efforts will dilute her inheritance."

"You misjudged her. She's not that self-centered. And Lester? Don't tell me you're worried about him as well."

"I am not."

"I'm glad," Archie said. "He's got a good head."

Well, he can thank his sister for that. After all, she arranged that for him when he was fourteen.

"Abby might have a heart of stone," he continued. "That

makes her great in business. Not so hot for living. I suppose I did that to her. My drive consumed me for too long. That's all she saw growing up, her role model. All she wanted to do was be like me, but she'd never acknowledge that."

My mind drifted to my own girls. What kind of role model was I? Morgan and I operated Harbor House; that was a plus. I made eggs, took special orders. Double plus. I occasionally, and with disturbing frequency, found myself in a tangled mess that often ended in unsolicited violence—maybe a black mark there. I read to them every night. Bonus points. Maybe it was time I grab the wheel of my life, before it was too late. Before I left an unintentional yet indelible impression on my daughters. But—?

"Right, honey?" Kathleen said, tossing me a conversational life preserver.

"Absolutely." I had no clue where the conversation was. Great Scott, what if I'd just said yes to a dog?

Kathleen continued, knowing full well I'd blanked out. "And when he's revisited those key players, we'll report back in three days."

We? Three days?

"That will be perfect," Bobbie Lee said. "Archie has chemo after that. Let's do dinner, and don't say no."

"I never say no to dinner," I said.

"I never say no to chemo," Archie quipped, and we all had a good laugh. A little comic relief goes a long way.

We eased back from the edge with idle talk. I reiterated that I thought I was close when I met with Jenna, and she thought she had the name of the couple who adopted Lisa's baby. But it wasn't to be.

"But it could have been," Bobbie Lee said. "And the next one might."

"Did you ever have the urge to find your birth parents?" I asked her.

"No," she said, as if puzzled by her own answer. "I mean, they gave me up. My adopted parents were wonderful. My mother said it was a private adoption. That the birth mother was young and didn't want a child. I totally get it."

"That's how we got our girls," Kathleen said. "We were lucky in that we met both birth mothers. Wonderful young women. They had no desire to raise a child."

"Exactly," Bobbie Lee said. "A win-win."

"That's what the parents who adopted from Ziegler were told," I said. "That the birth mother didn't want the child."

That brought a thud of silence. We all say something stupid sometimes, and I'd just taken my turn. We rounded out the evening discussing Harbor House, the dog in my future, and what a pity it was that cheese was so high in fat because we all could just live on it. As we approached the door to leave, Archie turned to me. "Have you been to her grave?"

"Whose grave?"

"Lisa's."

Had I missed something? Was I supposed to? I told him I had not.

"It's in Greenlawn. I put a new headstone on it some years ago. Go see it. Tomorrow. I'd like to know your thoughts on the epitaph."

Little pastry puff. He knew what he was doing. He wanted me to stand over Lisa's grave site, which would fill me with remorse and make me double down on my efforts to find his daughter. His comment would have its desired effect, but pity Archie, not me, for only a fool does not fear what he searches for.

CHAPTER 60

I hit Greenlawn the next morning, after my run. After I saw Morgan on the end of his dock, sitting with his legs crossed, facing the ascending sun that illuminated our houses and lavished our lives in glory, *and* after my date with my punching bag, which I was hitting harder and harder each day, an unidentifiable anger rising within me, *and* after I fixed eggs for the girls—cheese, onions, you know the deal—*and* after I fed Hadley III as she rubbed against my ankles, *and* after I read to Joy and Sophia under the coconut palm that needed trimming because Kathleen was afraid that a coconut would bonk someone in the head, *and* after I dropped by Harbor House—I haven't mentioned it much in this story, but Morgan was busier than ever there—*and* after Bonita took over with the girls, instructing me to stop fooling around and get rid of the bad guys in the world, *and* after my outdoor shower, my body bathed by sun and water, earth's twin mothers.

Only after those inconsequential yet otherworldly moments did I get in my truck and set out to view the grave site of Lisa Trowbridge.

I parked a few rows away from where, according to the

cemetery's website, I would find her headstone. Archie said he had changed the gravestone out years ago. I imagined that when Lisa died, it would have been her mother who had selected the tombstone. Archie would not have entered the equation.

I stuck a baseball cap on and ventured into the parched land. The grounds were well tended, but there was no shade in the area where Lisa was buried. I trudged over the flat land and couldn't help but notice the names and dates of those who were interred there. Most never knew each other while alive, yet here they slept for eternity, side by side. Some died old. Some died young. Some were remembered with poems and flowers. Others appeared not to be remembered at all. A child's grave had plastic toys by it.

I stood where Lisa's site was supposed to be but couldn't locate it. An older man with a straw hat was trimming around headstones with a gas trimmer. I got his attention. He shut his machine off. I told him I was looking for Lisa Trowbridge.

"She's over there." I looked to where he nodded, half expecting to see Lisa wearing a summer dress and holding a parasol. "See the flowers?" he added. "That's her. She gets fresh flowers every Monday."

"Whether needed or not?" I asked.

"Every Monday. I toss the old and replace them with the fresh ones."

"How long has that been going on?"

"I've been here close to thirty years. Every Monday."

"Do you know who sends them?" I asked, although I knew.

"Somebody who must have liked her and has money, wouldn't you say?"

The man must have been done, or it was break time, for instead of firing up his trimmer, he lumbered to a pickup truck. I stomped over to Lisa's grave. It was a simple headstone with her name, date of birth, and death date carved in stone.

On the ground above where she lay was a long flat stone with Christina Rossetti's "Remember" etched in it.

Remember me when I am gone away,
Gone far away into the silent land;
When you can no more hold me by the hand,
Nor I half turn to go yet turning stay.
Remember me when no more day by day
You tell me of our future that you planned:
Only remember me; you understand
It will be late to counsel then or pray.
Yet if you should forget me for a while
And afterwards remember, do not grieve:
For if the darkness and corruption leave
A vestige of the thoughts that once I had,
Better by far you should forget and smile
Than that you should remember and be sad.

Damn Archie.

CHAPTER 61

In *Institutes of Oratory*, Roman orator Quintilian of La Rioja noted that it is easier to stumble upon something by accident than to purposely set out to find it. If you catch that I've noted that in other stories, think not that I am lazy, but that I hold simple truths dear, and strive not to lose them in the clutter of my philosophies.

And so our story ends. Not by purpose or plot but by accident.

I spent the rest of the day with Morgan at Harbor House. We'd recently wound up three years of construction projects. My punch list was down to a few items. A bedroom door that scraped the ground. A second floor rear window that needed recaulking. A dresser and nightstand had come unassembled for one of the new guest rooms. I put them together and broke the boxes down for recycling.

I didn't think of Lisa. Of Archie or Bobbie Lee. The photographs. There was no Allison. No Jenna or Bree. No Georgy girl. My hands were too busy for my mind to get a word in. I did think of Clive. Lanelle called and told me he was being released. I was happy for him. And me. Every so often, a thought would flash through my mind. Something Jenna had said. Or Heather. Or Allison. I decided to pull out my notes that night and see if I had missed anything. But not until my world had gone quiet.

I left Harbor House and fixed dinner for five, as Morgan was joining us. More busy hands. I had not shared with Kathleen that I'd taken a sabbatical from the Lisa files, but she knew. She always knows.

After the girls were in bed and Morgan had crossed our dark, moon-shadowed lawn to his home, Kathleen announced she was going into the study to grade papers. As she left the screened porch, she dragged her hand across the top of my back. I wandered out to the end of the dock. When I arrived, my thoughts kept going over the bay, for like a rampant child who needs to run, my mind sought open space, unstructured words, and an unbiased landscape.

Whereas my mind might have been void of garbage, the dock was another matter. A pelican with serious digestive issues had splattered the decking. I'd meant to hose it off earlier, but it had slipped my mind. It was a winless battle, as the birds massively outnumbered me. So much for seeking a bolt of serendipity. I turned the spigot on and, as the red flashing channel marker kept a steady tempo, hosed off the dock. But there was only so much I could do.

I went back to the house, gathered my interview notes, and organized them chronologically. In the army, I played blindfolded chess. It forced me to see future moves, counter moves, and explore the consequences of those moves. I closed my eyes, thought of moves I might have missed, and fell asleep.

MIDDLE OF THE NIGHT a.m. My left eye popped open, then the right. Jenna Cappabianca was waiting for me. The Pophams. They'd adopted at the same time Lisa's baby was stolen. But they adopted a boy, and that revelation had tanked my victory. So close. Yet, like handshake and milkshake, their coincidences are meaningless.

A lot of people learned of Ziegler by word of mouth.

Why hadn't I followed up by talking with Elizabeth Popham? What if she knew of people who adopted during the time she did, which was around the time Lisa was under Ziegler's care?

Had I surrendered one foot from the finish line?

CHAPTER 62

Elizabeth Popham said she'd be glad to meet with me. She asked when. I said now. She said where. I said any place that was convenient for her. She was a volunteer docent at the Museum of Fine Arts and suggested we meet at the café there. I told her I'd be there in fifteen minutes. She said that was great, but they didn't open for another hour. We agreed to meet at that time.

A man and a woman manned the ticket counter when I entered the museum. They were in conversation with a third woman who stood to the side. The man asked if he could help me. I replied that I was looking for Elizabeth Popham.

"That's me," the woman behind him said. "You must be Jake."

Elizabeth Popham looked more like someone who donated to museums than someone who volunteered in them. Perhaps she did both. I thanked her for meeting me on such short notice. She waved me off, saying she was happy to and that it was hardly an inconvenience to her. We settled at a table in the café at the far end of the entrance hall.

"Wayne Ziegler," she said. "That was a long time ago. How I may be of assistance?"

I pretended not to hear her "long time" comment.

I hesitated. Do I tell her all? She likely never knew her child was stolen from his birth mother. That in all likelihood the birth mother was murdered for wanting her baby back. No way was I going to dump that on her. She might learn it someday, but not from me.

I explained that I was helping a friend who was searching for her birth mother. We had reason to believe she might have been in Ziegler's clinic around the time that Elizabeth adopted her son. I asked how she came to know about Ziegler and his services.

"If you're asking specifically how and when, I don't know. We just did. If you wanted a baby, there was this doctor who ran a clinic. Good reputation. Right here in town. You know," she said, as if it were common knowledge, "just go see him. Put your name on the list."

"And so you did?"

"My husband and I were unable to have children. We had no interest in waiting ten years on some adoption list. I remember him—Ziegler—saying that I should be prepared anytime. We were glad to have another option." She shrugged. "Felt lucky, really."

Jenna had told me that the Pophams became suspicious about the ease in which they adopted when the news of Ziegler broke. I asked about that.

"It's complicated," she bristled. "He was a positive influence in our lives. I have a son thanks to him. But my husband and I felt we needed to speak out and so we did."

"Because?"

She leveled her eye on me. "Because of that voice in the back of your head."

"Do you know of anyone who adopted around the period you did?" I tacked on the date that Lisa died.

"I can't be certain, but it sounds about the time that the Lakes adopted."

"The Lakes?"

"They lived down the street from us then. I lost track of them years ago. But Sandy, like me, was unable to get pregnant. They adopted a baby girl. I can't confirm the exact date, but it had to be pretty close to your time frame. You know he sometimes fudged the dates, right?"

Did I?

"Tell me."

"Something about protecting the mother. Never made much sense to me. Honestly? Probably should have asked more questions, but you know how it is. My son has a birth date that's at least a few weeks off from his delivery." She shrugged. "It's like that Three Dog Night song, you know—born in Oklahoma or Arizona, what does it matter?"

"Do you recall the name of the girl the Lakes adopted?" I asked.

"Yes and no. I don't recall her real first name; she always went by Jeri. Funny, right? The stuff you remember." She shrugged. "Sort of stuck with me, I guess. Not sure how or why that nickname came about."

I inquired if she had any pictures of her.

"No. But why not check with the high school?"

"Saint Petersburg High?"

"Go Green Devils."

"Do you know where Jeri Lake is now?"

"No idea."

"How about the couple who adopted her? Sandy Lake and her husband?"

"Deceased. Both she and her husband, and for the life of

me, I can't recall his name. It will come to me, you know, at two a.m. They moved away long ago."

"Where to?"

"Omaha. No-name husband got a job with an insurance company there. I believe they died in a private plane crash. You couldn't pay me to get in one of those tin buckets."

"How old do you think Jeri would have been when they moved?"

"Hmm, let's do the math. I'm pretty sure Jeri was in college when they left. So, what, twenty-five-some years ago? She went to UF. Everybody went to UF back then. Word was she dropped out. She was a bright girl. Real artistic. You know, the type who gets bored with formal education. Last I heard she was a stripper, but that was over ten years ago. So much for brains, right? Some club downtown. The name escapes me. I doubt she's there now. It's hardly a middle-age profession."

Had Archie's daughter once worked at the same club where he was to meet his wife?

"The Havana Club?" I said.

"Yeah, I think that's it. You familiar with it?"

I CALLED SAINT PETERSBURG High School and inquired if their yearbooks from the years I needed were available online. They were not. They also required an appointment with a librarian to view one. I made one for the following morning. I lobbied for that afternoon but was informed they were booked. I couldn't imagine how that could be, but I had no choice.

I curbed my initial enthusiasm. Just because Elizabeth Popham remembered an adoption from approximately the same time as Lisa Trowbridge was under Ziegler's care didn't make that child Archie's daughter. There could have been others during that period as well. I decided to hit the Havana

Club again that night. Maybe April had recalled more after our initial meeting. Maybe someone remembered a woman nick-named Jeri. I kept busy the rest of the day, but it did no good, for my thoughts had become obsessed with a wild and bizarre theory, and it flapped in my head like a flag in a hurricane.

CHAPTER 63

It had just stopped drizzling when I got out of the truck at the Havana Club. The air was warm and clammy and slowed my step.

I'd convinced myself that Jeri was Archie's daughter. My delusional optimism was based on the close birth date, but that wasn't the only reason. I'd drawn the line. After her, I was done, and I didn't want to fail. It was a long shot that anyone would remember her. The current cast members of the Havana Club weren't likely even alive during the time I was inquiring about. But stories last. "People like to spread juicy gossip," Elizabeth Popham had explained when I pressed her for how she remembered that Jeri Lake worked at the Havana Club. "I mean, if Jeri got a PhD in biology, no one would have said a thing. But pole dancing? That news travels."

Maybe Bobbie Lee would recall such a person. I made a mental note to ask her.

I paid the cover to the old man perched on a stool inside the front door. "Enjoy the show," he said, giving me the identical greeting he'd delivered the first time I was there. His speech was slow, and now I wondered if he had a mental impairment.

I surveyed the room. Lester and April were cuddled together in the same curved booth I had sat in with her last week. He must have decided to move his date up this week. I thought of leaving as I had no desire to blow her relationship with Lester. But Lester spotted me and I had no choice but to march over to their booth.

"You're just like everybody else." April said with a smug voice before I had a chance to say anything.

"Pardon me."

"They always come back."

"That's not what's happening here," I protested.

"Looks like it to me."

"I'm sorry," Lester said. "Do you two know each other?"

"I came in after I met you at Archie's house," I said. "I wanted to know if anyone remembered anything about Bobbie Lee." I thought that a better cover than admitting I was investigating him. "I hit a lot of people, including—"

"He threw out a lot of questions. It was a waste of time," April assured him.

"Why are you looking into Bobbie Lee?" Lester asked. "She hasn't worked here in years."

"I was just covering my bases. Getting to know the players before I dove into Archie's request."

I wasn't sure he bought that, but he went in a different direction.

"Abigail told me you paid her a visit. You never questioned me."

"I was led to believe that although Abigail might resent a third heir, you carried no such jealousy. That you were supportive of Archie's search for his daughter. Seeing as how I'm here, do you have a minute?"

"Why are you here?" Lester demanded.

"Just some follow-up questions."

"On Bobbie Lee?"

"On another person who might have worked here."

"I don't understand how that is going to help you."

"Indulge me," I said, sliding into the booth next to April. It would be easier to talk to Lester from there. The three of us made a comfy ménage à trois.

"You know, Mr. Travis," Lester said, "I wasn't too impressed with you when we met. Your manner has not improved."

"And that's something I promise to work on. I was hoping to wrap up my business with your father. Your boothmate might be able to help me out."

"I don't see how," April interjected.

"Five minutes," I said.

Lester flipped open a hand. "Let's get it over with. But I was never here."

"You have my word."

"Is it better than your manners?"

"You're going to have to take a chance on that."

Lester grunted. He likely realized that he might have a better chance of me keeping my mouth shut if he cooperated with me. April crossed her legs. Her right foot touched my leg, and she adjusted herself so it did not. She wore the same perfume she had when we'd previously met. Lilacs. After a rain. I didn't mention that the first time I told you about her. I don't want you to think I go around slathering after women, but my five senses have been tuned to their frequency since age twelve.

"My father said you're hitting the pavement pretty hard but haven't found any solid leads yet."

Do I push through with my questions in front of Lester? Why not? Nothing else had worked. "She might have worked here once," I said.

"Bobbie Lee?" he said. "She most definitely did. That's how they met. You didn't get that story? They usually lead with it."

"I meant his daughter."

"His daughter might have worked here as well?"

"It would have been some time ago. Her name was Jeri Lake. Jeri was not her first name. It was more of a nickname that everyone called her."

Lester chuckled. "What a small world."

April adjusted Lester's blue jacket, which was draped over her shoulders. While Lester and I talked, her eyes never left him. I wonder if he noticed that.

I looked at April. "Does that name ring a bell?"

"Sorry. Everyone here has at least two names. Probably a third they don't tell anyone about. How many years ago was this?"

"As few as ten, as many as twenty."

"You know how much turnover a place like this has over that period of time?" she said.

"If I recall, you heard of Bobbie Lee."

"You were lucky."

"I'm looking for luck again."

"Aren't we all?"

"Is there anyone around from then? The owner? Manager?"

"The current owner bought it four, maybe five years ago."

"And before that?"

"You can dig to China if you want. Owners. Managers. Girls. This place is a pass-through, not a destination."

"Would a customer remember?" I pleaded. "A vendor? Anyone with a sense of the history of the place?"

"We're not big on history here."

"My, my, Mr. Travis," Lester cut in. "You appear to be grasping at straws."

I let my breath out and leaned back. If someone had offered me five dollars at that point to forget about Lisa Trowbridge's daughter, I'd have taken it. Maybe April saw that on my face. Maybe she was holding back. Maybe she'd just thought of him. For a reason we'll never know, April said, "We can try Bernie."

"Who's Bernie?"

"The man at the door who collects the money. He's a bit slow but sweet as candy. He's been here forever. Hold tight a second."

She nudged Lester, who scooted out and stood. April grabbed her jacket with both hands, wiggled out of the booth, and walked toward the entrance. That left Lester and me.

"She covered pretty well," he said.

"Excuse me?"

"Macie. That line about you questioning the other girls, too. She told you, didn't she?"

Macie. I had never asked April what she told Lester her name was.

"I don't—"

"Cut the shit. Bobbie Lee told you I came here, and you dropped in to do a background check on me. What did Macie tell you?"

"It was early in my investigation. I was casting a wide net to get to know the players. Looking for a quick score."

He bounced his head. "If it weren't for the kids, I'd be out."

"You don't owe me an explanation."

"Don't flatter yourself. My wife thinks I'm an asshole. I think she's a bitch. Neither of us deserves that. We're nice people. We just can't be nice together."

"Some advice?"

"From you?" He snorted.

"Just a gut call."

"What the hell."

"You could do a lot worse than pulling off an Archie here."

"You don't even know her."

"Her eyes never leave you."

April approached the table with Bernie in tow.

"I'm going to hit the head," Lester said. He slid out of the booth. April wriggled in next to me. Bernie slopped into what I assumed was a warm spot left by Lester. His skeletonless body folded into the booth.

"Jake, this is Bernie. Bernie, Jake."

"What can I do for you, young man?" Bernie's eyes were wide and bland.

"I'm looking for a woman who worked here long ago. Went by the name Jeri Lake."

"I remember her. As fine as any woman who ever worked here."

CHAPTER 64

Here's the dictionary definition of hope: "A feeling of expectation and desire for a certain thing to happen. To cherish a desire with anticipation." Here's Emily Dickinson's take on it: "It perches in the soul, and sings the tune without the words and never stops at all." Bernie's casual comment was more than chirping hope. It was an a cappella chorus backed by 101 strings, blaring French horns, and rolling timpani. The only thing missing was the cymbal clash.

"Thirty-four years," Bernie said when I asked him how long he'd been working there. "Don't even know how many owners over that time."

"How many dogs, Bernie?" April said. "Our friend Jake here is just itching to get a dog."

"Three," he said, holding up three fingers. "I love dogs, but I don't like it when they die. But that's part of living, I guess."

Every owner had taken a look at Bernie and decided he was the person they trusted to stuff his shirt with money and turn it in at the end of the night. That spoke volumes about the man. Whatever Bernie lacked in executive functioning skills, he more than made up for in moral fortitude. I was anxious to know if he could pinpoint when Jeri Lake had worked here. And, more importantly, where she might have slipped off to.

April draped her arm around Bernie. "Jake here has a few questions for you, Bernie."

"Tell me about Jeri Lake," I said.

Bernie shot April a nervous look.

"It's okay," she told him. She glanced back at me. "We get a lot of crackpots wanting to know about our girls."

"I'm just trying to find a man's daughter who he never had the opportunity to know," I said.

Bernie nodded. "We get a lot of girls through here. Most of them real nice. More than a few come back to visit me."

"And do you recall Jeri?" I said, wondering if he'd spoken too soon when he indicated he remembered her. I tossed out the time she might have worked at the Havana Club in the event he was thinking of someone else. Maybe there was more than one Jeri Lake.

"That's about right," he said. "Cute girl. I remember her dimples. I know the time's right because that's when Duke—he was my dog then—started going lame. Had to carry him outside to do his business. She didn't go by Jeri when she was here, even though I always think of her as Jeri. She got herself a different name."

"What name was that?" I asked.

"I can't recall."

"Jenny? Geraldine?" I said, trying to jar his memory.

"No. No, not like that. A boy's name but spelled different for a girl that, for some reason, reminded me of the Civil War."

The cymbal player stood and spread her hands.

"What else?" I said. My voice was hollow.

"She was real nice. All our girls are nice, but she was special. Smart, know what I mean? Said she took the job so she had time to paint during the day. And, oh, I remember a story she told me. Said she had a dog growing up that loved to swim.

I like dogs. On my third right now. It's so sad when they die. She told me she couldn't keep her dog out of the water. When it died, she found it on the shore, right where the water meets the land. That's something you don't forget. That poor dog must have really loved the water."

Clash.

CHAPTER 65

I kept trying to convince myself that what I knew to be true couldn't be true. It was too bizarre. I would need to seek DNA confirmation, for one does not make such a revelation without ironclad certainty. And I would have gotten DNA, if the picture had not been so conclusive.

I hadn't said anything to Kathleen. Or Morgan. Or Garrett, who had flown back to Cleveland that morning. Part of the reason was I wanted to wait and see the picture in the yearbook. But that was an excuse. I needed a moment to envision the road ahead. What would I tell Archie? What unlucky words would be drafted to construct such a message? To deliver the blow. How would she react? I cursed myself for not seeing it earlier.

"Here we go," the librarian said the next morning, handing me a yearbook.

I opened it and flipped through the pages. Found the class mug shots. My finger traced the alphabetized names.

No.

No.

No.

Hello.

I slammed the book shut.

If they wanted to do DNA, that was between them. If it were me, I wouldn't waste my time.

The smile. The dimples. *Our mother used to tell us the gift of the brush ran in our hands.* How Archie even admitted she reminded him of Lisa. Jenna's comment about the similarities her adopted son had to a birth mother he never knew. *Lori never spent a second with him, yet he smiles like her. Cocks his head like hers, and I hear his voice, his intonations, in her voice.*

And the clowns. Someone, please tell me. What is it with the clowns?

CHAPTER 66

The girls, as I told you at the beginning, named the dog Woodruff. He became Woody before his first piddle on the screened porch, which was less than a minute after he bounded into the house, freaking out Hadley III, who went into hiding and has not been seen since. Woody was a frisky, fluffy goldendoodle who was stupid cute. When Patty the Duck left a mess in the yard, Woody rolled in it. I held him under the outdoor shower while Joy shampooed him, and I tried to pretend I wasn't having fun. Joy toweled Woody, and the puppy dashed off, no doubt searching for more duck shit.

Kathleen and I were heading over to Archie and Bobbie Lee's house. I'd called Archie and told him I was done searching for his daughter. He asked if I'd found her. I told him I was handing in my report. After that, despite his barrage of follow-up and increasingly irritable questions, I revealed nothing.

"K, time to scoot," I shouted.

"Five minutes," Kathleen answered from the bedroom.

That meant ten. Joy and Sophia were next door with Morgan. They'd recently discovered the freedom of running between the houses, each being a home to them. I craved a drink. I made a strong one and slouched out to the screened porch. A pelican squatted at the end of the dock. I'd have to hose it off when we got back. I'd tried everything—plastic owls, windsocks, pinwheels, you name it. Nothing deters the birds from defecating on the boards and handrail.

Woody ran around the corner of the yard—does the dog ever walk?—and chased a bird off the seawall. The dog spotted the pelican. He hesitated, for he'd never seen a dock in his puppy life. Without further thought, he launched himself, bounding down the hundred feet, yelping and barking in glee. The pelican took flight. Woody did a victory lap around the platform at the end of the dock, announcing his presence to the International Brotherhood of Shitting Birds. Buzz off, feather butts; this is my territory.

Uh. Look at that.

My bird-chasing, dock-hosing days were over. Pretty glad I convinced everyone to get a dog. Cleaning up after it was a small price to pay for a spotless dock. Good thinking, Jake. That's the way I remember it. And that's the way I will tell it for the rest of my life.

Kathleen popped onto the porch. "Ready, Freddy," she said. "I texted Morgan and told him we were going. Thank you, by the way."

"For what?"

"Hanging the painting in the girls' room. It looks nice there."

"Not too high?"

"Maybe just a tad?" she said, pinching two fingers together. "What do you think?"

I thought it was at the perfect height, or else I would not have hung it where I had.

"I'll lower it," I said. "Are you ready?"

After my trip to the library I'd told Kathleen, Morgan, and Garrett about what I'd discovered. What I feared to be true.

"Ready as I'll never be."

"I hear you."

"We're a hurricane, Jake. A named storm. After we pass, nothing will be the same. The date will be forever etched. That's how they'll remember us."

CHAPTER 67

Remember Jake's Rule Number One? Run away.

Can I do that?

"You cannot," Kathleen advised me when I voiced the question. We were crawling over the Tierra Verde Bridge as if in a funeral cortege, delaying the inevitable. She flipped the visor mirror up. It was its second round trip. Maybe the third. "How would that even play out?"

"I inform Archie it was a dead end," I said, arguing with my own thoughts as I spoke. "Did my best. Sorry."

"We could never face them again."

"Our absence grants them eternal tranquility."

"But to know and never say anything."

"What about it?"

"It's wrong, babe."

"Says who?"

"Says me."

"So what's the play? I review the events of the past few days. Let it dawn on them. Never come out and blurt it."

"I dunno," she said. "I think we should tell them separately. They deserve to find out in their own company. It will give them both a chance to be with their thoughts, if even for a brief time."

"I like that. Boy, boy, girl, girl?"

"Exactly." She flipped down the visor again, made a mindless swipe of her hand over her hair, and snapped it back.

"What will you tell her?" I said.

"I like our world."

"What's that got to do—?"

"A dog. A cat. A sometimes duck. A nanny who blabbers in a language foreign to us. Two girls the sun revolves around. A neighbor who is as much family as any of the above. Me lost in my silly literature, you torn between doing good at Harbor House and taking odd jobs for Yankee Conrad to quell your restless soul."

"Is that what I do?"

"We don't look for validation, do we?"

"We do not."

"Do we care what others think?"

"We do not."

"That's what we'll tell them. That they'll know. You and I know. It need never go further. An inner circle of four."

Well, plus Morgan and Garrett. It was probably not a good time to bring up Ben Franklin's quip that three people can keep a secret if two of them are dead.

"Agreed?" she asked, grasping for confirmation.

"Agreed."

"No guilt," she continued. She'd taken the lead, and I was fine with that. When the chips were down, she was really the stronger person. "No remorse. It changes everything. It changes nothing."

"It's a good line. But it's not our call, is it?"

"No. But don't underestimate the power of suggestion. Of support. Moods are contagious. Let them know we're fine with it."

"Fake it till you make it."

"Don't fake. Believe."

"Okay," I said. "We split when we get there."

"Any suggestions for that?"

"I'll tell Archie I want to see the painting that Bobbie Lee did. The one in his study."

"The angel clown thingy?"

"Pretty apparent from day one, wasn't it?"

"Don't go there," Kathleen reminded me. "It does no good. I'll tell Bobbie Lee I want to peek at her kitchen again. That we're thinking of remodeling."

"Ten minutes," I said. "Then bring her upstairs."

We were in their driveway. I wished the trip had taken longer. I put the truck in park and turned off the engine.

"At least her cough is gone," Kathleen said.

Here's something else I've picked up. When a woman has children, a part of her mind is forever thinking of those children. That upper room never sleeps. Never rests. It takes precedence over everything under the stars and all that lie beyond.

"We're lucky Sophia didn't get catch it," I added.

"There'll be another one. Ready to rock and roll?"

"Ready as I'll never be."

"On three. One, two—"

CHAPTER 68

Robert Penn Warren, in *All the King's Men*, said that man doesn't know if knowledge will save him or kill him. Was I to deliver salvation to Archie or a dagger to his heart?

Bobbie Lee swung open the door. She hugged Kathleen as we stepped inside. "It's so good to see you." She turned her attention to me. "Archie said you babbled on the phone, and you're not a babbler. He's worried you came up empty."

"I did not."

Her hand shot up to her mouth. "You found her?"

"I think so."

She touched my arm. "Oh my God. That is such good news." She raised a finger in the air. "Plus, he just got a favorable report from his doctors. A banner day, wouldn't you say?"

And about to get bannier.

"Follow me, kiddos," Bobbie Lee said. "The evening's warm, the wine is chilled, and you're the bearer of good news."

We followed her through the house and out the back door.

"Do you hear that song every day?" I said. Linda Ronstadt was back at it with "Long Long Time."

Bobbie Lee turned her head over her shoulder. "I know, right? That'll be Arch, though I like her as well. He told me he and Lisa listened to it all the time. I have to admit, I do feel"—she stopped, held up a hand, and pinched two fingers together —"just a teeny-weeny bit jealous."

"Maybe you and Archie can make this your song," I suggested.

"Think it works that way?"

"It works any way you want it to," I said, planting an idea that might echo and be useful later on.

"I suppose," she said with a shrug.

We arrived at the firepit. Even though it was a warm night, it was lit.

Archie stood and pumped my hand. "Good news, I trust?" he gushed.

"I believe so," I said.

"That's wonderful."

Should I have waited on DNA? What if I was wrong?

You can spin a cocoon around a conviction until it is so tight nothing can free it. I had one question to validate my cocoon, to seal their fate. Absent a conversational prompt, I blurted it out to Bobbie Lee.

"You mentioned when we first met that your parents died years ago. I never asked you the cause of their death. I apologize for my insensitivity in not inquiring how."

"You're so sweet," she said. "I certainly took no offense from the lack of further questions. They died in a private plane crash."

That's all she wrote, folks.

I was aware of Kathleen's eyes on me. I'd told her that if the answer went a different direction, we'd have to pull back. That would not be the case. Bobbie Lee's expected response brought neither relief nor trepidation, only the realization that there would be no easy way out.

"So you found her?" Archie jumped in. His voice was a mix of anticipation and annoyance at my digression.

"I believe so," I said. Should I ask Bobbie Lee if that was even her name? I was suffering a case of the jitters. Looking for a way to stall.

"What does that mean?" Archie demanded. "Did you find her or not?"

"You would need to do a DNA to test be positive, and—"

"That's not an issue. Is she receptive to it?"

"I haven't gotten that far yet."

"How far have you gotten?"

"I've—"

"Tell me about her."

"Arch," Bobbie Lee interjected. "They've barely sat down." She dipped her head to a charcuterie board. "You haven't even touched it, and I made sure to include a generous portion of summer sausage."

I reached in and snatched a piece of sausage, but it didn't taste anything like it had the last time.

Archie, who had been perched on the edge of his chair, leaned back. "I appreciate everything you've done," he said. "I know I'm not easy to work with. Ever since that letter came, it's been difficult. Dredging up memories that have lost their color, their edge. Wondering if she's out there, and if she is, does she care? What if she has no interest in me?

"After your latest news that Lisa was likely murdered, what would I tell her? I've begun to have second thoughts—don't get me wrong; I'm eager to meet her—but at what price? Will I be upending her life? Would it be better for her if she never knew that her mother was murdered?"

I took the opening.

"Those are valid concerns," I said. "You'll upset the status quo. There's certain to be unintended consequences."

"That can be said of nearly everything. Perhaps more so of

our undertaking, but to bury the information is unacceptable. She'll have to know what happened to her mother."

"We agree," Kathleen cut in. "I think Jake's merely stating that these things can be disruptive and to temper your expectations. You will be creating a before-and-after picture of your life. You will have feelings on both sides. That is natural."

"We've talked about that," Bobbie Lee said. "You can only anticipate so much. You just have to possess the confidence that you can handle what comes. Archie and I are very comfortable that we can manage whatever this new relationship brings."

Oh girl. You have no clue.

"Is she local?" Archie said. "Live in this area?"

"You could say that," I replied.

Kathleen coughed. It was time to move the evening along.

"I'd like to see the painting in your study," I said to Archie. "In a manner of speaking, it may be related to your daughter."

"I don't understand. Why don't—?"

"Indulge me," I said, rising to my feet. "I think I've earned that."

"No question about that," he said, standing up. "But how could that be?" The first tones of skepticism fringed his voice.

"Not necessarily related," I pedaled back my statement. "More like reminiscent. Let's take a look at it, shall we?"

Kathleen stood. "And I," she said to Bobbie Lee, "want to pick your brain on your kitchen. We're thinking of remodeling, and I love what you've done."

Archie and I started walking to the house. Kathleen was behind us, talking to Bobbie Lee, not letting her get a word in. We split in the kitchen, but not before Kathleen said, "We'll join you in a few."

I followed Archie up to his study, counting the steps along the way, wishing they took forever. Linda Ronstadt accompanied us with her song "Shattered" that Jimmy Webb wrote after

John Lennon died. But I didn't think Linda's magic was going to work any more than John Lennon was going to rise out of his grave. What is broken can be fixed, but what is shattered is lost. Archie's life was about to be shattered, for Archie Williams was doomed at both ends of love.

CHAPTER 69

"I can't imagine how that painting has anything to do with my daughter," Archie protested as we entered his study. He had clomped his feet on the way up, registering his distaste at my delay.

Then you're afraid to see what you see.

"Tell me why you like this painting, Archie. Because I've met your daughter, and I think she'll like it as well."

"You met her?"

"I have."

"For God's sake, man, what's going on here? Tell me about her."

"She's a remarkable woman. That bourbon bottle isn't empty, is it?"

"Never. Let's celebrate." He went to the bar cart and fixed two drinks. He handed me one. "To remarkable women." We clinked glasses. "I have one in my life; tell me about the other."

"About that," I said. I wandered over to the self-portrait of Bobbie Lee dressed as a clown with wings. "What do you like about this?" I asked, repeating my earlier question.

"I don't follow your thinking."

"Indulge me."

"You're big on that."

I took a patient sip of my drink.

"Fine," he spit out. "I like the subject matter. A female clown. With wings, to boot. Is she an angel or a clown? You're drawn to her even though you don't know what or who she is."

"And?" I prodded him.

"She's attractive. Even seductive."

"And?"

"What's this about?" he said with a hint of disgust.

"It's Bobbie Lee's self-portrait, right? She looks like Lisa."

He waved his hand. "I don't need that Freudian bullshit. That I married Bobbie Lee because she reminded me of Lisa or has certain facial traits she had. It's a coincidence, not a motivator."

"Was Lisa a good artist?"

He snorted. "She never got a chance. But she had talent, that's for sure."

"Her aunt Allison is also good. She said that talent ran in the family."

"I don't recall anything about that," he said impatiently.

I took a sip of my drink and remained silent, hoping the silence would speak for me. I wondered how Kathleen was getting along.

Archie said, "You indicated the painting is somehow related to my daughter. Reminiscent, I believe you said."

"Your daughter's about Bobbie Lee's age," I said.

He did the math in his head. "That's about right. Are you saying Bobbie Lee and I might have difficulties because my wife is about the same age as my daughter?"

If only.

"Not to be rude," he continued, "but that's hardly your concern. Don't get me wrong; I appreciate your counsel. But let's not create issues where they may not exist. Tell me about my daughter. Have you told her about me?"

"I have not, but she's aware that you're looking for her."

"Is she familiar with the Ziegler babies? Did you tell her?"

Easy now. Feed it out to him little by little.

"She is. And she knows she was adopted."

"What led you to her?"

"I caught a break. Found out who adopted her and what high school she went to. From there, I was able to track her down."

"Where did you meet her?"

"Here."

"Here? Is she still in the area?"

"She's here," I said.

Archie studied me. The first lines of anxiety crept into his face.

"You mean here, in Saint Petersburg?"

"Sure, Archie," I said dismissively. "That's what I mean."

"You're talking bullshit."

"She's *here*," I said for the second time, my voice cracking.

I hung my head and stared at my belt buckle. It wasn't aligned with the buttons on my shirt. Remember, I told you I did it one more time.

"No," Archie Williams said, his voice trembling. "No. No. God, man. What are you saying?"

He looked frail. Unbalanced. I reached out and clasped his sweating hand.

"It's a topsy-turvy world, Archie. It doesn't need to make sense to anyone other than you and Bobbie Lee. No one needs to know." I wished I could have done better, but I was just trying to hang on myself.

He looked at me with trepidation, his eyes wide with fear and anxiety. He opened his mouth as if to speak, but no words came forth.

"Your daughter's adoptive parents died in a plane crash. And she painted this picture."

His face turned a whiter shade of pale.

"Jake?" Kathleen called in a shaky voice from the hall outside the study. "Are you ready?"

"Ready."

Archie's daughter walked into the room.

EPILOGUE

Exit Interviews

C*lown who Archie saw the night he met Bobbie Lee*

Yeah, I remember him. I was walking down the street. It had been a bitch of a day. Two kid birthday parties and then some Knights of Columbus or something gig in the evening. They wanted dirty balloons—you know, like copulating balloons. The Shriners—that's who they were.

I was walking in sheets of rain, sipping Jim Beam from a flask. This guy's cruising slow. Nice car. Our eyes meet. I get it. I look like something out of *The Rocky Horror Picture Show*. I could feel the paint crawling down my face.

That's right. I did point my finger in the direction of the Havana Club. Why not? We all want someone to tell us what to do. He pulled into the side lot, just like I'd directed. Some rich guy looking for salvation in a pair of knockers. Who's to say it doesn't work that way?

Thanks for the audience. Everybody looks at a clown, but

no one ever listens to one. Even now, you just hear your voice in your head, not mine.

April

Jake Travis? Sure, I remember him. Scared Lester right out of my life. It never would have worked, though. A guy wants to think he found the girl next door on a pole. A girl wants to think a man walks through the door and nothing is ever the same. Both sides are losers. I know—look at Bobbie Lee. There's an exception to every rule, right?

Here's a tip: Don't look in the mirror and think that's you.

Lisa Trowbridge

Surprised to hear from me? I lobbied for a few lines. Why not?

I recognized him. Sitting behind the wheel. The boy who had taken my picture. What's he doing here? He's coming in pretty fast. Our eyes locked. He sped up. Why? What did I do? Is it because I know Little Strawberry's alive? I jumped back, but I was too late. I would never see my baby. My future was going to end right there. No Archie. No daughter. No me. I didn't even have time to cry.

Death is a great sorrow.

Dr. Wayne Ziegler

Disappeared? Is that what the cops said I did? They never searched for me, at least not hard, and I'll tell you why. They had nothing. Not one shred of evidence. I lived on Marathon Key for nine wonderful years.

The Cardinal Inn? A lot of women drove away from that place with their dream, their answered prayer swaddled in the back seat. If that were you, would you have asked questions?

April, Part Two

I get two entries? Cool. Doesn't happen often in life, though it did to me. I'm glad I can share it with you.

It was a year later. I'm at Trader Joe's buying flowers, and in strolls Lester. I got my daughter Charlotte on my hip. My hair's a hot mess, and I look like shit. Lester says he dropped by my house just as I was pulling out and followed me.

He tells me he's divorced. Left the company. Says he's going on a sailing trip, and will you come with me? Some private cruise his father and Bobbie Lee did and how much they loved it. Leaves from the Virgin Islands, where they live now. Don't ask me which one. He shows me a picture on his phone of Archie and Bobbie Lee, standing on the deck of a sailboat, their faces bright in the sun.

His question to me?

Hell yes. We leave next week.

ABOUT THE AUTHOR

Robert Lane is the author of the critically acclaimed Jake Travis novels. His books have won the Benjamin Franklin Award for Best New Voice: Fiction. He is also the recipient of the Eric Hoffer Award for Best Mystery as well as the Readers' Favorite Gold Medal for Best Mystery/Sleuth. Lane resides on the west coast of Florida. Learn more at robertlanebooks.com.

Receive a free copy of the Jake Travis series prequel, *Midnight on the Water.*

Equal parts mystery and love story, *Midnight on the Water* is the saga of how Jake and Kathleen meet and tumble into love. But a mob boss who fears Kathleen knows too much wants her silenced. Jake, Morgan, and Garrett take drastic action to save Kathleen's life and grant her a new identity. *Midnight on the Water* is available only to those on Robert Lane's mailing list. The newsletter contains reviews of books, music, and television shows across a wide range of genres. It also includes updates on the next Jake Travis novel.

Enjoy *Midnight on the Water.*

Be sure to read these highly praised Jake Travis novels:

The Second Letter

Cooler Than Blood

The Cardinal's Sin

The Gail Force

Naked We Came

A Beautiful Voice

The Elizabeth Walker Affair

A Different Way to Die

The Easy Way Out

Searching for Dali

Kiss it Goodbye

Visit Robert Lane's author page on Amazon.com: https://www.amazon.com/stores/Robert-Lane/author/B00HZ2254A

Follow Robert Lane on:

Facebook: https://www.facebook.com/RobertLaneBooks

Goodreads: https://www.goodreads.com/author/show/7790754.Robert_Lane

BookBub: https://www.bookbub.com/profile/robert-lane?list=about

Learn more and receive your free copy of *Midnight on The Water* at http://robertlanebooks.com.

www.ingramcontent.com/pod-product-compliance
Lightning Source LLC
LaVergne TN
LVHW100515110826
845146LV00002B/652

9798993329918